FERAL

ALPHA TIES II

NORA ASH

ABOUT THE AUTHOR

Nora Ash writes thrilling romance and sexy paranormal fantasy.

Visit her website to learn more about her upcoming books.

WWW.NORA-ASH.COM

ONE

LILLIAN

"Welcome, Miss Dorne. I am Dr. Simon Axell, and I will be your mentor these first few weeks."

I couldn't contain my beaming smile at the approaching alpha as I got to my feet. He was broad like his biology dictated, but for an alpha, he didn't make too intimidating a figure. The lab coat also helped.

"Thank you, Dr. Axell. It's such an honor to join your team. I've been following your work since I was a grad student."

It was true. I'd been quietly and nerdily fangirling over Dr. Axell's work in bio-research for years. When my old advisor had notified me of a position on his team, I'd leapt at the chance. He might be working with *"biological defense"* these days, rather than disease control as I'd majored in, but for Dr. Axell, I'd work in sewage disposal if I had to.

He returned my smile, albeit a bit more measured, and clasped my hand in a brief shake. "You come highly recommended—Professor Remmer is an old acquaintance of mine. He promised me you were one of the best bioanalysts in the country."

I did my best not to blush bright red at the praise— an unfortunate flaw of mine. Judging from the heat in my cheeks, I didn't luck out. *Damn it.* Not the most professional image to portray on my very first day.

At least if Dr Axell noticed, he graciously pretended he didn't.

"Professor Remmer has been very kind."

"I trust you've been granted a temporary access pass?" he asked, brushing off my bashfulness.

I nodded and held up the pass I'd been given by the receptionist upon arrival.

"Good. HR should have a permanent badge made out for you before the end of the week." Dr. Axell led me through the sliding doors behind reception, swiping his own badge to unlock them. "I'll get you introduced to a couple of key members of the team, and then we can go over the project itself. We are only two lead researchers with three support staffers, not counting the guards."

I nodded enthusiastically at him as we walked down long, white-painted corridors lined with metal on all surfaces and a strip of fluorescent lights guiding the way. I hadn't been informed of what exactly I'd be working on, except that it was *"biodefense,"* highly classified and sanctioned by the Ministry of Defense, even if it was run by a private corporation—SilverCorp.

I'd done as much research as I could on my new employer, but nowhere had there been any records of what exactly they worked with, so I was more than a little curious. Especially after I'd been sworn in by government agents in black suits and stern faces to keep a strict non-disclosure agreement. Suffice it to say, I was pretty much expecting to walk into a *Men in Black* situation when I arrived at the heavily guarded compound earlier this morning.

The long hallway we were following didn't do much to dissuade my overactive imagination, with the way our shoes made the metal flooring echo ominously and the smell of disinfectants in the air, but when Dr. Axell finally opened a door and ushered me into a small staff room, I was utterly disappointed.

It smelled like coffee and looked exactly like any break room you'd see in millions of companies across the country. No extraterrestrials in sight—only a lone beta male in a lab coat eating a sandwich by the large, white table in the middle of the room. A newspaper lay sprawled next to his sandwich wrapper, opened to an article about the stock market, as far as I could tell.

"Dr. Urwin," Dr. Axell began, "I want you to meet our new bioanalyst, Miss Lillian Dorne. Miss Dorne, this is Dr. Dave Urwin. You will mainly be running tests on my data, but occasionally you'll also need to help Dr. Urwin—he's responsible for the female subjects."

The beta got to his feet and extended a hand toward me. "A pleasure, Miss Dorne."

"Likewise." I smiled and shook it as I looked around the small break room, doing my best not to pinch myself. This high spec research facility, so important it was under government protection and unsearchable on the web—was now my actual workplace. I wasn't even thirty yet and I'd already reached the pinnacle of my dreams.

Since I'd left high school with a 4.0 GPA, I'd dreamt of working in a place like this, under a man like Simon Axell, and here I was.

The only thing that could have made today any better was if this did in fact turn out to be a secret government department for intergalactic diplomacy.

"Female test subjects?" I asked, turning from Dr. Urwin to my mentor. "Am I to understand that the research is in human trials, at this stage?"

"Very observant, Lillian." Dr. Axell smiled as he handed me my coffee. "That will do you well here. And yes, indeed it does. Are you keen to learn about the project?"

So no aliens, then. I nodded nevertheless. "Very."

"Well, since it looks like our support staff are working through lunch today, why don't I take you down to my department and I'll give you an introduction to the project as a whole and what I'm working with right now? Bring a cup of coffee—there are no biohazards." Another smile as he nodded toward the coffee machine in the corner of the room. "I know you come from disease control."

I grimaced at the thought of what bringing a cup of coffee into the lab could have done at my previous job and quickly poured myself a mug. As much as I'd loved my former field, being able to keep caffeinated while working would be a nice and unexpected bonus.

Dr. Axell poured himself a cup as well, and then led me out the door with a nod to the beta doctor by the table.

"We've been working on developing a way for our most specialized troops to gain an edge in combat," Dr. Axell explained as we walked further down the corridor. When he came to a thick door, he swiped it with his card and pressed in a code before it opened with a heavy clonk. On the other side, a spiral staircase led underground.

"It's undeniable that our very best troops are alphas, which has given us a unique angle from which to approach the problem of improvement. My team and I are working on using the biological imperative that separates alpha males from the rest of society to enhance our subjects' combat skills. Bluntly put, we found a way to purify the alpha instincts within the males. The results have been very promising so far, but not without their drawbacks."

I frowned as I followed the doctor down the stairs and through another set of password protected doors. I'd been quite shielded in my academic cocoon—most alphas who advanced in academia had learned to control their more animalistic impulses early on, to be able to excel within a dynamic that cherished mind over physique.

That didn't mean I hadn't seen the other side of them. No woman could live in ignorance of the latent aggression within the part of the male species we knew as alphas. These large men, whose biology had marked them as the leaders of society, the warriors and protectors, were known for their dominance and ruthless aggression toward anyone who didn't bend to their will. It was a predicament largely ignored by polite society—something no one spoke of, but quietly accepted. We craved their leadership at an instinctive level, but many alphas abused their superior strength and the benefits it got them.

I may have been shielded from the worst of them—the ones who terrorized the city streets at night and took whatever and whoever they pleased—but that certainly didn't mean the idea of *enhancing* their alpha instincts didn't fill me with dread.

"Forgive me—what do you mean by purifying their instincts?" I asked as I stepped through the final door after Dr. Axell. I was going to elaborate, but just as the door slid closed behind me with an audible *click*, my eyes adjusted to the bright light in the room spread out below us and I stopped cold.

"It was a quite simple process, once we perfected the formula," Dr. Axell said, that easy smile still on his face as he turned to look at me. "In its essence, we've created a serum that will turn any alpha injected with enough of it feral."

I stared mutely into the room below. We were up a few steps from the main room, which gave me a perfect view of the lab and every person in it.

Two young men in white lab coats were walking from one subject to another, noting down numbers on charts.

And all along both walls and curved around a big, glass-paned room in the center, was cage after cage of imprisoned alphas.

TWO

LILLIAN

"They're... they're all in cages?" I asked, not quite believing my own eyes.

"Well, cells. Trust me, things would go south rather quickly if they weren't safely detained. Have you ever seen a feral alpha?"

I shook my head, mutely watching the nearest caged and buck naked man pace restlessly behind the bars of his prison, his muscles flexing as he stared at the nearby lab-coated staff member scribbling notes on his chart. He looked like a wild animal searching for a way to get at his captor.

"And they agreed to this... this arrangement?"

Dr. Axell glanced at me, for a moment appearing startled. Then his trademark smile spread across his face once more. "Oh, of course. Forgive me, I didn't consider how this would look to a newcomer. These test subjects were all imprisoned on death row—their lives were forfeit. Instead of getting the needle, they come here and help the society they turned their backs on learn how to better defend our borders. I'm sure you agree that this is far the better option for these wretched souls?"

Hesitantly, I nodded. If the only other option for these men was death, there wasn't much of a choice.

"Come, I want to show you our most promising subject." Dr. Axell walked down the few steps to the concrete floor below, leaving me to follow. "He was a Navy SEAL before he came here, and his physical tests are off the charts. They all become superior fighters once they're feral, but Subject 351 is something else entirely. We've shown his results to the Minister of Defense, and they are very hopeful he will be the key to improving the armed forces."

We walked to the far end of the large room, past cell after cell of naked and pacing alphas. Each and every one of them snarled when Dr. Axell passed, the sound and overwhelming scent of them making every hair on my body stand on end as I fought back my own primal instincts to show my throat in submission.

It was a ridiculous urge, of course, a leftover defense from before civilization made us all rein in our animal instincts and substitute them with rules and manners. I'd felt the brush of those instincts before—of course I had. Every man, woman, and child who'd ever been around an alpha had, but I'd never experienced anything as strong as this. The sheer density of testosterone in the air made my heart pick up speed, preparing my body to flee.

"It's a bit overwhelming in the beginning," Dr. Axell said, undoubtedly when he picked up on my scent of fear. "Every beta male on the team has been through it. It gets easier. Just remember they're behind bars—there's nothing they can do to you. You're the one in charge."

I gave him a grateful, but fleeting smile in acknowledgement, yet didn't manage to keep my eyes off the predators we passed. That's what they were, I realized. Predators. No longer fully human.

"What have you done to them to... to turn them feral?" I asked, aware my voice was squeaky with pent-up anxiety. Dr. Axell was polite enough to ignore it.

"Once a day, we give them a serum we've developed specifically for this purpose. It increases the activity in the medulla oblongata, forcing their primal instincts to the forefront. It doesn't fully erase their humanity—they're still capable of using tools, and to some degree, solving puzzles and performing simple tasks like showering and opening doors. We've yet to have anyone speak while the serum is still strong in their veins, but toward nighttime when it begins to wear off, most are capable of expressing basic needs and wants using some language." He stopped in front of the last cell on the left side of the room, smiling broadly at its occupant. "Ah, and here he is. Our most prized specimen. Miss Dorne, this is Subject 351. He's twenty-six, and a former Navy SEAL at six foot ten and two-hundred ninety-one pounds."

I peeked in the cell from my hiding-spot behind Dr. Axell's shoulder, and bit my lip at the sight of the man inside. All alphas were larger than beta males, but it was quite obvious even from a quick glance that the nearly three hundred pounds on this one was pure muscle. His body looked like it'd been carved from granite, with bulging muscles from his shoulders down his arms and pecs leading down to two hard rows of stacked abs and a prominent "V." I quickly averted my gaze when my eyes caught sight of what hung below his hips, forcing back my immediate blush.

Instead of pacing like the other alphas, he was sitting at the far concrete wall of his cell, his head leaned back and his eyes closed. When I looked closer, I could see several scars crisscrossing his skin. A few of them looked fresh.

"What's happened to him?" I asked, indicating the scars.

The moment I spoke, the alpha's eyes snapped open. His icy, blue-green eyes swept from me to Dr. Axell, and his lip curled up in a snarl that had me retreating a step before I caught myself.

"We have to test their fighting prowess on a regular basis," Dr. Axell explained. "Sometimes they sustain injuries, but they are of course treated instantly."

"Oh." That sounded plausible enough. I forced my eyes away from the scars and pressed down the sense of discomfort churning in my gut. He wasn't a good man, I reminded myself. And a few scars were a far better option than getting the needle, even for a former soldier of his obvious ability.

"You said the serum has drawbacks?" I asked, not taking my eyes off the alpha as he slowly got to his feet. His gaze was locked on Dr. Axell, and his stance was obviously defensive. How the alpha researcher reined in his own instincts was a mystery to me, but apart from a slight scent of aggression emanating from the man by my side, he didn't seem to be fazed in the slightest.

"Yes. As much as it purifies their alpha nature, it obviously also enhances their dominance and disregard for following orders. Not exactly prized qualities in what we hope will be the nation's most elite soldiers." Dr. Axell took a step closer to the cage and the alpha within reacted instantly. His snarl grew to a roar as he launched himself at the bars, barging against them with his shoulder so hard they shook. When unsuccessful, he started pacing instead, as close to the bars as he could without touching them, a look of absolute murder in his eyes as he stared Dr. Axell down.

"W-what are you working on to pacify them?" I asked, doing my best not to let on how hard my heart was pounding after the feral alpha's display of aggression.

"It's more about control than pacification," Dr. Axell said. He cocked his head while he watched the alpha pace, still seemingly unfazed by the threat of violence emanating from the man. "We've worked on a lot of solutions, but when it comes right down to it, there is only one thing that can be used to control any alpha on the planet. Even a feral one. A mate."

I blinked and finally wrested my gaze from the feral alpha to stare dumbfounded at Dr. Axell. "W-what? He has a *mate*? There are rules for mated pairings, even in cases of violent crime." Only in the most extreme cases was a criminal sentenced to death row if he'd taken a mate, because it was deemed too cruel a punishment for the—often innocent—surviving spouse to lose her mate before his time. There'd only been three cases in the past decade where a mated alpha had been sentenced to death, as far as I could recall, and that'd made waves across the country because in all three cases, their mates had been accomplices.

"No, he does not. None of them do." Dr. Axell returned my gaze with a calming smile. "Not yet. But it is our working theory that if we can get them to claim a mate while in this state, they will be much easier to control. We keep the woman with us, safe and sound, and her alpha will obey every command given."

"But..." About a thousand questions tumbled

through my brain, but I found it hard to word any of them. An esteemed researcher like Dr. Simon Axell would never break the strict codes of conduct every person employed within the sciences swore an oath to uphold, and I didn't want him to think I was accusing him of doing anything of the sort. Yet this...

"How will you find the women to bond with these men?" I finally asked.

"We already have." Dr. Axell nodded toward where the central, glass-paned room curved around. When we'd entered, I'd noticed a door leading out of the room on that side. "Inmates at several women's prisons across the country were given the option of shortening their sentences by taking part in this research. Those who accepted were given a physical before they arrived. Every one was deemed in a fitting physical state to participate. Don't worry, Miss Dorne. Everything is above board. I would never ask fellow researchers to partake in anything that could harm their careers."

"I wasn't implying that—"

He put a hand on my shoulder. "I know, my dear. And I want you to feel safe in confiding any concerns that may arise during your employment here. We take the welfare of our employees, as well as our test subjects, seriously."

I offered him a brief smile of gratitude that he responded to with a quick squeeze before he removed his hand and turned away from the caged alpha still pacing in his cell. "Now, if you will come with me. I'll show you your work station. You won't often have need to come down to the lab, but on occasion, someone will forget to jot down the relevant numbers in the reports you'll be given. If that's the case, you can always come down and read them off the cells. Just be careful not to come within reach of the bars."

I nodded shakily, my gut clenching at the thought of being close enough to one of the feral alphas that they might reach through the bars and grab me. One final look at the still-pacing 351 made it very obvious I wouldn't like the outcome of an encounter like that.

THREE

LILLIAN

I settled into a rhythm at my new job quickly enough. My colleagues were friendly, if a bit aloof, like most researchers tended to be. I was the most junior member of the team, and a newcomer, so I didn't mind too much that I spent most of my time alone by my computer. I was determined to prove myself the best analyst Dr. Axell had ever employed, hopeful that I'd improve my standing with the accomplished alpha enough that he'd eventually consider me part of his core team.

So I worked overtime hours from my second week, staying later than anyone else to catch up on the pile of work that'd been accumulating while they didn't have an analyst employed. Spreadsheets and bio measures haunted my dreams.

It was a full month into my employment before I had to return to the lab.

It was past 8 PM Friday night, and I was the last employee left in the whole compound, save the guards patrolling the upper layers and surrounding grounds. I'd decided to run the last few numbers on the latest test results from Subject 351. But as I sat yawning in front of the computer screen, staring at numbers that slowly began to look like ants to my tired eyes, I realized Dr. Axell had forgotten to fill in the alpha's daily calorie intake for this past week. Either I had to wait until Monday to get the numbers, or... I had to go read them off his chart myself.

A small jolt of nerves made me grimace. I'd been in plenty of labs before—that this one contained several aggressive alphas really shouldn't make me flinch like an intern. They were safely locked up. It didn't matter that I'd be the only staff member down there—not if I wanted to get this report done for Dr. Axell to hand over first thing Monday morning.

After only a moment's hesitation, I snatched pen and paper off my desk and made my way to the lab. Impressing my new boss was far more important than the dumb animal instincts nagging at my spine at the prospect of being all alone in a room full of alphas.

The lab was only half-lit when I stepped in through the sliding door after having swiped my card on the scanner. I briefly considered flicking the bright fluorescent lights on to make it easier to see the numbers on

351's chart, but a quick glance at the nearest cages made me decide against it.

In contrast to when last I'd been here, the alphas within view weren't pacing restlessly. Instead, they all seemed to be in some state of rest, and I didn't want to disturb them.

I walked as quietly as I could down the left row of cells, but even though I didn't go unnoticed, no one growled at my presence. A few got to their feet to watch me as I passed their cage, alert but unaggressive. I scented the air and blushed at my own lapse into primitive instincts. I was usually much better at ignoring the small, primal urge to smell for pheromones that always jabbed at the base part of my brain when around alphas—but then again, it wasn't often I found myself surrounded by this many of them.

Despite the heavy smell of disinfectant in the air and the relative calmness of the lab's inhabitants, the bitter note of alpha aggression still hung above it all, a silent reminder of the much different atmosphere the other staff members saw during regular working hours. Faint as it was, it still wreaked havoc on my nerves, and I sped up on my way to 351's cell. The sooner I got this over with, the sooner I'd be able to get out of here.

Subject 351 sat against the near wall when I got to his cage. His eyes snapped open when I stopped in front of the door where Dr. Axell's notes were attached to the concrete separating his cell from the next.

"Hey," I said, feeling halfway stupid talking to a feral alpha who'd likely rip me apart if he got the chance —but also too uncomfortable under his dark stare to pretend like I didn't notice him. Besides, the sound of my own voice calmed my frayed nerves, if only a little. "I just need to get your stats for the week—Dr. Axell forgot to complete them."

He didn't respond, obviously, but he didn't move closer to the bars either. I relaxed a little and pulled out my notepad, intent on getting the task done.

Dr. Axell's writing wasn't the most legible at the best of times, and in the dim lab, I had to squint and lean in to decipher the numbers and notes he'd scrawled on the alpha's file for the week. I was so absorbed in my efforts that I didn't realize I'd taken a step closer to the bars—nor did I notice the alpha getting to his feet. Only when I took another step and my shoulder brushed against the metal did I notice what I'd done—and by then, it was too late.

A large hand, with strength to rival a freight train, closed around my upper arm. *Hard.*

I shrieked and flailed, dropping my notepad and pen. My heart pounded in my throat so hard I thought I might throw it up, and I pushed at the bars in a vain attempt at getting free. I might as well have tried to dislodge a boulder.

"*Key!*" The snarled word hardly sounded human.

"I-I don't have any keys!" I whimpered. "Please, you're hurting me!"

The alpha growled and pulled me closer, slamming the full length of my body up against the bars in the process. I whimpered as pain lanced through me at the impact, and the errant thought, *"I'm going to die,"* flashed through my brain with merciless clarity.

But when Subject 351 grabbed at me through the bars with his free hand, it wasn't to tear me in half. He held me firmly in place, stopping me from squirming, and then pushed his hand into my lab coat's nearest pocket. The material slid across my body at his violent rummaging, and I bit back an undignified gasp when his large hand basically rubbed right across my private parts.

The alpha didn't give two shits about what was underneath my clothes, though. Another growl, triumphant this time, vibrated from his chest when he pulled out what he'd been after—my pass.

So that's what he meant by "key."

"I don't have access to the cells," I said, hoping with everything I had that I was right. There was no reason for me to have clearance to unlock the cages, but the entire lab might be under the same security level. "Please, just let me go."

He didn't. He kept his grip on me as he shifted behind the bars, moving so he could push his arm out of the cage and slap my keycard against the card reader attached to the door. It beeped, flashing a red light, and relief flooded through me all the way from my toes. A relief that was instantly squashed when the alpha roared, clearly furious, and clenched his hand so hard around my arm the bones creaked.

"*Ow, stop!*"

My pained cry died on a wheeze when he slammed me back against the bars and snarled, "*Open!*"

"I-I can't. Please, I'm telling you the truth. I don't have clearance." I twisted a little to try and look at him, and hopefully plead with whatever humanity was left within him. However, actually *looking* at him this close did nothing to calm my own racing heart. He was so big, his bulging muscles tensed with unleashed fury, and there was hatred painted all over his carved features. Under different circumstances—mainly not being trapped and reasonably certain I was about to lose an arm to his anger—I might have found him very handsome, even if he was very clearly all *alpha*. He had even features with high cheekbones and full lips that were currently pulled into a snarl, dark, buzz-cut hair, and the most startling pale, blue-green eyes. However, right then, all I could feel for the man was fear. Sick, gut-wrenching *fear*.

"Please. Don't hurt me. I haven't done anything to you."

He growled low in his throat in response and tugged hard at my white lab coat. "*Always hurt.*"

I wasn't sure if he meant I was like the other people in lab coats, and therefore he wanted to hurt me, or if they hurt him. Regardless, I knew distinguishing myself from the people he undoubtedly blamed for locking him up in here was my only shot at getting out of this mess in one piece.

"I'm not them. I only run the data through a computer. You've never seen me down here because I don't... I'm not part of the hands-on research. I just do my job," I babbled, twisting further to catch his gaze.

"Once. With *him*." The way he spat the last word out, there was no mistaking the loathing.

"Dr. Axell?" I blinked, remembering my first day—surprised my brief visit had even registered with him.

The alpha snarled furiously in response, and I whimpered and braced for being slammed against the bars again. But the impact never came.

I raised my gaze to plead with him once more, finally managing to catch those piercing eyes of his—and felt the words die on my lips. An odd buzz at the base of my spine made me shiver as I stared into what looked like two perfect flecks of ice.

His growl cut off like someone had flicked a switch, and I vaguely noticed the small gasp that escaped his lips before his pupils blew wide, and something entirely primal welled up from deep within my core in imme-diate and entirely involuntary response.

It felt like electricity snapped through my veins

instead of blood, hardening my nipples into painful peaks within the confines of my sensible cotton bra— and down low, an unmistakable heat began to radiate up through my abdomen.

What... the hell?

There was nothing sexual about being threatened with dismemberment from a feral alpha—a fact I'd been completely on board with not two seconds ago. So why was my body suddenly responding to the huge man as if... as if I wanted to...?

The deepest blush of my entire life flooded up from the tips of my toes and covered my body when I realized exactly what kind of ideas my body seemed to have gotten just from looking into his now darkened eyes. A *test subject!* How entirely inappropriate!

I flinched, trying to distance myself from the source of my perverted urges. To my surprise, he let go this time, letting me slip out of his grip as he continued to stare at me with a mix of confusion and... something else I couldn't put my finger on.

I scrambled a few steps back, breathing hard as if I'd just run a mile. I felt like it, too. Shaking like a leaf, I turned to leave—to put as much distance between us as I could.

"Key."

I looked back up at him at the sound of his now much softer voice. He was reaching through the bars for me, my pass in his upturned palm. *Fuck.* I couldn't very well leave the lab without it.

Hesitantly, I took a step back toward him, keeping my eyes on him to make sure he wouldn't snatch me again.

The difference on his sharp features was like night and day. Before, he'd been a mountain of unleashed fury. Now, he looked like he was trying to appear smaller, as if he was... trying not to scare me? There wasn't an ounce of the previous anger on his face, just that intense stare of his as he looked at me unblinkingly.

Slowly, I edged closer until I was exactly close enough to reach out and snatch my card out of his hand.

He didn't try to grasp me again, only looked at me as I quickly stepped out of reach once more.

"Thank... you," I said, not entirely sure why I was thanking the man who'd just tried to pull my arm off. Or whatever it was he'd been doing. It dawned on me that he hadn't actually harmed me nearly as much as he could have, should he have wanted to. Sure, I'd be sporting some pretty nasty bruises tomorrow, but I could have been dead on the floor for whoever fed the test subjects over the weekend to find.

The alpha didn't say anything, but I could feel his eyes on my back as I made my way out of the lab.

FOUR

LILLIAN

Subject 351 didn't leave my thoughts the entire weekend. I couldn't get his haunting eyes out of my mind, and, at night when I tossed and turned in my bed, I dreamt of him. They were disturbing dreams, filled with darkness and feral snarls, but despite the terror I felt as I slept, come morning I'd be aching and wet between the legs.

The shame from that particular bit was the worst part.

I'd never had this strong a reaction to an alpha before. Sure, I could appreciate them on screen as attractive on that primal level that spoke solely to the most primitive instincts in my body, but as soon as a male switched on the alpha aggression in person, all I felt was fear. I wasn't like the women who flung themselves at any alpha who sniffed in their direction—I'd never seen the attraction of their dominance. They just scared me.

Sure, I could work with an alpha fine, as long as he was perfectly well-behaved—like Dr. Axell. But anything more than that?

I shuddered as memories I'd long ago repressed threatened to spill into my conscious mind. My step-dad had been an alpha, and he hadn't liked taking care of another man's child. I'd learned from an early age that it was best to give the aggressive ones a wide berth, and the well-mannered a cautious eye.

So why the hell did 351 make me toss and turn all nights with... with *yearning*, like a damn cat in heat?

These thoughts were still tumbling around in my head when I made it to work Monday morning, tired and disheveled from yet another bad night to finish up the report I hadn't managed to complete on Friday.

My colleagues chatted quietly about a new female test subject they'd secured, while I stared blankly at 351's test results. My coffee sat next to me untouched despite my fatigue. Perhaps that was why I blurted out, "What do you do to them? During the tests?"

"Beg your pardon?" Dr. Axell looked at me over his shoulder, eyebrows raised in question.

"It's just, it would be useful for me to know exactly what these figures are referring to," I quickly added. Which was true, I sternly told myself. It was purely to help me do my job better. Not because the echo of the feral alpha's voice growling out, *"Always hurts,"* had been playing on a loop all weekend.

"That's a fair point." Dr. Axell turned back to Dr. Urwin. "I guess it wouldn't hurt to let her oversee today's tests?"

The other doctor smiled—I was pretty sure for the first time since I'd worked there. He looked genuinely excited. "Yes, I think it would be brilliant to have a fresh pair of eyes on today's proceedings. We have procured a very interesting female candidate. I'm expecting great results today. You're very welcome to shadow, Lillian."

THE TEST TOOK place in the circular room placed in the center of the lab.

Inside was a donut-shaped room with glass panes facing the central room. Dr. Axell flicked the lights on behind the glass and revealed a sterile-white floor and ceiling, and what looked like a padded bench or narrow table. It was roughly hip-height, with four legs and a flat surface.

Nothing else was inside the room except a heavy steel door with a grid on the far side.

I sat down in the chair Dr. Axell indicated for mc, frowning at the empty room. "What's that piece of equipment for?"

He glanced at me, a little surprised. "You do know how alphas claim their mates, right?"

My frown deepened. "They give them a claiming mark. But why—?" My voice died when I recalled the circumstances in which such a mark was usually placed. "*Oh.*" Really wish I'd thought of that before I'd accepted the offer to shadow their work!

Flushed, I looked back at the room. This was for science—it was no more awkward than mixing bacteria in a test tube. "Ah, why not... give them a bed?"

Dr. Axell snorted. "We tried that. Once. It got destroyed during the first test. This is much more practical. And sturdy."

The steel door inside the test room clanked and was pulled open, and I frowned again at the state of the woman Dr. Urwin dragged in with him.

She was naked, which wasn't particularly shocking after being reminded of what was going to happen—but everything else about her, from her wild look to her unkempt appearance, made my breath catch.

Aside from her knotted hair and wild eyes, she was a pretty woman in her late twenties. She wailed hollowly as Dr. Urwin pulled her through the door and placed her face-down on the bench, but instead of struggling against him she arched her back and pushed her backside up and out, moaning pitifully.

"What's the matter with her?" I asked, a little

alarmed at the poor woman's seemingly complete lack of awareness.

"She's Presenting," Dr. Axell said, and I frowned at the small smirk on his face. It was gone before I could fully process it. "We treat the females with heat-inducing hormones now. In the beginning we didn't, and it was surprisingly difficult to get the male subjects to mount. They were too busy trying to break free to care much about whichever female we wanted them to bond with. This particular female has been kept in this state for five days, until she naturally ovulated. It is our hope that the extra allure of her enhanced scent will finally get us a completed mating claim."

Females. I knew he was simply using scientific terms for his test subjects, but the way that word depersonalized them bothered me. True, we called alphas males, but that woman in there was no different from any other of her gender. No different from me.

The snick of metal as steel cuffs slid out of the mating bench and locked around the woman's wrists pulled my attention to more pressing matters.

Dr. Urwin bent behind her, ignoring her attempts at enticing him to mount her, and spread her legs so her ankles could be secured in steel cuffs attached to the bench's sturdy legs. Moments later he joined Dr. Axell and I to observe, offering me a polite nod as if nothing was out of the ordinary here. Which I guess it wasn't, for them. They did this every day.

Something nagged at me, like a pesky gnat nibbling at the back of my conscience as I watched the hapless woman sob quietly into the bench she was bent over. It seemed so... so wrong. To put a human being through this much distress in the name of science.

I had to remind myself that she'd agreed to this to lower her prison sentence, and that in the end, this entire research study was for the protection of the country.

Loud bangs of flesh against metal and growls drowned out the woman's sobs. Both Dr. Urwin and Dr. Axell sat up straighter.

"Showtime," Dr. Axell mumbled just as the steel door burst open and the furious alpha's growl vibrated off the glass separating us from the two test subjects.

I recognized him the second my eyes landed on him. 351. The man, the *alpha*, I hadn't been able to get off my mind all weekend. Three burly guards wearing padded armor and masks to cover their noses shoved him into the room with metal poles attached to steel collars around his neck and arms. Once they'd shoved the naked alpha far enough into the room, they detached the poles with practiced expertise and slammed the door shut behind him.

The feral alpha turned around at the door faster than I'd thought humanly possible, but it was too late. His fist impacted with the door instead of the man who'd been pushing him in via the collar around his neck.

Snarling in fury, he drew his nails down the door as if they were claws. The sound cut through my brain and made me grit my teeth.

"Is it good to have him this agitated before the... the mating?" I gave the poor woman on the bench a pitying glance. If I'd been locked in a room with an alpha of 351's size and current fury level, I'd have wet myself from fear. I didn't know what she'd done to land herself in prison, but part of me hoped it had been truly terrible. The thought of someone having to go through what was in store for her due to too many parking tickets made my insides twist—even if she seemed to want it pretty badly.

"It helps—anger is such a primal response, it makes the transition to mating easier. Don't worry, once he catches a whiff of the female, he'll funnel all that aggression into something far more useful," Dr. Axell said. "351 has done this many times before. He knows the routine."

I don't know why that statement made my discomfort at the scene unfolding in front of us even greater, but it did. I frowned at the feral alpha as he paced in front of the door, the sound of his angry growl unwavering.

Despite Dr. Axell's reassurance, for the longest time 351 didn't seem to even notice the woman moaning pitiful pleas for him to mount her. He only paced and growled without taking his eyes off the door, like a tormented animal in a cage, for the better part of ten minutes.

"Well, this is unusual," Dr. Urwin finally said. "She's definitely giving off the right scent—we nearly had an incident with one of the guards on the way here."

"Maybe we just need to catch his attention by other means," Dr. Axell murmured. He leaned forward and pressed a button on the panel in front of his chair. A loud beep blared through the room, making me jump nearly a foot out of my chair.

On the other side of the glass, 351 whipped around, all his corded muscles tensing. But it had the desired effect—he finally seemed to notice the tied-up woman on the bench. His growl lessened a little, though it still remained a constant rumble as he circled her with a cautious look. When he walked around the other side of her so his front faced the windows, it was quite obvious his body was beginning to respond to her scent.

I paled at the sheer size of him, too gobsmacked to do the decent thing and avert my gaze. The intimidating pole of flesh between his thighs looked as thick around as a Pringles can, with maybe half the length. Wincing in sympathy with the trapped woman, I instinctively crossed my legs.

She, however, didn't seem to have any hesitations. Realizing she'd finally gained the alpha's attention, she lifted up her backside as much as her restraints would allow and emitted a keening sound that made Dr. Axell shift uncomfortably next to me. I glanced at him out of the corner of my eye and noticed the notepad covering his lap. Apparently even esteemed men of science weren't entirely above the laws of biology—at least not this close to a woman in heat.

But on the other side of the glass, 351 seemed to be hesitating. After circling the breeding stand twice, he pulled away and returned to the door to resume his pacing.

"What the—?" Dr. Axell pressed the button again, sending another blaring beep through the room. The feral alpha swung around and snarled at the window separating us from the room—and then froze, eyes locked on me.

"C-can he see us?" I asked, unable to take my eyes off the alpha on the other side of the glass as he slowly walked across the room, shoulders hunched in a defensive posture and that icy gaze not moving from mine. For some reason, a wave of guilt gnawed at my gut.

"Yes, they can see through the glass, but not hear us," Dr. Urwin said.

I don't know why I reached forward and put my hand on the glass—maybe it was an apology, though I didn't know why I felt so guilty. Maybe it was just to support myself from the woozy feeling rolling through my body from 351's unwavering stare.

The feral alpha came all the way up to the window —and placed his hand on the glass opposite mine.

"What on Earth is he doing?" Dr. Axell growled, irritation clear in his voice. He reached forward and hit the button again, sending a blaring beep into the air.

I jumped again at the unexpected sound—and 351 *snapped*.

I could see it in his eyes, the second that sound echoed through the room. They went pitch-black like a predator's, anything remotely human on his otherwise so handsome features disappearing in the blink of an eye. Fury so intense it made the blood freeze in my veins radiated off the huge alpha as he turned his attention toward Dr. Axell. And then he attacked.

The window vibrated as the wild alpha pounded on the glass with both fists, the strength in his coiled muscles unleashing blow after blow on the only barrier separating us from the feral beast.

The first crack in what I was sure was meant to be unbreakable glass made me shriek, and even Dr. Urwin began to look pretty worried.

"Dr. Axell, maybe we should..."

Dr. Axell nodded, irritation still clear on his features as he glared at the attacking alpha. The scent of alpha aggression rolled off him in waves, which didn't exactly help calm down my wildly beating heart. He leaned forward and pressed another button—a microphone.

"We need the heaviest dose of tranquilizer. And bring stun guns, just in case."

Only a few seconds later, the door behind 351 burst open. He turned around, ready to launch himself through the opening, but the newcomers were prepared. Two darts pierced his flesh before he could take a step toward them, one in his chest and one in his thigh. He wobbled, growling furiously as he fought against the tranquilizer, but it was no use. With a small whine he turned halfway, catching my eyes once more. In his gaze I saw fear and a sorrow so deep it made my heart clench.

Then his sea-colored eyes closed and he slid to the floor with a thud. Out cold.

I shook as I watched the armed men drag his unconscious body out of the room, fighting against the tears stinging my eyes.

As frightening as I'd found his fury, that look haunted me long after the heavy steel door closed, leaving only the sobbing woman tied to the breeding post behind.

FIVE

LILLIAN

"Here, I think we could all use a cup of coffee right about now."

I gave Dr. Urwin a grateful smile as he offered me a steaming mug. "Thank you."

The low sobbing from the woman still tied up on the other side of the windows made me look back at him and Dr. Axell. "Shouldn't she be untied?"

"That would be cruel." Dr. Axell clicked a couple of buttons on the control panel, but what they were supposed to do I couldn't tell—as far as I could see, nothing happened. "Her heat won't break before she's taken a knot, not at this stage. We will have to use another alpha subject to complete the test. A pity—we were hoping to have 351 pair-bonded by the end of the day."

"The experiment can still be repeated with a

different female, if proven successful with another male," Dr. Urwin pointed out. "May I suggest subject 287?"

"My thoughts exactly," Dr. Axell said as he leaned back in his chair. "He should be with us in a moment."

He was right. It hadn't been a minute before the steel door flew open and another snarling alpha was shoved into the room by long poles attached to metal rings around his neck and biceps. But instead of turning around to attack the men as soon as the poles were detached, like 351 had done, his wild gaze immediately zeroed in on the woman on the breeding bench. His nostrils flared as he scented the air, and a deep, rich growl sounding nothing like the fury he'd initially displayed emanated from his chest.

The woman on the bench keened loud and shrilly in response, bucking her hips what little she could.

The alpha was by her in a second, scenting her as he bent between her spread thighs.

I did my best to fight back the furious blush I could feel spreading over my entire face at the intimate display. A sentiment that was only strengthened when he—finding her more than ready—without delay mounted her and shoved his brutal cock up inside her dripping opening in one, smooth movement. All the way to the hilt.

The woman *screamed* and tried to both escape the invasion and spear herself deeper on his girth at the

same time. Her hands locked in steel manacles clawed
and clenched at air, but there was nothing she could do
one way or the other.

I'd never seen sex like that. I knew video clips and
images of alpha matings could be found on the inter-
net, but I'd never had the nerve to search for them.
And this... this was so much worse than seeing it on a
screen. Even though the thick glass panel separated us
from the pair, knowing that they knew we were
watching them made the heat in my cheeks flame all
the hotter. Every thrust made me clench my hands
around the edge of my seat, wishing I was anywhere
but here. The woman's cries and screams rang loud
and shrill, and I winced in sympathy at the way her
brutalized sex clung to the alpha's impossible girth. He
wasn't as huge as 351, but plenty big enough to make
my pelvis clench for every wet *thwack* of his flesh
against hers.

It lasted for nearly twenty agonizing minutes.

I'd somehow managed to almost regain my professional composure when the poor woman's hoarse cries
suddenly took on a different tone. She'd long-since given
up struggling, but without warning she let out a stran-
gled yelp and tried to lurch forward. The restraints and
the alpha's hands on her hips kept her securely locked in
placc, but that didn't stop her frantic struggling nor her
desperate whimpers.

"What's happening?" I asked, my worry for the

woman strapped into the breeding post returning with renewed vigor. "Is he hurting her?"

"He's about to knot her. A female will always struggle a bit, especially with a new alpha. Once he's popped it inside is when he'll hopefully put a claiming mark on her." Dr. Axell didn't look to my side, so I couldn't decipher his expression, but I very much hoped the unmistakable excitement in his voice was purely from a scientific standpoint.

Of course. The knot. I don't know why I hadn't been expecting it—it was an unavoidable fact of alpha matings—the fist-sized swelling at the bottom of an alpha's member that inflated at the end of a mating to increase the chance of fertilization. It was an entirely different thing to learn about such matters from a textbook than it was to see it in person. Part of me wanted to look away, but morbid curiosity kept me staring at the pair as the alpha's knot finally swelled enough to make a tie.

The final, brutal thrust into the woman's body was marked by a bloodcurdling howl from her, and a deep groan of pleasure from him. They both stilled—the woman still panting and sobbing while her body twitched as if in cramps, the alpha moaning in release.

We all stared at him with bated breaths, waiting for the moment he'd lay claim to the woman he'd just fucked for all she was worth, but apart from occasionally rocking his pelvis a little and making her jerk and whimper, he didn't move. In fact, for someone who was still intimately connected to said woman, he seemed remarkably uninterested in her, now he'd spilled his seed.

"Sonuvabitch," Dr. Axell growled next to me. "How is he not claiming her? She's fucking ripe as a peach!"

I blinked, not expecting that kind of language from a man with Dr. Axell's academic achievements. He seemed to remember himself and cleared his throat. "Right. Well, I must apologize that we didn't manage to show you the next step of the research. Clearly we're still missing a key factor in making these alphas bond with the females we offer them. We will have to run some tests on her pheromone levels and perhaps look for more precise chemical markers.

"But before we get that far, I'd be interested in your observations of this experiment. Your analytical skills are without question."

I bit the inside of my cheek. It was what I'd always wanted—to be asked to contribute to the scientific method of a significant research study, but... the fact that they'd missed something that seemed so obvious to me made me kind of hesitant. "Well... I mean, aren't pair bonds meant to be... very special? I've always heard how an alpha simply knows when his intended mate is near. It seems to me you're trying to force a bond without taking into consideration what the subjects might want. Perhaps this is one thing nature never intended for us to replicate in a lab."

Dr. Urwin scoffed. "My dear girl, an alpha's urge to claim a mate is a purely biological response, nothing more. As such, all we need to reach our goal is to find the right triggers."

I blinked, taken aback by the patronizing tone. But when I looked at Dr. Axell, expecting him to put his colleague in place, all I got from him was a small head shake and a wry smile. "I do think you've watched one too many romantic movies, Miss Dorne. Trust me— alpha instincts have nothing to do with love. They're about possession, desire... procreation. A feral alpha will not be able to even play pretend when it comes to claiming a female."

I dug my nails into my palms to force myself to return his gaze. There was something... different in it. As if there was just a glimmer of someone else behind his professional mask—someone who spoke about alpha instincts so confidently because perhaps, deep down, he also felt them. The thought made my stomach lurch, and I gave in to the instincts at the back of my conscious- ness murmuring about the dangers of provoking an alpha. I dropped my eyes and felt my shoulders slump forward without my conscious choice, displaying subservient body language even as my mind still seethed with the rude dismissal.

Dr. Axell patted my knee with a large hand, lingering for just a second before he pulled it back—but it was long enough for every muscle in my body to freeze.

He'd reacted to my body language like an alpha would —giving me silent praise for falling in line with a touch. It was so inappropriate and so far from anything I could ever have expected from a man with Dr. Axell's reputation. I stared mutely at my now hand-free knee, halfway expecting an apology. Hoping for it with all I was.

It never came.

Seemingly happy with my submission, Dr. Axell turned to Dr. Urwin and began discussing parameters for a new line of tests as if I wasn't even there.

I sat for a moment longer until the stinging in my eyes became too much to bear. Silently, I left the room and walked back to my empty work station.

It was silly to cry, I knew that, but no matter how many times I told myself that, I couldn't will the tears away. Dr. Axell had been my idol for so many years. Working for him had been a lifelong dream of mine, and yet in the end.... In the end, he was just like the rest of them. An alpha. A ruthless man who sought to bend anyone who disagreed with him to his will.

And in my eagerness to please him, I'd pushed my own ethical objections to his methods aside, trusting that he knew best. I'd been so damn stupid. How had *I,* of all people, let an alpha's charm and dominance pull the wool over my eyes?

Christ, I'd... I'd watched a woman get violated right in front of me, and I'd done nothing to stop it.

I'D NOT BEEN DOWN in the section of the underground lab where the female subjects were kept. Most of my analysis was of the males' data, and so there hadn't been any reason to venture into that area.

There probably wasn't any reason to tonight, either, I told myself as I walked along the empty corridors long after everyone else had gone home for the night. But despite the urge to turn around, go back to my work station, and—ideally—forget all about what I'd witnessed earlier today, I kept walking.

I needed to see that she was all right before I'd be able to sleep tonight for the guilt gnawing at my gut.

The female subjects were kept in a long cell block on the eastern side of the facility. They were locked in individual cells along a narrow hallway, but unlike the males, they weren't separated from each other by thick concrete walls. They each had an area that was shielded from their fellow inmates, where a mattress and restroom facilities were located, but the rest of each small cell was only separated from their immediate neighbors by bars.

I found the female subject—A642, as the paperwork attached to the cell door revealed—curled up on her mattress, which had been dragged over to the bars between her cell and her neighbor to the left. The woman on the other side of the bars was stroking her still-messy hair and mumbling soothingly. She quieted when I stopped in front of the cell, shooting me a disgusted look.

"Is she all right?" I asked when A642 didn't so much as move to acknowledge my presence.

"What do you care?" her neighbor spat.

I opened my mouth, but nothing came out. What did I care—beyond making myself feel better? If she was okay—which so far not much pointed toward—then what? Could I really just be on my merry way, content in the knowledge that what I'd witnessed would happen to all of these women?

"I brought this," I said, holding out a pack of ice wrapped in a towel. "For the..." No delicate way of saying it. "The swelling."

A642's neighbor begrudgingly accepted the offering. Once in her hand, she nudged gently at the curled-up woman. "Hey. Gloria. Take this. It's for your pussy. It'll make it feel better."

I fought back a blush at the inmate's candid language. We were so far past embarrassment over frank word choices.

I sat down on the concrete floor by the separation between the two women's cells as Gloria sluggishly pushed the ice pack between her legs before curling back up again. But this time, she was looking at me from underneath her tangled hair.

Her dark eyes were red from crying, and I couldn't blame her for the accusation I saw burning behind the dull look of despair.

"I saw you there. You are one of *them*," she said, her voice not much more than a hoarse croak. "What do you want?"

"I... came to see how you were doing," I said.

"How do you think I'm doing?" she spat. "How would you feel after being locked up and forced into heat for five days with no release? Or after having some feral beast of a man mate you like a bitch? You people are monsters."

"I thought you volunteered for this study," I said. Even to my own ears, it sounded like the worst attempt at excusing what was inexcusable.

Gloria muttered something in Spanish and didn't answer.

"We do," her neighbor said. "We were told we can knock up to ten years off our sentence if we participate in this study. Let an alpha fuck us now and then— maybe even meet a nice one who'll provide for us once we're released. They never said what they'd be like. They never said what they did to them." She visibly shuddered and pulled her legs up so she could curl in on herself. "They treat us like we're nothing more than lab rats. *You* treat us like lab rats."

I couldn't blame her. I was pretty sure if I'd been tied up at that breeding post and at the mercy of one of the feral alphas, I'd want to curl up and hide, too.

"I didn't know," I said, hating myself for sounding like such a sad apologist. "Today was... it was the first time I saw what... what happens here."

"You're new," Gloria said dully. "You'll get used to it, or you'll disappear."

"I won't." I shook my head, determination welling up in my chest. "I'll go to the press, if I have to."

The neighbor woman snorted. "The press? You think anyone gives a shit about criminals being treated like breeding stock? This isn't Mattenburg. No one cares."

"I care," I said, wrapping my fingers around the bars separating me from the two women inside. "I'll help you. This isn't right."

Gloria shook her head. "Don't. No one here will take your help. The alternative is being sent back to prison, and believe me—it's not better than here."

"Really?" I blinked. It wasn't that the prison system had the best reputation, but I'd kind of assumed it would beat being hauled in to mate with feral alphas whenever the doctors saw fit.

Gloria's neighbor shrugged. "At least there's always enough food. And for ten years, I'll take a lot of knots. Even if it's in front of Dr. Pervert and his team. If anyone would take your help, it'd be the alphas."

"They have even more to lose," I said, dropping my gaze when 351's haunting eyes flickered before my mind's eye. "If I intervene, they'll go back on death row."

The woman shrugged before returning her attention to Gloria. "Seems to me they're already dead. Nothing human left in them, anyway. If it were me, I'd rather the needle."

SIX

LILLIAN

Some of the alphas were sleeping when I entered the lab, but my footfalls as I passed their cages woke them. The sound of shifting bodies followed me as they raised their heads to follow, a wariness in their eyes that spoke of broken humanity.

From what the women had seen of them, I could understand why they'd think there was nothing remotely human left in these men. They were little more than savages during the day, when the drugs they were given were at their most potent. But later...

I remembered 351's gravelly voice as he rasped out the word *key*.

They were still human, behind the serum. And though they belonged on death row, it didn't mean they should be treated like animals. The women might see this facility as the lesser of two evils, as much as they hated it, but the alphas might not. Even if death was their only alternative, maybe some of them would still rather die with dignity than be forced to act like mindless beasts.

That was the mantra I kept repeating in my head over and over as I walked to the very last cage. As much as being around these men set every instinct in my body on edge, I still had a professional duty to ensure their humane treatment.

351 didn't move when I stopped in front of his cell, but I could feel his eyes on me from the shadows by the far wall.

"Hey," I whispered. "It's... it's me." I don't know why I thought adding that in would do any good, but I didn't know what else to say. How *did* you break the ice with a feral alpha you'd so far only met under less than ideal circumstances?

Movement from within made me bite my lip, but the knot of tension in my stomach turned to icy horror when the alpha came to the front of the cage and I could finally see his face.

His lip was split and there was a gash of dried blood across one prominent cheekbone. Bruises marred his strong body, visible even in the low light, and when he wrapped his hands around the bars, I could see scrapes along his knuckles.

"What happened to you?" I gasped, too horrified to remember to keep a safe amount of space between myself and the bars. I closed the distance to the cell to gently trace the wounds on his hands. They looked defensive.

The alpha didn't respond, but when I reached up to inspect the damage to his face, he closed his eyes and pressed his head against the bars, giving me easier access.

Someone had beaten him. I didn't know if they'd let another test subject at him or if the guards had hurt him, but the truth was too obvious to ignore. They'd done this to punish him for his unwillingness to cooperate in the breeding room.

"They're monsters."

It was only when he opened those piercing blue-green eyes to look at me I realized I'd spoken out loud.

"I'm so sorry."

351 unwrapped his hand from the bars and reached out toward me. I flinched on instinct, but he only stroked his abused fingers clumsily over my arm. Trying to comfort *me*.

I set my jaw as I looked at him, grim determination settling in deep in my gut. "I'll be back in a bit."

The good thing about working in a lab as well-stocked as this was that finding rubbing alcohol and oint-ments was a breeze. I was back at 351's cell within five minutes, arms full of medical supplies, and saw him waiting for me by the bars.

"Sit with me," I said as I sank down to the floor in

front of his cell, scooting close enough to reach him with ease.

He obeyed slowly, eying the bottles I'd brought with caution.

"It's to clean your wounds," I explained, trying to ignore the twinge in my chest when I realized why he was so wary of a woman in a lab coat bringing medical supplies to his cage. "Rubbing alcohol and some ointment for your bruises, nothing else." I held up the two containers for him to see.

He still didn't look entirely trusting of the bottles, but when I poured some of the alcohol on a piece of cotton, he let me dab it on his skin. It had to have hurt, but he didn't so much as flinch as I cleaned every laceration I could see. When I was done with his face and the scrapes on his knuckles, I placed the used piece of cotton in the discarded pile next to the ointment. "Do you have any more cuts or scrapes? Or can we continue with the bruises?"

He was still for a moment, staring at me with obvious hesitance. But after a few moments, he twisted around, turning his back to me. His heavy muscles flexed and bulged, tensed and ready for violence, but he still turned. For a short moment I didn't know if I was more shocked or awed that he trusted me enough to have his back turned to me... but then I saw them.

Several long, red gashes of broken skin marred the

middle of his back. Tell-tale wounds from a lash. He'd been whipped. Brutally.

"Who did this?" The anger in my voice manifested in my hands as well. I had to take several deep breaths before I could steady them enough to apply the rubbing alcohol to the deep lacerations.

He still didn't move under my careful touches, but I could feel the tension in his hard muscles as I gently brushed my free hand against his unbroken skin. I didn't think about it—it was an instinctual urge to soothe the pain laid bare in front of me, despite his silent endurance. His skin was warm and surprisingly soft underneath my fingers. I kept them there while I dabbed cleaning solution in his deep lash marks, mumbling soothingly when his muscles twinged with the pain. It took far too long to clean them all, shaking as my hands were, but he sat patiently through it until I finally put the bottle of rubbing alcohol down.

"If you turn back around, I'll take care of the bruises," I said, my voice hoarse with barely restrained emotion. The tears that had been threatening to escape ever since I saw his damaged back stung in my eyes. I wasn't sure why seeing the alpha like this hurt so much. The shock of realizing exactly how ruthless Dr. Axell truly was was a shock, but this... it felt so... personal, somehow. Like *I* was the one he'd had beaten, not a criminal alpha on death row.

351 turned around to face me once more, and the

look in his eyes made me lower mine as something warm and confusing pressed against the inside of my chest. There was so much tenderness in his blue-green gaze. It felt... so intimate, like he... *knew* me somehow.

Fumbling, I reached for the lotion meant for bruises. It was ridiculous, of course. I may have empathy for what had happened to him, perhaps even on a personal level and not just professional, but there was no reason to start reading anything more into it. And this man... He was deep in his instincts. Of course he would see a young woman caring for his wounds as an intimate gesture and react appropriately. It didn't mean *I* had any excuse to lose my damn mind. I had a job to do.

Biting the inside of my cheek to steel myself, I looked back up at him, focusing on his bruises instead of the look in his eyes as I poured lotion on a fresh piece of cotton and reached in through the bars to dab it on his discolored skin.

It was a quicker job than caring for his scrapes and cuts, and I breathed a quiet sigh of relief when I could finally put the used bit of cotton in the discarded pile with the others and screw the lid back on the bottle of lotion. But before I could stand up, the feral alpha reached a hand through the bars—slowly, as to not startle me—and brushed his warm, scraped fingers against my cheek.

"Thank you." His voice was rough, and the hesitant

way his soft lips formed around the words spoke of how infrequently he used it.

I couldn't help the rush of warmth and pity and anger that coursed through my veins as I felt his gentle caress and looked back up at him. I could *see* him—the man behind the feral beast, struggling to break through the haze from the chemicals they'd given him. His lips parted, to say more I realized, but he couldn't find the words. Frustrated, he growled and pulled his hand from my face, clenching it around one of the bars.

That's when I knew, with unequivocal certainty, that I had to save him, no matter the cost.

SEVEN

LILLIAN

It was four days before the handheld RFID copier I'd ordered off eBay was delivered to my home address, but it gave me enough time to prepare my plan.

It was simple, in the end. I'd bought clothes and a lab coat in a size I thought would fit a man of 351's stature and kept them in my locker at work. The security team was used to me leaving late and didn't give me any second glances. As long as the feral alpha could pass for just another researcher who happened to leave at the same time as me, he could be swiped out on my card and hopefully shouldn't draw any attention.

The only pinch point was in getting him out of his cell. That's where the RFID copier came in play.

I spent the day after my eBay delivery trailing after Dr. Urwin and Dr. Axell—the only two people on our team I was sure had access to the cells. Just before lunch

I saw Dr. Urwin put down his card by the coffeemaker while he had his lunch at the break room table along with Dr. Axell, Dr. Miller, and Kenneth, the main lab assistant.

My heart rate spiked at the sight of the unguarded card, and I covertly glanced over my shoulder to make sure no one was looking this way. Thankfully, they were all deeply engrossed in conversation about what sounded like the potential to control the alpha who'd mounted the woman in front of me earlier in the week if she conceived his child.

I suppressed a shudder at the thought of using an innocent baby like that and turned my attention back to the card.

Careful to keep my body between the men at the table and the coffee counter, I slipped my card copier out of my handbag and snatched the card up under the guise of grabbing a mug.

The process took less than two seconds. Very anti-climactic. Which didn't stop me from elbowing the coffeepot and sending it flying to the floor with a loud bang when Dr. Urwin said, "Miss Dorne?"

"Oh, goddammit!" I groaned. Thankfully the pot didn't shatter. "Sorry! Having a clumsy day here." I shot the table my best *"frazzled female"* smile and bent for the pot.

"Happens to us all," Dr. Urwin chuckled. "You all right?"

"Uh-huh." I picked up the coffee pot and gave it a little shake. "And so's our friend here. Can't have a research team with no caffeine supply."

"True," Dr. Urwin said, a wide grin on his lips. "Once you've gotten your food and coffee, come over. We're discussing a potential new plan for our alpha problem and would love your input. I reckon a naturally produced child will bind an alpha almost as tightly as a mate, but Dr. Axell says otherwise."

THE ONLY THING the discussion about whether or not using a child against one of the imprisoned alphas did was strengthen my resolve to get 351 out as soon as possible. It was my hope that, once he was out, I would be able to somehow use his testimony to uncover what horrors SilverCorp committed in the government's name. If he ever regained his full humanity again.

I knew he was able to speak a few words at night, when the drug they used on the alphas wore off a little, but I had no way of knowing the long-term effects. It seemed Dr. Axell and his team hadn't been too bothered, seeing as all their male test subjects were on death row anyway.

Hopefully 351 would be able to find enough words to help me convince one of the big news networks to spread the word of the abuse going on in this lab.

It seemed like forever before the clock on my computer finally showed five o'clock, marking the time where most of the team went home. I waited two hours longer before I grabbed my clipboard and a pen and started down the hallway. Under the guise of needing to check up on numbers, I walked through the entire ground floor of the facility, ensuring no one was there except me, the locked up women, and the alphas.

Thankfully, it seemed no one else had decided to work overtime today. If I wanted to break 351 out, now was the time.

With my heart pounding in my throat, I hurried to my locker and got the bag of men's clothing out. I double checked my newly made copy of David's swipe card was safe in my handbag, took a deep breath—and made my way back to the lab.

The alphas looked up at my arrival, a couple of them getting to their feet to pace, but most of them ignored me after they saw who I was. Clearly, after I'd been down here enough times that they'd gotten used to my scent, they'd all written me off as a non-threat.

351, however, got to his feet and walked to the front of his cell when he saw me, a pleased look on his handsome face.

"Hey," I said as I stopped in front of his cage.

He didn't answer, but he did reach one hand out between the bars, palm up. A clear encouragement for me to put my hand in his.

I bit my lip, fighting back the flush of heat in my cheeks at the gesture. I wasn't entirely sure if he was just being friendly, or if me tending to him earlier in the week had given him some unfortunate ideas about my intentions.

It took everything I had not to glance down his naked body as I placed the bag of clothes in his outstretched hand rather than my own palm. "Here. Put this on."

He didn't move, staring at me rather than the bag in his hand.

"It's clothes," I explained, trying to fight back the adrenaline threatening to take over my nervous system. "Please, put it on. Quickly. You remember how, right?"

Those piercing green-blue eyes flickered from me to the bag. Slowly, he pulled it in through the bars and opened it.

"We have to hurry," I said, even though no one would be down here until morning. But I wanted to get out of there as quickly as humanly possible, before my heart exploded from stress. The sooner I had Silver-Corp's facility in my rearview mirror, the sooner I could breathe again.

"Lab coat last," I said as 351 pulled out the contents of the bag. "Pants first." I hadn't bothered with under-wear or socks, deeming them unnecessary hindrances to a quick escape. If 351 cared or even noticed, he didn't show it. Fumbling a bit, he managed to pull the gray pants on, even doing up the zipper and the button, though the shirt seemed to cause him more problems.

"Come here," I said when it became obvious he had very little care for which button was meant to go in which button hole.

The alpha obeyed, and I reached through the bars to undo the crooked buttons and then slip them through the right holes. My fingers skimmed over his warm chest as I worked, and he made a humming noise deep in his throat in response that had my cheeks flushing again. I was suddenly aware of how near he was, despite the bars separating us. Close enough that I could smell his alpha scent. It wasn't unpleasant, somewhat to my surprise. I'd always found the smell of alpha unsettling, my biology reacting to the primal notes of dominance without my consent.

But on 351, it was oddly comforting to my frayed nerves. I inhaled a little deeper, breathing in the calming scent of him to steady my racing heart.

The feral alpha's humming noise turned deeper as he leaned his head closer to the bars until it was right above mine, and then he drew in a deep breath through his nose.

Scenting me.

I flew back from the bars, eyes wide. "Don't you even think about it!"

He gave me a puzzled look, and I bit the inside of my cheek to force my focus back on what was important.

He couldn't help it—he was a feral alpha, and from his point of view, I was just a female trying to get close to him. It wasn't odd that he would... scent me.

Even if such behavior was appallingly crude in civilized society.

Scenting a female was basically how alphas used to check if she was ready to mate. No civilized alpha would be so obvious about his instincts these days, though. We were all *supposed* to respect privacy and verbal consent, but as I looked at the feral alpha who'd only followed his basic instincts, I couldn't help but wonder how many of the supposed civilized alphas just pretended they didn't do the same. How good was their control over their instincts, when it came down to it?

With an effort of will, I pushed the thoughts from my mind. Right now was really not the time to contemplate such issues.

"Put your shoes on," I snapped at the alpha, and got a warning growl in return. *Right.* He didn't like getting bossed around. "Please."

His eyes narrowed as he watched me, without making any attempt at the shoes. Some of the softness in his gaze had disappeared, replaced by caution.

"I'm breaking you out of here," I said, unable to control the urgency I felt from penetrating my voice. I fumbled in my bag for the key card and held it up. "I got a key that works. But we have to hurry."

The change that came over him made my breath

hitch in my throat. The same alpha who'd pulled me against the bars of his cell hard enough to leave bruises in order to get at my key card was back, and it wasn't until I saw the cold, hard calculation in his icy gaze that I fully realized how different he'd been around me since that day. All of a sudden, the thought of actually letting this three-hundred-pound feral man out seemed a lot less appealing.

But I'd already committed to this.

Taking a deep breath, I motioned at the shoes once more before I reached out and swiped my new card over the lock.

It beeped, flashing green, and a mechanic clink rung through the air between us.

He pushed the door open in the blink of an eye, and I only barely managed to stumble back and out of harm's way from his huge bulk of muscle as he stepped out of the cell and into the lab, eyes glued to the far exit. Clearly locked on his target, he started toward it.

"Wait!" I grabbed his arm.

The alpha stopped abruptly, and I could feel every muscle in his body tense underneath my palm in response to my touch. He whipped around, and I staggered back and quickly removed my hand from him again, sure I was about to feel the impact of those bulging muscles straining against the cheap shirt I'd bought for him. But he only stared at me.

"Y-you can't just storm up there. There are guards.

Armed guards. Please, put on the shoes and lab coat and just follow me. Quietly." I pointed back at the discarded shoes and white clothes in his cell, doing my best not to show him the burst of anxiety his nearness caused me. Having solid steel bars between us had been a pretty good safety net. "I'll help you, but you have to trust me. Okay?"

351 made a low growling noise, but to my relief he returned to his cell, shoved his large feet into the shoes, and pulled the lab coat on.

The transformation from wild alpha to smoking-hot doctor look-alike was pretty damn convincing.

The errant thought made me blink, my cheeks heating slightly, but I forced it away as quickly as it'd reared its disturbing head. Now was definitely not the time for inappropriate fantasies about the man I was trying to save.

"Come. Stay by my side—and keep quiet," I said, squaring my shoulders as I started toward the exit.

The alpha followed me—or rather, he walked beside me, but just a half-step ahead. *Typical alpha—incapable of letting someone else take the lead.* I shot his shoulder an annoyed glare, but at least he wasn't storming ahead like I'd halfway feared.

The other alphas were much more alert this time— they all got to their feet and stared after us, hands wrapped around the bars to their cells, but didn't make a sound. Instead they formed a silent guard, as if they knew their own fates depended on the outcome of our escape.

They might have been murderers, locked away on death row for their crimes before they were shipped to this facility, but my heart still twanged uncomfortably at leaving them behind. No one, not even the most dangerous of prisoners, deserved to have their voice taken away and their bodies beaten bloody if they stood up to their abusers. And these men... whatever they'd been before, they weren't that anymore. Dr. Axell and his team had made sure there was nothing left of what had made them human.

But 351's compliance only lasted until we reached the stairs. With a low grunt, he put a large hand on my shoulder, stopping me from ascending the steps. Then, without a care for my startled protests, he took them two at a time and smacked his hand against the door's release button.

"No, wait!" I called, flashes of his hulking form leaping through the hallways and bursting out into the reception area like a wild beast playing through my mind in rapid-fire bursts. "You have to wait f—"

My voiced died when the door swung open—and the alpha immediately sunk into a defensive crouch, his lips pulling back in a furious snarl. But before he could leap forward, three *thuck thuck thucks* whistled through the air. I stared, wide-eyed at the three black-feathered darts sticking out from his chest. My heart pounded in my throat, realization setting in even as my conscious mind tried to deny it. *No, no, no!*

351 roared in absolute fury and staggered forward, intent on taking down whoever had shot him, but whatever they'd injected him with was obviously fast-working. He only managed two steps before he sunk to the ground in a heap.

"No!" I cried out. The Goliath of a man twitched once before he went still, his eyelids sliding shut. I sprinted up the stairs, not thinking about the danger, and threw myself down by his side. I frantically pulled the darts from his chest. *Oh, God, what did they inject him with?*

"Well, well, well," a familiar voice sneered from the doorway. "I can't say I'm surprised, but it is still a disappointment."

I looked up from the unmoving alpha to the doorway. Dr. Axell stood in the middle of it, flanked by armed guards, and behind them I could just make out Dr. Urwin's features.

"You had such potential," he continued before he turned to the guards with a dramatic sigh. "Take him away."

"What did you do to him?" I spat.

"Relax, sweetheart. He's just knocked out. He's much too valuable to kill, even though he's sorely testing my patience these days." His cool eyes narrowed as they returned to me. "*You,* however... I can't say I'm not disappointed I'll lose such a fine data analyst, but you *are* replaceable."

I swallowed thickly and steeled myself as the guards came forward to hoist the passed-out alpha up. He was so big, it took all three of them to carry him off.

As much as my heart ached for the feral alpha and the fate that awaited him, I had to focus on my own situation now. I'd known there was a very real risk involved in trying to break one of Dr. Axell's test subjects free— and now I had to face it.

"Are you going to kill me, then?" I asked with far more bravery than I felt. On the inside, my heart felt like it was trying to escape through my throat and my stomach was a hollow pit.

Dr. Urwin scoffed. "Hardly. We'll hand you over to the authorities. You tried to sabotage a project funded by the Ministry of Defense."

"Of course, death might be preferable to being tried for treason," Dr. Axell mused. "But maybe they'll go easier on a dumb female who thinks with her ovaries."

I blanched. Somehow, while I'd prepared my plan, I'd never thought of what would happen to me if they handed me over to the authorities. I'd thought they might kill me, or—best-case scenario—I'd get turned over to the police and I'd end up with a petty charge and a ruined career. But in between those two extremes, I'd not considered the ties to the Ministry of Defense.

Yes, they would undoubtedly try me for treason.

"Please. Don't. J-just kill me if you have to. But don't... They'll send me to Ezban." It wasn't that I wanted to die—not by a long shot. But... there were worse fates than death. Being labeled a traitor to your country was definitely one of them.

"If you didn't want to go to Ezban, you shouldn't have let your bleeding heart get in the way of a fucking government-stamped research project, should you?" Dr. Axell snarled. "Fucking women. We let you into the sciences, and this is the reward we get. It's going to take us *weeks* to get 351 back in line now, all because of what? He makes your pussy tingle, is that it?"

"You torture them!" I snapped. "He disobeyed you, and you beat him bloody. You've taken their voices, their humanity! It's not right, and you know it."

"Their *humanity,*" he sneered. "They were hardly human to begin with. Do you know what 351 did? He murdered his commanding officer while out on assignment in the desert. He's a war criminal, and *you* tried to release him into the public. That one?" He pointed at the nearest caged alpha, who bared his teeth at the doctor. "Raped and killed five children below the age of twelve before they caught him. Trust me, they deserve every damn thing coming their way. And so do you. Now *get up.*"

The world seemed to twist below me, centering on the black pit in my stomach as my indignant anger at what they'd done to these men faded to the background.

Imminent fear for my own life set in instead. The few stories that ever made it out of Ezban made it very obvious that any other fate was better than being sent there. The nation had no concern for the wellbeing of traitors and war criminals. Anyone with even a shred of sanity would choose death over what awaited them there. "Please, don't turn me in. There has to be another way."

"I don't think so. You tried to ruin my research after I let you onto my team—I have no pity for you." Dr. Axell said, disdain clear in his voice. But when he stepped forward to grab me, Dr. Urwin raised his hand.

"Hang on a moment."

Dr. Axell turned to his colleague, eyebrows raised in question.

"You saw how 351 acted around her on the video surveillance," the beta male said as he gave me a coldly calculating look. "He seems interested in her. Perhaps, if Miss Dorne is certain she would rather find another solution to this predicament she's put us in, she would be willing to test out the theory she suggested during the mating trial she overlooked."

I blinked, my brain taking a few moments to zero in on what he was referring to. Then I remembered my thoughts on them trying to force a mating bond. "You're kidding? You think he'd claim *me?*"

Dr. Urwin shrugged. "Perhaps. Perhaps not. I'd be curious enough to test it out to perhaps overlook your transgressions, seeing as no other female has had any non-sexual, positive reaction from 351 yet."

"Hm, that is a good point," Dr. Axell conceded. "It would at least be worth a trial, now that the opportunity has presented itself." He looked down at me. "But of course, if you don't want to..."

"No, I'll..." I swallowed thickly and forced the images of Gloria tied to the breeding post out of my mind. Whatever happened in that room, it would be better than going to Ezban. "I'll do it."

EIGHT

LILLIAN

"We had another female employee in the early stages of the project," Dr. Urwin said when I handed him the signed contract allowing SilverCorp full discretion over my body for the next year. It stipulated that I was to allow matings with alphas of the research team's choosing, and that I agreed to not hold SilverCorp or its agents responsible for any and all bodily harm that may occur under their care.

Despite its content, I didn't hesitate to sign it. Not even when I read the part where a "successful bonding" meant the contract would be extended indefinitely.

"She also got swept up in her feminine emotions and tried to smuggle pictures of what goes on here out to the press," Dr. Urwin continued as he looked over my signature. "It was before we had an easy supply of female inmates for our alphas, so we struck a similar bargain with her—her cunt in return for not turning her in to the feds. I must say, it is a disappointment to see an educated mind lose all sense of reasoning to irrational emotions. It makes it hard to argue against the alphas who suggest your gender belongs at home, barefoot and pregnant.

"And then you go and prove them right *again,* after Dr. Axell hired you against his better judgement not to take on any more females for this project. I guess he was right—no amount of accolades can make up for the softness between your legs. He's been watching you, you know. The security cameras in 351's cell captured all your sweet little moments with him. When we saw you tending to him after his failed mating, we knew it was only a matter of time before you betrayed SilverCorp."

"What happened to her? The other woman?" I asked. Taking his bait wouldn't help me now.

"Oh, it was very unfortunate." Dr. Urwin motioned with one arm for me to walk out of his small office. I obeyed, following his directions down the narrow corridor until we came to another locked steel door. "It was before we began forcing heats on our female subjects, or tying them down. So instead of submitting to her first alpha, she tried to fight him off. Stupid woman. He predictably went into a rage and killed her before we could intervene." He gave me a small smile devoid of emotion as he swiped his access card over the lock and pushed the door open. "But you have nothing to worry about. We have had no fatalities since we implemented the heat treatments."

I blanched as he stepped aside to allow me into the room, and I finally saw what was inside. It was a small room, clad in tiles and white paint, with a fluorescent light flickering in the ceiling. And by the far wall stood a narrow, padded examination bench with leather restraints attached.

Dr. Urwin scoffed at my obvious horror. "Don't give me that look. They're to keep you from hurting yourself once the drugs set in. We're not barbarians."

I arched an eyebrow at him, but if he even saw the irony, he ignored it. Apparently, in his mind, violating a tied-down woman yourself versus letting a feral alpha do it was entirely different.

He sat down by a small desk I hadn't even noticed, seeing how the bench and restraints took up my whole focus, and rummaged through a drawer for some paperwork. "Please take off your lab coat and roll up your right sleeve before you lie down," he said as he began making notes on the form he'd procured. "I'll be with you in a moment."

I took a deep breath, steadying my thudding heartbeat before I walked over to the bench and shrugged out of my lab coat. There something poetically final about seeing the white fabric pooling on the floor —almost like a metaphor for how I'd thrown away my life to help the alpha who'd made my conscience resurface. I wasn't a scientist anymore. I was a test subject.

But at least I'd done everything I could to help. No matter what happened to me during the next year, I knew I could live with myself once they finally released me. If I hadn't tried to save him, I would never have been able to look myself in the mirror again.

Even if he was a war criminal.

At least I knew there was no chance he or any other alpha they'd make me mate with would claim me. It was just one year, and then I'd be free. And who knew, maybe if I was smart enough, I'd somehow be able to gather enough evidence during my time as a test subject to take them down once I was out.

Once I was lying stiffly on the bench, Dr. Urwin rolled on his chair across the concrete floor to my head. In his now gloved hand was a syringe containing a yellow liquid.

"I'm going to inject you with a heat trigger now. Depending on how your body reacts, in one to four hours you will begin to sweat and you will experience vaginal and uterine cramping, as your body begins to prepare for mounting. Most females will continue on to the next stage on their own at this point, but some require further stimulation. If that is the case for you, I will provide you with alpha-scented cloth. The next stage is marked by a flush of slickness from your vaginal opening, and often aggressive behavior if a mounting isn't imminent.

"This is also the stage when I will restrain you, to keep you from causing harm to yourself or others. You may or may not feel the need to start nesting, but since this is a clinical procedure, we unfortunately cannot allow our subjects to engage in such urges. Needless to say, you will be very aggressively searching for an appropriate mate at this point. Because 351 will be incapacitated for at least the next six to eight hours, regrettably this stage will be prolonged.

"Once he is deemed ready to complete a mating, I will lead you to the breeding room and the trial will commence." Dr. Urwin reached for my upper arm, quickly wiping it with rubbing alcohol, and then jabbed the needle into my skin.

I gritted my teeth to not flinch away, but he clearly had a lot of practice. He'd pressed the plunger down and removed the needle before I'd even fully processed everything he'd explained.

"Nesting?" I asked. It was the only part of a woman's biological response to her chosen alpha I wasn't at least somewhat familiar with. It wasn't a subject I'd studied in great depth, but there had been a class or two back in my early days of college about what happened if a woman Presented to an alpha. Of course, I certainly hadn't had any classes about *forcing* a woman into heat. It wasn't exactly something polite people discussed.

"Some women get the urge to prepare a space for the offspring her body assumes will be produced after tying with her alpha during a heat. Some don't. We haven't seen it much here—the circumstances aren't exactly ideal, you might say. Mostly it happens for a Presenting woman if she is already in the comfort of her own home, with an alpha she has established an intimate relationship with beforehand." Dr. Urwin rolled his chair back over to his desk, his gaze already on the papers there. "May I suggest you try to relax until the drugs kick in? You won't get the opportunity again for a while."

I LAY on the padded bench for the better part of two hours, staring at the ceiling with nothing to do but worry about what was in store for me once 351 regained consciousness. All-too-vivid images of the brutal mating I'd seen take place between Gloria and 287 played on repeat before my mind's eye. The longer I lay there, the more impossible it became to shut them out. Flashes of the thick pole of flesh I'd seen between 351's thighs in that same room, and his bulging muscle as he pounded on the window separating us, made me shiver. He was so much stronger than me... so much bigger... And that primal fury in his gaze as he'd stared down the other alpha by my side... I shivered again and fidgeted when heat seemed to pour through my veins in thick, languid pulses.

"Ah, I see you're beginning to take." Dr. Urwin looked up from his papers, undoubtedly having been alerted by my fidgeting. He rolled his chair over by my bench once more, his expression calm and clinical as he pulled a small penlight from his pocket and shone it into my eyes.

"Pupils are dilating nicely," he said as I squinted. "And your temperature is rising," he continued after testing my forehead with the back of his hand. "Once you start to get too hot, do feel free to strip down. You will be much more comfortable."

"I'm not taking off my clothes!" I protested as I clasped my arms across my chest.

"Suit yourself," he said, not even bothering to look at me as he rolled back to his desk. "I've yet to see a female last through the second stage while still dressed."

Forty-five minutes later, I was starting to see his point.

It was so goddamn hot. I was sweating buckets as I paced around the small room, trying to fan air down my drenched shirt. It didn't help matters at all that my abdomen would infrequently make me curl in on myself with deep spasms, and despite the very un-sexy situation, a distinct throbbing from down below was making it harder and harder not to press a hand between my thighs to ease the tension.

I shot an angry glare at the back of Dr. Urwin's head as I passed him on my sixth-hundredth round. He was still working away as if he didn't have a care in the world, completely disregarding my mounting levels of discomfort.

"How much longer?" I growled without stopping. I knew if I didn't keep pacing, it wouldn't be long before I was forced to acknowledge the insistent throbbing between my thighs. As if on cue, a cramp made me groan and lean forward, supporting my hands on my knees to ride out the tremor.

Dr. Urwin turned then, giving me a long, evaluating look. "It shouldn't be much longer. Any slick yet?"

If I hadn't already been so hot, I might have flushed from the intimate question—but right then, I didn't care about what was proper. All I cared about was that I was so damn *hot,* and my clothes felt too constrictive as they stuck to my sweat-covered body—and that I wanted this to be over already!

"No," I said, shooting him an accusatory glare from my bent-over position. "Just buckets and buckets of sweat. This can't be fucking natural! Are you sure you haven't messed up the formula of whatever was in that injection? I feel terrible!"

"I did warn you," he mumbled as he reached for my forehead. I swatted his hand away—just the thought of him touching me made my skin crawl. I frowned when that realization set in—along with the sudden dawning that I wasn't worried about their plans anymore. I was just really, really... *irritated.*

"Mhm," Dr. Urwin hummed. "I think it's time we move on to the next stage. Last chance if you want to strip before we have to put the restraints on."

I shot him another glare, but the thought of being tied down and wrapped up in my restricting clothes finally made me give up the last remnants of dignity.

With a demonstrative huff, I turned my back to my —former—colleague and shrugged out of my soaked shirt. It was such an immediate relief to get the clingy fabric off my overheated body, the last of my self-consciousness faded to nothing. Eager to cool down as much as possible, I unclasped my bra and made quick work of my pants zipper and button, kicking off shoes and socks before I could shed them and my panties.

There was a moment's relief as I stood naked on the cold floor next to the pile of discarded clothes. It felt glorious to no longer have the soaked garments clinging to my hypersensitive skin, and even though I was still much too hot, at least I wasn't also wrapped up.

"Please lay back on the bench."

I turned my head toward Dr. Urwin, my upper lip curling in a snarl at him. He wasn't who I needed, so why the fuck was he here?

Dr. Urwin's eyebrows shot up in amusement, and I

blinked when I realized what I'd done. I'd... *snarled?* Like an animal. And what the hell was up with the errant thoughts about... about *needing* someone?

As much as I wanted to deny it, I knew exactly where those thoughts came from. Images of that alpha mounting Gloria played before my mind's eye and resonated deep in my core. My abdomen twinged with longing.

Fuck.

Without a word, I walked over to the bench and lay down. I didn't resist when Dr. Urwin placed the leather cuffs around my wrists and ankles, securing me to the padded surface.

I lay there for what felt like forever, sweating and waiting for the mounting pressure in my abdomen to finally break, but no matter how much I writhed on the bench and squeezed my thighs together to alleviate the need to be touched between them, nothing happened. It soon got to a point where, as much as I had dreaded their plans to force me into mating heat, I was desperate for it to finally sweep me away, because this... this was agony.

"How much longer?" I finally whined at Dr. Urwin, who at least hadn't gone back to his stupid desk this time. He was watching over me as I squirmed in my restraints, eyebrows furrowed.

"It should have broken now," he said. "I think it's

time we give you some stimulants to push you over the edge. I'll be back in a moment."

I whimpered pitifully when he left the room, not wanting to be left alone. As frustrated and irritated as I was, the moment he closed the door behind him and I was all alone, all I wanted was for him to return.

The flickering fluorescent light reflected off the white walls, somehow enhancing the sterile scent of disinfectant and the rattle of the chains tying my leather cuffs to the bed every time I fidgeted. While Dr. Urwin had been there, it'd been easier to pretend this was just a normal research project—that I was participating for the sake of scientific progress. Not tied up and waiting for a huge alpha murderer to penetrate me like a feral beast.

I breathed in deeply, doing my best to ignore the twinges from my abdomen as I focused on that look in 351's eyes that'd made me risk all to save him in the first place. That sense of humanity behind his primitive instincts I'd seen when he touched my cheek to thank me for caring for his injuries.

But no matter how hard I tried, I couldn't get his wild eyes and huge cock when he was locked in the breeding room out of my thoughts. He was an alpha through and through, and unless his humanity managed to surface, nothing was going to save me from the monstrous girth between his legs.

Thankfully Dr. Urwin was back within a few minutes, a piece of cloth in his hand, and my increasing panic instantly eased some just from his presence. As much as he'd irritated me earlier, and as much as I should probably have despised him for what he was about to do to me, I only felt relief. At least I wouldn't be alone in the medical-scented room with only my own anxious thoughts for company. And besides, as much as I was dreading what he was going to let happen to me, at least he'd stopped me from being sent to Ezban.

"All right," he said, placing the cloth over my nose. "Take a few deep breaths of this. It's laced with 351's scent from his last rut—it should push you over the edge."

I'd heard about such cloths before. Single women sometimes purchased pieces of fabric soaked in alpha sweat to enhance their private pleasure sessions. I'd never been among them, finding the idea of sniffing an alpha's sweat far more disgusting than erotic, but as I carefully smelled the cloth pressed against my nostrils, something... something *weird* happened to my body.

The scent of man and musk and *sex* filled my lungs, and a full-body shudder passed through my limbs before I could even comprehend how intoxicatingly *amazing* the smell of that cloth was. I sucked in another greedy gulp, and another, intent on inhaling as much of that wonderful scent as I could. My nipples hardened to aching points while I mewled and rubbed my face against the piece of fabric and fought against the restraints because all I wanted, all I needed, was more of that smell. I wanted to roll in it, rub my pussy against it...

The errant thought made me realize the growing heat south of my bellybutton and the powerful throb that had my clit twitching for every one of my heartbeats. *God,* I needed to be touched!

Aching to feel friction against my aching nub of nerves, *any* friction, I kicked my legs uselessly against the ankle restraints and tried to rub my spread thighs against each other to sate the increasing desperation growing there.

"Ah, modern women," Dr. Urwin sighed somewhere above me. I was too preoccupied with sniffing the piece of cloth to pay much attention to where. "You try to pretend like you want independence and a nice beta husband to settle down with, but when it comes right down to it, every one of you would much rather spread your legs for a primitive alpha." He sounded bitter, but before my brain could fully process his tone, his hand came down between my legs, smacking against my swollen labia and aching clit. I squealed at the sharp sting, and then moaned brokenly when he began rubbing his fingertips against my stiff little bud.

Fuck, it felt *so good.* Some distant part of my mind railed against his touch—this wasn't professional, and he wasn't the man I wanted to touch me there, but... *oh,* it felt amazing. Every instinct in my body ached for a release—somehow, I knew deep down that that would ease my suffering.

"Please, don't stop," I whimpered, not moving my head from the delicious scent of alpha pressed against my nose.

Dr. Urwin snorted, but didn't pause the firm pressure against my most sensitive spot. "Do you have any idea how you look, spread open and panting like a bitch in heat?" he growled, a mocking tone in his voice, but also an edge of frustration. "You're a woman of science, and right now, you'd like nothing more than to be shoved into that feral alpha's cage so you can offer your cunt to him. Isn't that right? Heck, I bet you'd happily let Dr. Axell mount you. I've seen the looks you give him—the big alpha boss. Everyone's always fawning over him and his brilliance. I bet if he'd offered, you'd have let him tie you to the breeding post after hours even without the drugs.

"Would you like to know why he's not the one servicing you, instead of the lowly beta doctor you'd never look twice at if you had the choice?" Dr. Urwin paused long enough to push the hood of my clit back, and then grabbed the bared little nub between thumb and index finger, squeezing viciously.

The unprotected touch directly to the cluster of hypersensitive nerves sent me off the bed with a yowl. Only the restraints kept me from falling to the floor. I arched up as high as I could, squirming and screaming incoherently as raw, electric jolts of sensation crackled through my poor clit and made every muscle in my body jerk. It hurt so *good,* I didn't know if I wanted to beg him to stop or to do it harder.

"It turns out, Dr. Axell, for all his brilliance and all his derogatory comments about women and their instincts, is as much a slave to his primal self as the poor bastards we have locked up downstairs. Seeing you like this... all tied down with that pretty little cunt winking like crazy, begging for a nice, thick dick? He'd mount you himself, and then probably kill you once he was done. The esteemed doctor doesn't like to be reminded that, when it comes right down to it, he's just like the feral beasts we poke and prod all day."

I probably should have been more concerned with what he was saying, but I didn't have it in me to focus on anything but the excruciating pleasure being forced into my abused clit. For every pinch, the tension deep inside of my abdomen grew. I writhed mindlessly, blindly searching for relief. And, just as the pressure right behind my pelvic bone became unbearable... it broke.

A flush of sticky liquid rushed out of my frantically spasming core, covering my thighs and the medical bench below me. My body arched as high as the restraints allowed while waves of euphoria rolled through my pelvis, taking me closer and closer to that elusive peak... until the abuse against my pulsing clit abruptly stopped.

I cried out in frustration, thrashing against my restraints. "No! *More!* Please!"

Dr. Urwin gave me a small smirk as he stepped away from the bench. He sniffed the hand he'd had between my thighs and gave an appreciative hum. "There's no need. You're ready for your alpha. But don't worry—once he's awake, you'll get all the sex you can stand."

NINE

LILLIAN

It was several more hours before Dr. Urwin's phone rang, slicing through my own personal hell with a sharp ring.

I whimpered as the sound cut through my feverish brain, causing echoes of pain to vibrate through my already aching body. Everything was too hot, too *loud*, and the fluorescent light mounted on the ceiling above me hurt my eyes whenever I tried to open them.

I didn't know what time it was, but knew it had to be the middle of the night or early morning. Every muscle in my body ached from the frequent cramps shuddering through me, and I was so exhausted I was barely lucid— but that wasn't the worst part.

No, the worst part was the dull, unrelenting *yearning* deep inside. My blood burned with brutal need, and no matter how much I squirmed and begged for relief from the cruel beta who'd tied me down, he hadn't so much as glanced my way since he'd forced my pussy to soak the surface under my backside.

This was worse than any illness I'd ever suffered, including the unpleasant week of swine flu back in college. Though this time, I knew what would cure me.

"Is the alpha ready?"

The alpha.

Dr. Urwin's voice rang through my brain as loudly as the phone had, and I keened in desperation at hearing him say that word out loud: *alpha. My* alpha—the man who would finally end my torment.

"Yes, that's her," Dr. Urwin chuckled into the phone. "Just as ripe as a two-dollar whore. If you get him prepped, I'll take her to the lab. This slut's gagging for a fat knot."

DESPITE MY DESPERATION TO slake the fire between my legs, fear muted by need rolled through me when Dr. Urwin fastened first my wrists and then my ankles to the breeding post. I was bent over by the hips and stretched out with my hands tied so far away from my body I wasn't able to move my torso more than an inch. My feet were spread wide, and the hard legs of the bench in front of me ensured I couldn't squirm my hips.

I was completely helpless, and more vulnerable than a woman ever should be.

Dr. Urwin finished tying me to the breeding post and slipped a padded roll underneath my hips, forcing my arse up and out and exposing my flushed sex to the the room. "There we go, all ready for some dick, huh?" he said cheerfully, stroking his palm against my swollen pussy before cupping it.

I mewled despite myself and tried to push out against the stimulation, even though the small sliver of sanity still left hated him with the fiery passion of a thousand suns. He might have saved me from Ezban, but ever since my heat broke and I Presented in the small examination room, any pretense of profession-alism had vanished. He mocked me, mocked my biolog-ical response to the drugs he'd given me as if it was somehow a betrayal of my entire gender and the scien-tific method, too.

The worst part was that part of me agreed. Maybe logically, if I'd had the capacity for such a thing, I wouldn't have. But as I stood tied up and bent over with my intimate parts on full display, and all I wanted was for someone—anyone—to mount me... the shame of what basic biology had reduced me to was too much to bear.

When Dr. Urwin dipped a digit into my opening and began to shallowly thrust it in and out, I bit back on my pleas for more and turned my head to the side.

Trying to find something to focus on that would distract me from my humiliation.

But what I found to focus on only made everything so much worse.

Behind the panes of glass, in the observation room, Dr. Axell sat. Looking at me. He had his hand wrapped around his thick alpha cock, stroking it slowly.

The look of him... of his bloated cock in his hand and the look of excitement on his face, there was no more pretending that this was for the greater good of science. I hadn't been saved from Ezban in the hopes that 351 would claim me as a mate and help further their research.

I was first and foremost here because they wanted revenge for my attempt at putting a stop to their inhumane methods.

Being forced into a heat that had me desperate to be violated by the same hulking alpha I'd tried to save was my punishment. Not my redemption.

When Dr. Axell saw me looking with horrified disgust, he gave me a lecherous smirk and leaned forward to press one of the buttons on the panel in front of him.

"I think it's time our rebellious little analyst meets her new lover. Finish her up and let's get on with the show. It's been a long night for us all." His voice rang through the test room from a speaker somewhere high above me, sending shivers of unease through my aching body.

"Is he right, sweetheart?" Dr. Urwin said from behind me, his tone mocking. "You ready for your big, bad alpha to come satisfy your greedy little cunt?" He slipped his finger out of me, and I whined at the loss.

He chuckled in response. "I guess so. Best get you oiled up so you can take him without ripping, eh?" Cool liquid trickled down my slit, finding every nook and cranny as it dripped inside of me. "You might be wet as swamp back here, but we've had more than one first-timer tear for the knot. Turns out ferals don't care if you're screaming in pleasure or agony, but it's so much work to stitch you back up once he's done wearing you like a sock puppet."

"You're disgusting," I hissed—only it came out more like a needy whimper.

Dr. Urwin snorted, patted my arse and then leaned in over me so his lips brushed against my ear. "It's shocking, isn't it? Realizing that us lowly beta men love watching a poor little female getting screwed to pieces? I bet your previous beta lovers have treated you ever so gently... and told you how much they *respected* you while they slow-fucked your twat, because they knew that's what you expected of them. That's the only reason why any of you little cunts let a beta mount you, isn't it? Because you know you can control us with what's between your legs. We're not scary or violent. And we'd never hold you down while we rape-fuck your tight little hole until you scream for mercy.

"Well, let me tell you a little secret, *Miss Dorne:* Every single one of your beta boyfriends have fantasized about fucking you on a bench just like this one, with your legs spread and your hands tied down so you can't fight back. We *all* fantasize about it as we make sweet, gentle love to you and ask you if you've come yet.

"And now here you are... tied up like a sacrificial lamb and gagging for a thick cock to destroy your pretty little pussy as roughly as possible. I'd almost call that poetic justice, wouldn't you?"

I wanted to bite back—to call him sick, to yell at him for abusing his position to quite obviously torment women for his own twisted sense of revenge. But all his taunts did was make my pussy gush with need as I couldn't help but picture 351 forcing himself inside of me... finally sating my aching body.

"Please," I gasped, surrendering to the humiliation. "Please. Bring him to me. I need... *Please!"*

Dr. Urwin snorted as he walked away from me and rapped his knuckles against the door. "Oh, you'll get him all right, slut. And my guess, it'll take you roughly three seconds before you start begging us to get him off you again. Should be fun—I always love it when they scream."

Guards I hadn't known were present opened the metal door and let the doctor out. It slammed shut behind him with an echoing thud, leaving me alone in the small room.

Was it morning already? Or were those guards the same men who'd pointed their guns at 351 and I what felt like a lifetime ago?

Would they watch my humiliation, too?

I pressed my face against the padded surface of the bench, unwilling to look at Dr. Axell behind the glass panes—the esteemed doctor I'd spent so many years looking up to, never knowing what kind of a monster truly lay beneath the surface.

I waited in silence under the bright light, the only sound in the room my own ragged breathing for several minutes. My body ached from the artificial heat, cramps rolling through my abdomen in uneasy waves, and I fidgeted to try and get comfortable in my restraints. Not that I could—I was strapped down too tightly to move more than half an inch to each side. The sweat dripped off my heated skin in fat droplets and pooled on the padding underneath me, making me stick to the surface. And all the while, my sex clenched helplessly around nothing, the desperation to be mounted and filled over-shadowing the rest of my discomfort.

Thuds from somewhere on the other side of the door pulled my attention away from my misery and into the present. I turned my head to face it, my breathing picking up speed at a muted *roar*.

He was here.

TEN

LILLIAN

My pussy gushed a new rivulet of slick at the sound of the enraged alpha, even as I whimpered with fear. My body didn't care about my traumatic childhood and ingrained terror at even the thought of being at the mercy of a feral alpha—it simply recognized the sound of an approaching male strong enough to finally quell my suffering and ensured my readiness to receive him.

Another roar, this time much closer, was followed by a loud *bang* as the door swung open and a heavily restrained 351 was shoved into the room with metal poles attached to the bands of metal encircling his neck and arms. He fought like a wild animal despite the restraints, trying to twist back and grab at the men controlling the poles. When I caught a glimpse of his eyes, I shuddered in primal fear. They were pitch black, any humanity that may have been present completely overshadowed by *rage*.

A man not wielding a pole stepped halfway into the room and aimed a taser gun at the feral alpha. He pressed the trigger and 351 jerked once, his resistance coming to an abrupt halt as he dropped to his knees.

The guards reacted quickly, detaching the poles and slamming the door shut—and then I was alone with the wild man.

351 shook his head, his lip pulling up in a deep snarl as he regained control of his muscles. He was on his feet in the blink of an eye, and the room reverberated when he threw the full weight of his body against the now locked door, roaring in rage as he tore at the metal with fingers hooked like claws.

I gasped in a small, panicked breath as even my wanton pussy tensed with fear. As much as my body needed him, there was no mistaking the absolute fury currently in control of the alpha. The only thing he seemed interested in right now was to *maim*—and I was the only breakable target within reach.

At the sound of my gasp, the alpha froze, and he whipped his head around to locate the source of the noise. Black eyes bored into mine, and I tried to shrink into the bench with a whimper of fear. But there was nowhere for me to hide.

His roar quieted to a deep, rich growl—like a stalking panther rounding on its trapped prey.

"D-don't h-hurt m-me," I pleaded, because that was the only thing I could do. "P-please, please. Don't—don't h-hurt me!"

If he even heard my words, it was clear he didn't understand them. His upper lip pulled back in a snarl again as he took in my quivering form strapped to the breeding bench, and he took two long steps toward me. But before he came close enough to touch me, his nostrils flared wide and he froze to the spot.

He'd finally caught the scent of my heat.

Black eyes roamed over my body again as he scented the air more deeply.

When he growled again, it had a distinctly different tone than before—deeper—and my pussy responded in kind.

I groaned at the spasm in my abdomen, and moaned at the rush of liquid gushing down my inner thighs and dripping on the floor.

Even though my heart was still pounding in terror, my body recognized the alpha's shifting interests.

Strong fingers twisted into the manacles shackling my wrists to the bench. 351 pulled at the metal, his muscles bulging with the effort, but they didn't give.

I looked up at him, confused at his intent, and flinched when he snarled with irritation at his inability to break them.

The movement caught his attention, and his darkened gaze returned to me. His pupils were still blown, but there was more than just anger in his eyes now. A heat that had my breath catching in my throat radiated from the black pools—and when I glanced between his thighs, I saw the unmistakable proof as to why.

Despite my body's eager shiver of delight at the sight of the gruesome cock jutting straight up in evidence that the feral alpha was no longer interested in fighting, I couldn't help but whimper with horror.

It was so impossibly *big,* the head alone easily the same size as my own fist. Oil or not, there was no way I'd be able to take that—there was just no way.

The alpha either didn't notice or didn't care about my terrified stare. His gaze swept over my body once more, taking in my naked flesh stretched out for his use, and a pleased rumble escaped his throat.

When he bent over me, I shuddered with equal parts fear and yearning, but I wasn't prepared for my body's reaction when he pressed his nose against the side of my neck and sniffed.

Me hips jerked backward of their own accord, trying to push up to present my flushed opening to the alpha scenting me for readiness to mate. This time, my whimper was long and needy.

351's only response was to lick at my neck, lapping at my sweat and tasting my skin while he breathed in my scent. Slowly, he moved down my body, licking at my shoulders and neck as he shifted next to the bench for ease of access until, finally, he moved around the back to stand between my spread legs.

I was shaking at this point, my fear of his brutal size nearly lost to the fog of hormonal bliss. My instincts, forced to the forefront by the artificial heat, relished in the alpha's attention. He was so big, and *strong,* and I could practically taste his pheromones in the air as he scented me. They made the panicked voice in my head die to an indistinct murmur and the urge to mate overtake my frazzled mind.

When his tongue lapped at the small of my back, I keened pathetically and rolled my hips the small bit my restraints allowed, trying to make him focus on where I needed him the most.

It worked.

The heat from his breath brushed against my drenched opening as he slid down in a crouch behind me, followed by his big, warm hands as he grabbed a hold of my ass.

"Alpha," I moaned, wishing with everything I was that he would mount me and finally end my torment.

The feral man growled again, making my pussy gush for him. When he dragged his tongue up through my folds to taste my offering, I nearly passed out.

"Ooooh! Yes!" I groaned, and—when he did it again — *"Please!"*

But 351 seemed in no rush. Despite my more and

more desperate whimpers and pleas, he kept licking at my drenched sex, forcing sharp crackles of bone-shattering pleasure through my swollen clit every time he caught it with his tongue.

I struggled against my restraints, writhing mindlessly for his lips and tongue while he lapped at my sodden folds and buzzing clit. Pleasure rose from my toes up through my straining legs, threatening to throw me over a cliff I hadn't known was so close, but in the core of my being, I knew it was all wrong. I wanted relief, needed it more than the air filling my lungs in pained gasps, but not from a sharp, superficial release brought on by having my clit manipulated.

He was my alpha. There was only one way he would be able to end my torment.

"Please, please fuck me—*oh!* Oh, God, please, alpha... take me. I need you. *Please!*" My voice wasn't my own, pleasure-addled hormones making it much rougher than I'd ever sounded before. And, when he sucked my clit into his mouth in response, a growl I'd never even known I could produce ripped from my throat.

"*No!* Don't! Not like this!" I thrashed against the sharp shocks of pleasure, fighting back the rising tide threatening to overcome me. "I don't... I can't! *Inside!* Please! I need you *inside! Now!*"

I don't know if it was my words or my growl, but finally, he heard me.

The alpha growled deep in his throat in response, releasing my tormented clit. I felt him shift behind me, saw his shadow loom over my back when I desperately craned my neck to look at him. Huge, rough hands grabbed my hips, jerking at me as if to shift me into position. The strain on my shoulders and wrists from where the manacles held me in place made me grit my teeth, but when something hot and *huge* nudged at my weeping sex, all thoughts of discomfort evaporated.

"Yes, yes, yes!" I chanted as I tried to arch my back and push myself down his cock, but the manacles kept me locked in place.

Not that the alpha needed my assistance.

Firm, heavy pressure pushed against my opening. My pussy gaped open in welcome, the steady drip of fluids from my core and liberal helping of oil easing my lower lips apart around his fat cock head. But even the rich amounts of lubrication didn't change his size.

My pussy yawned open as wide as it could, desperate to allow him inside. Only he didn't fit. His tip kissed my pink tunnel, but the girth of his head caught in my opening.

I mewled in frustration—but I needn't have.

With a growl, the alpha dug his fingertips deep into my hips and *shoved*.

The pressure rose to the unbearable when he bore down on my opening with all his weight, but it only lasted a second before my pussy caved. White-hot relief mixed with agony as his thick cock head barreled into my unprotected pussy, forcing it much too wide in one, rough push.

I shrieked, clawing at the padded bench in an instinctive attempt to get away from the brutal intrusion, but his grip along with the manacles forced me to stay put. There was nothing I could do but endure.

The feral alpha didn't pause to let me get accustomed to his size, either. Once his head popped inside my horrifically dilated opening, he rolled his hips and shoved home with far more strength than my body could ever hope to counter.

Despite the obvious force he put behind that first thrust, he sank into me excruciatingly slowly while the depths of my pussy struggled desperately to open wide enough for his massive cock.

A deep groan and the wet smack of his heavy balls against my burning pussy lips and forcefully bared clit announced his victory over my violently trembling body.

Mercifully, once he was certain he had conquered my depths, he stilled for a moment while my pussy clutched fitfully at his full length, squeezing it in hard little pulses as my aching channel tried to accept the vicious stretch.

It was only then, as my mind disconnected from the roil of sensation in my body, I registered with distant wonder that the throbbing pain between my legs hadn't been caused by any ripping. No, it was the agony of tautly stretched muscles and a deeply feminine sensation of being invaded so brutally that my body was completely at the alpha's mercy. No woman would voluntarily allow her most sacred depths to be rendered this vulnerable by a near-stranger, and the physical shock of having it forced upon me mixed with the ache of penetration.

But *underneath* it...

Endorphins and adrenaline danced in my veins, threatening to drown out the pain until nothing but the sweet, mind-shattering ecstasy remained.

He was finally *inside* me. The aching, clenching emptiness was finally filled, and I *knew*—despite everything, I knew this man would sate my desperate yearning.

When the alpha moved, my consciousness snapped back into my body as quickly and brutally as a punch to the jaw.

His monstrous cock dragged against my still-trembling channel, making my tight sheath cling to his girth as he pulled halfway out, only to reverse the movement with a punishing snap of his hips.

I cried out at once again being filled so harshly all the way to my womb, but this time the alpha didn't give me any respite. With a roar that drowned out my frantic sobbing, the feral man took me with every ounce of his strength, fucking my helplessly gaped pussy faster, harder.

It hurt. It hurt so goddamn much I screamed for him to stop, but I didn't mean it. Because for each push into my weeping core, that thick, horrific cock of his ground against every nerve ending inside me, pummeling my G-spot and giving me exactly what every inch of my body knew I needed more than air. *"Pleasure"* was not strong enough to describe the bone-deep flood of ecstasy forced through my pelvis for every one of his hard thrusts.

His deep groans and growls blended with my screams and the constant, wet *thwack* of his thighs against my upturned ass and hamstrings. Again and again he pummeled my pussy, forcing me higher on waves of pain-addled bliss until finally, and without warning, my pussy surrendered.

Electric currents rocked through my pelvis, down my thighs, and up my abdomen, drawing blazing trails of heat in their wake. I wasn't even aware of what was happening until my body arched up as high as it could go for the manacles tying me down, and blinding plea-sure exploded through every nerve ending and behind my eyes. Foaming at the mouth like a rabid dog, I screamed in release while my body convulsed on the alpha's hard cock.

And through it all, he kept fucking me like a man possessed, giving me every single inch of thick meat until my pussy was gagging and drooling from exhaustion. Milking and squeezing him in a desperate attempt to bring forth his own release so the assault could end.

It wasn't until after several minutes of that torturous, blissful orgasm my weeping sex finally gave up. Every strained muscle in my core shuddered one final time, and then relaxed.

I lay still in shocked silence, only capable of gasping for air as suddenly, the alpha's presence inside me no longer hurt. He'd finally fucked the last ounce of resistance out of my pussy.

I moaned softly in between gasps for air as a calm unlike any other settled over me. His thrusts felt so good now... Soothing, even though his cock forced pleasure to rise deep inside once more, like a lazy serpent uncoiling.

I couldn't do anything to meet his thrusts, couldn't move my body to clench around him and hurry the building climax along. But he was alpha... he was meant to dominate my body. Own it.

I don't know how long he mated me after my first orgasm, but I was almost at my second when my blissed-out mind began to wither at the edges. Something was starting to hurt again.

Confused, I whimpered underneath the huge man, trying to gather my focus. Something was stretching my opening again, trying to force it even wider for every thrust.

I whined in protest and tried to wriggle away, but

there was no escape, and my sex was far too worn to put up any resistance.

The stretching at my entrance grew and grew, until the alpha's thrusts shortened to slow, grinding strokes that forced the swelling at my entrance deeper.

His knot. He was trying to *knot* me.

That snapped me out of it.

I opened my mouth to wail out a plea for mercy, but it came too late.

Growling with effort, the feral alpha shoved home one final time, popping the brutal knot inside my already gaping lips.

My yowl rang through the room, wild and shrill. It was to much, *too much!* Too *big!*

Large arms wrapped around my waist, holding me close as the massive man pressed his body down on top of me, holding me down so I couldn't dislocate my joints while I struggled. I was so lost to the insanity coursing through my body from where his knot kept swelling, grinding mercilessly against my G-spot, I didn't notice his teeth around the back of my neck before he bit down.

Hard.

I mewled, shocked confusion flooding my mind the second before the strongest endorphins I'd ever experienced hit my brainstem and my body went lax.

I was faintly aware he was still rocking inside me, grinding faraway pleasure out of my G-spot that trembled through my limbs. I didn't feel it, though. Not really.

All I felt as I lay knotted underneath the feral alpha was his teeth piercing my skin as he placed his mating mark on my neck.

Claiming me as his for eternity.

ELEVEN
LILLIAN

Everything hurt.

Every muscle in my body, but especially the back of my neck and between my legs, ached, and I was so exhausted all I wanted to do was curl up and sleep until the pain went away.

But a furious growl rolled like thunder around me, and an urgent *twang* from behind my ribs made instincts buried somewhere in the fog of my brain fight against the yearning for sleep.

"Jesus fuck, tranq the sonuvabitch again so we can check he didn't injure her! She's barely conscious," someone rasped from far away. It sounded familiar and made my hackles raise. I groaned in protest and tried to shake my head clear of the fog, even if my eyelids refused to open.

I moaned in agony at the sharp pang in my neck,

which was immediately followed by a *roar* and the unmistakable sounds of flesh hitting something hard. Groans of pain followed.

The panic in my chest finally made me force my eyes open, and I saw the blurry outline of a huge, naked alpha fighting against men with metal rods. They were shocking him with the ends of the rods, but he kept fighting and snarling, eyes locked on me.

I whimpered in panic as my chest constricted. He couldn't get hurt—he couldn't—

Three darts bored into the alpha's neck. His next roar came out as a groan—and then he sank to the floor in a heap.

"No!" I croaked.

A small jab at the side of my neck was the only response to my distress—and then everything turned black.

———

THE NEXT TIME consciousness returned to my fuzzy head, it wasn't the delicate ache in my body that first presented itself. No, it was a weird sensation in my chest, somewhere behind my ribs. As if *something* was hooked there, tethering me.

Only then did I notice the heavy warmth cocooning me from all sides, pressing me down against a sparsely cushioned surface. It was all-pervasive and penetrated deep into my muscles, easing the tension in them.

I twitched, the tether in my chest giving an odd lurch, almost as if it were *alive* somehow, my eyes popping open with a start. What the hell—?

A rumbling vibrated through me from the heavy mass resting against my back, followed by strong bands of warmth clamping tighter around my body until I couldn't move my limbs.

Trapped.

I fought against the pressure keeping me down, disorientation and panic starting to set in as the tether in my chest lurched again.

Something flesh-colored maybe three inches from my face blocked my vision of my surroundings, but I could make out the surface I was getting pressed into—a bare mattress.

Another low rumble rippled by my ear—a scolding noise—and the weight on top of me shifted a little before teeth clamped shut around the back of my neck, making my body go lax without my consent.

That was when everything that'd happened last night came back to me.

351.

351 was wrapped around my back, pressing me into a mattress.

I wanted to shout at him to get off me, but his jaws

around my neck made it come out as a pathetic whimper instead.

The alpha snarled, a questioning note to it this time, and somehow I knew he was checking if I'd calmed down.

I drew in a shuddering breath, but the panic in my brain was well and truly gone, washed away in the rush of endorphins his bite had released.

"Please. Let go," I whispered. "It hurts."

It did—pangs of tenderness radiated from where his teeth were still locked against my skin. He was aggravating the wound from last night, I dimly realized. Where he'd bitten me after he knotted me.

He'd broken the skin...

He'd... he'd put a *claiming* mark on me! I was his... *mate!*

My brain tried to push another panic attack on me at that particular thought, but the alpha's bite didn't allow it to. Thanks to the trigger points he'd clamped, I was forced to accept the grim reality of what had happened to me.

Flashes of the brutal mating, of my forced heat, and Dr. Axell's lewd delight as he watched us made their way to the forefront of my mind, and I finally became aware of the dull throbbing between my legs, the conclusive proof that this wasn't all some horrid nightmare.

351, perhaps sensing my horror as everything came back to me in vivid detail, finally released my neck and instead dragged his tongue over the impressions of his teeth in slow, languid licks.

I tensed against the expected pain, but it didn't agitate my wound. Instead, it felt... oddly soothing.

The tether in my chest hummed pleasantly, as if in agreement. And then the most calming sound I'd ever heard reverberated from him, through my back, and into the length of my body. It penetrated my very bones, liquefying my muscles and shielding my psyche from the trauma creeping in. I had no idea why, but something about that sound blanketed me in bliss, as if... as if it was somehow connected to my very soul. It wasn't anything like his other growls. It was softer. Gentler. Almost like... like a *purr*.

I blinked dazedly at the mattress when some faraway part of my mind still capable of analysis put the pieces together. It *was* a purr. An alpha purr. The sound they would produce for their mates and offspring in their most private, intimate moments.

And he was doing it for *me*.

I lay underneath the feral alpha as he licked my nape and purred for me, letting him soothe me into a state of complete and utter peace. He was so warm and strong on top of me, shielding and protecting me. Some faraway part of my mind understood that the vibrations of his purr were lulling me into accepting my situation, that he was forcing a biological response from my body I had no way of controlling. But right then, I truly didn't care. He was warm and strong and would care for me, and I'd never felt better or more relaxed in my entire life. So I closed my eyes and let my mind wander, content to pretend everything was okay for as long as I could.

IT LASTED until the pressure in my bladder finally became too great to bear.

I forced my eyelids open again, the fuzzy sensation of true calm making it hard to do, and poked 351's arm. "You need to move."

Only a small octave change in his purr let me know he'd even heard me, because he didn't move so much as a muscle.

"Seriously." I pushed at his arm again, squirming to get free. "I need to pee. Please, get up."

His purr cut off with an annoyed huff, but he rolled off me just enough that I could scramble up into a seated position.

The loss of his body heat made me shiver in the comparatively frigid air, but I was too desperate to care much. "Where's the bathr—"

Which was when I remembered where we were... and what the facilities were like.

I stared at the stainless steel toilet bowl attached to the back wall of 351's cell. Then I looked at him.

He was resting on his side on the mattress, blue gaze

not so much as hinting that he understood—or cared about—my current dilemma.

I glanced back at the toilet. "Uh... Could you... turn around, please?"

351 didn't respond, and when I looked back at him, he was just staring at me as if I'd not said anything.

Too desperate to wait until the alpha got my intentions through his thick skull, I got up and walked to the toilet, praying he would have enough civility left to do the decent thing and look away when a lady was about to pop a squat in his cell.

One glance back in his direction told me I had no such luck.

"Seriously, turn around!" I hissed, any vestiges of my previous calm dissipating at the prospect of having a captive audience for this.

351 growled, a disapproving frown marring his forehead.

"Ugh, just..." I bit my lip to stop myself from yelling at him—from the look on his face, he was moments away from reasserting his dominance over the disrespectful female making demands of him.

Deciding against testing him, I drew in a deep breath and—studiously avoiding his green-blue gaze— did my business as quickly as I could.

Perhaps it shouldn't have been mortifying, in light of what else I'd been made to do in front of an audience lately, but it was. Something about squatting over a steel toilet bowl in the corner of a cell drove home the inhumanity of my situation, and 351's unconcerned stare didn't help.

I was truly a test subject now, no better than an animal in the eyes of my captors.

No better than the alpha whose very humanity they'd stolen.

I didn't return to him on the mattress after. Now that he'd stopped purring, there was nothing preventing the harsh reality of my situation from settling in full-force. Despite goosebumps spreading on my skin without his body heat to keep me warm, I skirted the mattress and went over to the bars to peer out, keeping my arms across my chest and pelvis to preserve just a modicum of modesty.

Not that anyone was there. The lab was desolate. Because it was the weekend, I realized. They'd all gone home to their families and hobbies, to get refreshed for the next work week, leaving the lab rats behind.

I shuddered and steadied myself against the bars as memories of doing the same came rushing back. I'd gone home night after night to my apartment, to make dinner and unwind with a silly TV show. And all the while, people had been imprisoned here. Like animals.

I glanced over my shoulder as the feral alpha got up and walked over to me, perhaps sensing my distress again.

"Can you talk?" I asked, biting my lip when he

wrapped an arm around my midsection and pulled me back against him. His heat was comforting, but right then, I'd have given anything to just be able to talk with him. Discuss what we'd been through—to feel even halfway human again.

His only response was to nuzzle at the bite mark at my neck, an unmistakably possessive growl rising in his chest.

There was nothing human about him right now.

I swallowed thickly to push back the tears stinging in my eyes.

"Don't bother. We gave him a double dose while you were both knocked out—to ensure the claiming takes good and proper."

I jolted at the unexpected voice, but only managed to catch a glimpse of Dr. Urwin as he sauntered up to the bars, because 351 *ripped* me behind him with a furious snarl.

"He won't be able to form words for at least twelve more hours. May I suggest you don't agitate him in the meantime? He'll be deep in his instincts, and a newly mated alpha can get quite *assertive* with his female until he's certain she has submitted to him fully."

351 growled, releasing his grip on me so he could pace in front of the bars, keeping his body between me and our captor without ever taking his eyes off him. His evcry aggressive move underscored Dr. Urwin's point.

"What are you going to do to us?" I managed, despite my throat feeling too tight to produce words.

"We will continue with the next stage of our research," he said with infuriating calm. "We need to know what demands we can put on him now that he has a mate he'll want to keep safe, and which trigger points will be most efficient in ensuring his compliance."

"So you'll torture us."

"No, not torture. Whatever you may think, this is a scientific study. We will provide stressors and stimuli, true, but for a much higher purpose than something as base as commonplace torture. We are truly grateful to you, Lillian—without your suggestion that creating a pair-bond requires more than just physical attraction, we would not have had this opportunity." He sounded like his regular self, absorbed in his study—as if I was still capable of discussing scientific method after everything they'd done to me.

"You won't get away with this."

Dr. Urwin regarded me coolly. "There's nothing to *get away with*. You signed yourself over to this study willingly, if you remember, just like all the other women. And thanks to you, we have a breakthrough that will improve the nation's defense. You will be with us until your death, Lillian. I appreciate it will take some time for you to acclimate to your new life, but I suggest you try to do so as quickly as possible. Most women eventually find contentment with the alpha who has claimed them. Perhaps, despite the circumstances, you will too."

"Do you think I've forgotten what you said to me?" I hissed. "What you did?" How dare he try to pretend he hadn't said horrible things to me while he'd rubbed me between my legs? As if he could fool me into believing he was nothing more than a scientist, and I his willing test subject. Nothing about last night had been professional.

"Ah. Yes. I admit, we did not expect success from your mating." He gave me a thin smile past 351's shoulder as the alpha stalked between us, growling a low, continuous threat. "But since it did... it is only prudent that you be treated in the same manner as our other test subjects."

"How comforting." I hadn't forgotten 351's deep lash marks, or Gloria huddled on the mattress in her cell.

"May I suggest you spend the weekend coming to terms with things? Monday we will have more tests for you both, and they will be best faced with a refreshed mind." Dr. Urwin snapped open a slot in the door, and I only noticed the tray of food he'd brought when he pushed it through. "You both slept through the earlier feedings, so I have increased your evening portions. Try not to make it a habit—we don't usually coddle our test subjects."

Feedings.

He truly saw us as lab rats.

"Enjoy your night, Lillian."

I stared at his back as he walked away from the cell, until the angle of the bars didn't allow me to see further.

Only when he was completely out of sight did 351 lower his hackles and turn his attention to the food.

It looked like a hefty portion of some form of stew, and next to it was an empty plastic cup.

351 took the tray and placed it next to the mattress. He grabbed the cup, along with one he had stashed by the concrete wall, went over to the small stainless steel sink next to the toilet, and filled both.

I watched him quietly as he set up, surprised he remembered the function of such things *and* that he was setting a place for me as well, a gesture made all the more clear when he finally crouched next to the tray of food and looked up at me expectantly.

A small part of my mind was too busy having a breakdown to contemplate such things as food, but the larger—and more rational part—was starving.

"So we're just gonna sit here, butt-naked, and eat stew with our hands, then?" I said as I reluctantly knelt down on the mattress by his side. "But I guess this isn't the sort of establishment to provide silverware, huh?" Or pants.

I drew in a deep breath as I looked at the food. It didn't smell overly appealing, and I wasn't keen on lowering my arms from my naked body to start eating with my fingers... but then, I'd already had to pee while being ogled like a zoo exhibit, so what did it matter if he saw my breasts while I ate? It was quite clear that the sooner I gave up on my dreams of humane treatment, the sooner I'd be able to get my bearings back and perhaps try to find a way out of this mess.

Only that thought—the faint hope that I'd be able to find a way out somehow—allowed me to push down the panic attack that kept trying to take over. With a deep breath, I moved my hand from my chest and reached for the tray.

351's immediate growl made me snap it back. "I'm sorry, I didn't—do you want to eat first?"

He huffed as if irritated with my question and reached for the food himself. Only instead of scooping it to his own mouth, he offered me not only his now food-laden fingers, but also the first bite.

"No, that's okay, I can eat on my—" Another growl, angrier this time, shut me right up. I glanced up at him and gulped at the impatience painted across his ruthlessly handsome face.

Apparently, I was getting hand-fed.

Hesitantly, I parted my lips.

His growl quieted, and then he more or less shoved his fingers into my mouth.

I did my best not to gag, partly from the force of it, and partly from the gross taste of unseasoned mush violating my tongue.

"Thanks," I choked out. "I can take it from here, though—you need to eat too."

Another growl made me grimace and obediently open my mouth for a second scoop of stew.

351 fed me until I was well and truly full—nearly half the portion of the giant mountain of food—and my gag reflex was threatening rebellion. Only then did he relent, turning his attention to his own hunger as I sagged on the mattress in faint relief. I didn't know much about alpha mating rituals, but clearly he had some dumb animal instinct to feed what he considered his female.

I curled up in fetal position with my back to 351 and let my fingertips ghost over the still-sore bite on my nape. From what little I knew about alpha matings, they were supposed to be very special. Like... gaining a soulmate. At least, for the couples entering into it voluntarily. I'd heard a few rumors, urban legends, really, about alphas forcing a mating bond on a woman after raping them. But I'd never put much stock into such gossip—it seemed so far-fetched that anyone, even the most vicious of alphas, would corrupt a bond meant to be so pure.

As I touched my own claiming mark, it dawned on me that perhaps what alphas had told us about their claims wasn't entirely true. I didn't feel my soul singing, nor did I feel any special bond to the alpha who'd fucked me raw while I'd been tied down. I just felt...

I cut myself off before I delved into the emotions

welling behind the thin veil of willpower I was currently using to keep myself together. If I started delving into my emotions, I'd lose the grasp on my sanity.

I lay in silence, doing my best to think of absolutely nothing until 351 was finally done eating. He pushed away the tray with a shriek of metal on concrete, and then the mattress dipped as he lay down behind me. He curved his body against my back and slung one of his huge arms around my midriff.

I closed my eyes as I involuntarily relaxed upon making contact with his warmth. Clearly the lab was kept at a comfortable temperature for alphas, as they ran hotter than the rest of us.

He wrapped me up in the cocoon of his warmth and bulky protection, and I couldn't help my amused snort at the fact that the feral alpha locked away for treason and murder was apparently a big cuddler.

351 rumbled in response and buried his face in my hair.

I tried to ignore the way he sniffed at me, drawing in lungfuls of my scent, and focused on the warmth of his embrace instead. Like before, I knew that as long as I didn't think—as long as I just focused on the comfort of his heat, I'd be able to keep it together until I was able to process what had happened to me.

Only that wasn't what the alpha had in mind.

I'd managed to doze off into light sleep when 351 cupped one of my breasts, startling me awake.

I bit my lip as his thick fingers brushed over my nipple, shooting sensation through my body as his hard pole of flesh rose against my back.

I thought about pushing him away, but knew I'd never be able to fight him off if he was determined.

It took everything I had to keep my breathing slow and steady as he plucked at my nipple. I pretended I was still sleeping, knowing that was the only defense I had.

I didn't blame him for what he'd done to me last night. He wasn't in control—the bastards drugging him out of his mind had made sure of that—and even now, as I lay stiff, heart pounding with increasing fear as his hands further explored my body, I didn't blame him. But that didn't stop the tears from trickling down my cheeks when he found the softness between my legs and—seemingly without effort—pried my thighs apart.

His first touch to my clit shot a bolt of sensation through my pelvis sharp enough to make me jolt. All pretenses of sleep fled at the tremble he inspired in my body.

351 rumbled against my ear, his mouth pressing to my jaw and then down the back of my neck toward my mark as he stroked me.

I wasn't ready for it, my folds still dry and closed like reluctant petals, and my mind was blank with mounting panic. His touch was too raw against my bud of nerves, too direct.

"It hurts!" I gasped, finally breaking through the panic at the too-intense rubbing of my most sensitive spot. My hands moved to his of their own accord, grasping onto his wrist to still his movements.

Teeth clamped shut around my nape, so immediate and mercilessly I didn't even flinch before my body went lax.

351 growled approvingly, never releasing his grasp on my neck, and let his fingers press in harder against my clit.

Unable to resist this time, let alone stop him, I whimpered pleadingly as he rubbed it slowly again and again, coaxing it out from its protective hood despite my hips jerking in protest. Only when it was fully swollen against his touch did he finally relent, sliding his two fingers lower between my flushed lips, spreading them apart until he reached my entrance.

I grimaced against the expected pain of dry penetration when he dipped them inside, but the stretch was slick and felt... good.

He pumped his finger into me a few times, the lewd sounds emitting from my sex making me draw a shuddering breath just as he returned his focus to my clit.

This time, there was no pain.

I jerked and moaned when he rubbed his now dripping wet fingers across my little bud, zings of ecstasy shooting through my pelvis.

God, it felt... I panted and groaned as he rubbed me

hard and fast, my body tensing despite his strong jaw keeping me still, and I knew what was coming.

My orgasm rocked through me, making me arch against the alpha as I moaned in pleasure. It came in short, hard pulses, flooding my mind until I finally collapsed onto the mattress in an exhausted heap. 351 released his grip on my neck and pulled back.

Endorphins danced in my blood as I let my hooded gaze meet his.

He stared down at me, green-blue eyes dark with desire, and for a moment I was filled with gratitude that he had ensured my pleasure despite my initial reluctance. He could have easily torn into me like the savage beast he was.

He didn't let me bask in gratitude for long.

Apparently content he'd prepared me enough, he pushed me to my stomach, and before I could think to crawl away, he settled his huge bulk between my spread thighs, trapping me with a firm grip on my hips.

A rough yank, and I was on my knees, and my heart burst into overdrive when his huge cock pressed right up against my splayed nether lips.

TWELVE

351

His female whimpered, the fragrance of her fear sharp enough to pierce the delicious aroma of her desire.

He growled, frustrated that his attempt to calm her had failed, and pushed her head down to the mattress, clamping his hand around the back of her neck in the way that made females relax.

She twitched, fighting his hold, but finally succumbed with a small whine.

There.

She was dripping between her legs as he pushed his blunt cock against her silky softness, her body ready and flowering open despite her reluctance to submit.

Why did she fight him? She was *his!* His to take, his to mate—his to calm with his strength and virility.

Grunting with equal amounts of raw lust and frustration, he penetrated her weeping opening and was immediately greeted with the tight, wet heat of her cunt pulsing frantically around the rim of his cock head.

He groaned with overwhelming pleasure and tightened his hold on the little thing's neck when she squealed and lurched forward. Holding her firmly in place, he gritted his teeth and pushed through her body's resistance, forcing his cock all the way in until her bottom smacked against his hips and he'd impaled her completely.

She babbled something—he couldn't focus on her words through the bliss ringing in his ears—and reached back, attempting to push at his stomach.

The alpha growled, a flash of irritation that she still refused to submit completely burning through his pleasure—and fueling it.

But she could fight if she wanted—he had her conquered now, and it was only a matter of time before she realized that too. Time, and a hard enough rutting to settle her end of their fresh pair-bond. He could feel her in his chest where the bond was hooked, her fear and uncertainty, and he knew with every instinct in his body that she needed to surrender before the bond would be satisfied.

Roaring, he snapped his hips, eliciting another howl from the small woman as her left hand clawed feebly at his abs. He grabbed it and forced it to the mattress next to where he had her neck pinned, using his hold to gain even deeper access to her fluttering core.

And then, *finally*, he fucked her. Thoroughly.

She wasn't as wet and open as the last time he'd been inside of her, wasn't in heat like before, but though her cunt clutched painfully tight on him for every thrust, it was only a few moments before the slick between her thighs allowed him to rut her as fast and hard as his cock needed. It was as if her body knew how to open for her alpha now and only needed a reminder before it obeyed. The first time had been a battle for every thrust, until his knot had hooked behind her pelvic bone.

Finally, some long minutes of excruciating pleasure later, she stopped fighting.

He growled in triumph when her body stopped straining against his hold, her muscles softening under his hands. He released her neck and wrists to finally grab at her hips. She'd submitted, even if reluctantly so —it was time to reward her with what they both craved.

But when he picked up the pace, his female moaned hoarsely—and then she widened her legs and arched her back, pushing back against his aggression with the smallest of movements.

True surrender.

He wasn't prepared for the rush of mind-shattering ecstasy splintering through his head in response. Black desire darkened his vision, his knot swelling hard and fast. It was instinct alone that let him push it past her straining lips before it became too engorged.

She *screamed,* the pain stronger in her voice than when he'd first penetrated her, and he had to clamp his arms and legs around her and push her bucking body against the mattress with the bulk of his own torso to stop her from lurching forward in her desperation to escape his knot.

Grunting at the electric currents of rapture sparking up his spine as he began to come in powerful spurts, he rocked his hips forward, ensuring his still-swelling knot pushed through the tight spot in her pelvis that caused her to sob and shake in the prison of his arms.

He felt it the second his tie locked where it was supposed to, like a puzzle piece snapping into place.

And so did she.

She jolted hard underneath him, a gasp escaping her in a dry croak—and then her cunt clamped down tight, snapping shut around him like a vise.

They groaned together as her pink inners locked on his knot, the pleasure so strong he could hardly move. But he did, knowing what she needed from her alpha.

Gritting his teeth, he ground his hips against her, forcing his knot into the ribbed flesh along her frontal wall fluttering against his pulsing girth.

The little female screamed again, but this time, there was no pain lancing through his ears.

She jerked and bucked uselessly, but it wasn't to escape his brutal penetration. Her body ground on his knot, riding it hard as a rough orgasm tore through her small frame. Her cunt gushed for him, making the rocking motion draining his cock for its seed slick and smooth.

HER CLIMAX LASTED A LONG WHILE, peaking and ebbing like waves on the ocean as her cunt forced pleasurable shivers almost too intense to bear through his engorged cock.

He groaned with her when her tight heat pulsed on him yet again, crooning praise when she gushed another trickle of slick to ease the coupling.

Though he searched the dazed echoes of his memories, he could think of nothing that had felt like this—like being buried balls-deep in the woman he'd known was his mate since they'd first locked eyes. And nothing else ever would.

It wasn't a conscious thought, but an instinctive knowledge that went all the way to his marrow. *They'd* punished him for rejecting another, but no pain could ever compare to the primal knowledge of having found his mate at last.

When she finally stilled, her tears dry on her cheeks and her whimpers of pleasure fading to deep, shuddering breaths, his knot finally released its tie on her battered depths.

In their bond, he felt her exhaustion and the sweet song of her satiation, but as the silence spread in their cell, he sensed a dull flicker of her fear pulse unpleasantly in their bond as well.

He rutted her again then, his body heavy on her back and his cock hard between her thighs, knotting her deeply when she surrendered her pleasure to him once more.

And again. And again. And again, until finally, some long hours later, there was nothing but submission humming through her end of their bond.

THIRTEEN

LILLIAN

The next time I woke up, it was definitely my aching muscles that first grabbed my attention.

I groaned at the dull throbbing between my thighs, wincing as I tried to move into a more comfortable position.

A questioning grunt sounded next to my ear, the warm, heavy press on top of me moving slightly to accommodate me.

I stilled, even as my heart quickened as 351 rubbed his nose against the side of my head, a lump of panic forming in my hoarse throat. "Please. Please, don't. It hurts so much. Please."

351 made a noise of displeasure, then clamped his jaws around the base of my nape. It wasn't hard enough to agitate the scabs from his claiming bite; just enough

that the trigger points there sent a calming rush of endorphins through my blood.

It helped quell my mounting panic just enough. I breathed raggedly, but deeply underneath him, forcing oxygen through my lungs until he deemed me calm enough and finally let go again.

"Food." His voice was rough, barely more than a growl, but it was a word.

Despite his still huge and naked body on top of mine, an overpowering rush of relief crashed over me. His humanity was returning.

"Y-yes. I'm hungry," I said.

He grunted and lifted off me, exposing my skin to the cool air. Goosebumps immediately crawled up my arms and down my torso at the loss of his heat, but I still breathed easier without his closeness and scent filling my nostrils.

There had been pleasure when he mounted me, but it had come with a lot of pain. On some level, I would almost have preferred it to just be agony and nothing else, because then it would have been easier to deal with. Now...

I forced myself to turn over so I could keep a wary eye on 351 as he crouched down to pick up a tray by the cell door. Breakfast must have arrived while I was out cold.

Some might call what he'd done to me last night rape. I might have too, were it not for the pleasure that had coursed through me with every rough thrust 351 made into my protesting core. But despite everything, despite how much his brutal cock had hurt me, the fact that he had ensured my body's enjoyment meant I couldn't ignore what I'd known since the first time he took me: he was a slave to his instincts. If I'd had no choice in what happened to me, he'd had even less.

At least I'd signed the contract that landed me here of my own free will. He'd had no say when they stripped him of his humanity.

But that didn't mean I didn't shrink back when he walked back to the mattress, tray in hand, and the hugeness of him reminded my aching body of the strength and ferociousness he'd taken me with while I'd howled and sobbed for mercy.

351 frowned down at me, clearly displeased, and I clasped my hand to the back of my neck with an involuntary whimper.

But instead of forcing me into submission again, he set the tray in front of me and went to fill our cups from the sink, and I breathed a shaky sigh of relief. Perhaps the return of his speech, however limited, meant he was capable of fighting whatever primitive alpha instincts were telling him to put his female in her place.

He returned with our now filled cups, placing mine on the floor next to my end of the mattress before he sat down on the other side of the tray.

"Thank you," I whispered.

351 grunted. "Eat."

Seemed I was allowed to feed myself today, then.

I picked up one of the chunks of bread and carefully dipped it into what looked like leftover stew from yesterday, making sure not to brush against the alpha's hands as he dove in.

We ate in silence, but even though I made sure to keep my eyes on the food, I could feel his gaze on me the whole time. When I finally dared a glance at his face, it became clear that he was studying me. His eyes tracked every move I made, every flutter of my hands as I tried to stop them from shaking.

"Why?"

I drew in a sharp breath at the unexpected sharpness of his voice cracking between us.

"Why... help? Risk..." he growled, clearly irritated with his limited vocabulary.

"They were hurting you," I said, flashes of his bloodied back finally easing my hands' trembling. The reminder that I was in here because I had tried to put a stop to the horrors I'd seen somehow soothed me. Despite everything, it had been worth it, because I couldn't have turned my back on this. "All of you, the women too. I couldn't let them continue."

"Dumb." The word was spoken with so much anger, my heart picked up speed in another uneasy pitter-patter. "In danger. Can't protect."

"I know I can't protect anyone when I'm in here too,

but I couldn't have gone to the media without proof. Pictures wouldn't have been enough, they had to see—"

"No," he interrupted me, agitation drawing his lip up in a silent snarl. "Females don't protect. *I* protect! Mate."

"Oh." I swallowed hard. I guessed now was as good a time as any to straighten a few things out. "Look, I know... I know you can't help being all wrapped up in instincts. It's not your fault—it's the drugs. Like I couldn't help... the heat. They drugged me too. What happened between us. The... the bite. It wasn't our decision. I know that, and deep down you must too. I am not your mate. Not really. We didn't choose—"

"*I* choose," he growled, something dark flashing in the depths of his eyes that made me recoil as my heart slammed into my throat. But I wasn't quick enough, and he snatched me by the neck before I could get off the mattress. His big hand closed around the top part of my throat and jaw, squeezing just tight enough to labor my breathing.

I gasped and clawed at his hand with my fingers, the panic I'd managed to settle since the return of his speech ramping up tenfold as I stared wide-eyed at the furious alpha.

"Mate," he snarled, blazing eyes narrowed. "*Mine.*" And then he reached out with his free hand and touched my chest exactly where the *thing* buried behind my ribs was squirming anxiously.

"Bond."

I blinked, my frantic clawing at his fingers around my throat stilling. "B-bond?"

"*Bond,*" he repeated, voice firm as he touched his hand to his own chest right underneath his heart. "Mate."

The mating bond.

I'd always thought it was a metaphoric bond—a feeling. A promise.

But the thing in my chest—that was physical. There was something *there* that hadn't been there before. Like a hook, or a... a rope.

A bond.

I stared mutely at his hand fisted against his chest in the exact spot where I could feel it behind my own ribs.

Our mating bond.

"Why?" I croaked, fighting back tears I didn't fully understand. It was as if up until then I'd thought there was some sort of escape clause—some possibility that what had happened to me wasn't permanent. As if him claiming me while we were both drugged out of our minds would mean we weren't truly mated. Not in the real sense. Not... not for *life.*

But the physicality of it—of suddenly understanding that the thing I'd felt in my chest since waking up after our first mating was his bond. His claim on my body. On my *life*... The finality of it came crashing in over me until I felt like I was drowning, the only thing keeping me above water the strength of his hand against my windpipe forcing me to feel every breath wheezing in and out of my lungs.

"You *chose* this? *Why?*"

"*Mine,*" he repeated, as if that was all the explanation needed.

"*No!*" I snarled, the panic inside of me melting into rage. I clawed at his hand, gritting my teeth with the effort of freeing myself. "I'm not something you own! I don't want a *mate!* Let go of me!"

Fury so intense it overshadowed my own blazed in his eyes as he got to his feet in the blink of an eye, taking me with him by my throat. But before the sharp pull on my neck became painful, he threw me down on the mattress on my back.

"*Mine,*" he ground out as he stood above me, muscles bulging in response to the fury in his eyes.

And that was when I saw it.

The mass of flesh between his thighs was hardening rapidly, expanding into an angry, flushed pole.

All my anger withered at the sight, pure terror overtaking me instead. My poor sex clenched at the sight, pangs of agony resounding deep in my abused abdomen.

"No..."

He fell on top of me, immobilizing my frantic attempts at crawling backward and away as he pinned my body to the mattress with his huge bulk.

"No, please!" I beat at his shoulders to get him off

me, but I might as well have been smacking a rock for all the reaction I got. Ignoring me as if I had no more strength than a newborn kitten, 351 forced my thighs apart and seated his hips between them, letting that brutal cock head kiss my still swollen opening.

"*Submit,*" he growled, the anger in his eyes even more prominent in his gravelly voice. "*Now!*"

"I will, I will!" I gasped, forcing myself to stop fighting. "Just please, don't. I beg you, please—it hurts so much!"

He frowned at me, eyes still narrowed. "Hurts?"

"Y-you're too big," I whispered, the first tingles of relief that he wasn't forcing his way in yet calming my frantic heart just a smidge.

"Fits," he growled, rocking his hips so the broad pole trapped between us slid up between my lower lips, rubbing over my clit.

The wet sound it made made me realize I was slickening up for him again, as if my body didn't care that another rutting like yesterday's would likely leave me with a permanent limp.

I grimaced. "You hurt me. I'm sore, and I don't want it again. Please."

351 growled, but didn't advance, which gave me enough time to think of another defense for my poor, swollen nethers.

"We can't keep having sex—my birth control will be

out of my system soon. I-If you take me again, I might become pregnant."

The first glimmer of true hesitance showed on his face. "Pregnant?"

"Yes. W-we can't let that happen. You don't know what they'd do to a baby here. Please."

The alpha above me moved a hand between our bodies, placing it over my stomach in a protective gesture that made an odd sensation of warmth hum in the bond hooked in my chest.

When he looked at me again, the darkness in his eyes was gone. "Don't fight. Submit."

"I am, "I whispered.

"No." It was a small growl. "I... need... you. You fight, I need. Pregnant. Submit. I need you... less."

Oh. I stared at him wide-eyed when it dawned on me what he was trying to say. Flashes of my stepdad and how only cowering and begging forgiveness would pull him out of his rages filled my mind. My mother had called it his *alpha mood* when she'd dabbed witch hazel on my bruises after he'd left to cool off at the nearest bar.

It would seem that for 351, challenging his dominance brought out other kinds of urges.

So that was why he'd been so rough last night. I'd fought him.

"How?" I croaked.

Instead of answering, he bent his mouth to my

throat, forcing my head back so he could close his teeth around it.

I lay still, heart pounding in my chest as he growled low, showing me his dominance over my existence.

I closed my eyes and thought of how I'd promised myself to never let an alpha dominate me the way my mother had let my stepdad dominate her. He'd ruled her life, and mine along with it.

I kept my eyes squeezed shut while the alpha who'd claimed me as his mate brought his hand to his cock and stroked himself to release, his teeth remaining clamped around my throat while I tried not to cry.

FOURTEEN

351

The weekends when his captors only showed up with food and the lab outside his cell was otherwise abandoned had been their own form of torture up until now.

While he was allowed rest and not injected with whatever the fuck they used to suppress his mind during the week, it was also the time when there was nothing to do. Nothing but to wait for them to return and resume their twisted experiments.

He rubbed the stubble on his skull with both hands as he paced back and forth in front of the bars of his prison, trying to force the fog around his mind to lift completely. It was useless, of course. It had only worked for his first few weeks on the drugs—these days, coming back from them was getting harder and harder.

He glanced at the female curled up at the far end of the cell. She'd dragged the mattress over so she could lean against the wall, and was now watching him warily as she sat with her arms wrapped around her knees.

Animal urges stirred at the base of his spine and transferred to his cock, and he grunted as he forced his gaze from her again. She was the reason he *had* to come back this time. Every instinct in his body was roaring to flip her over and fuck her raw again, the memory of her sweet cunt clamping and milking him through the night enough for the fog to thicken over his mind.

If they'd been anywhere else, he wouldn't have bothered to fight against his natural urge to solidify their bond until it was ironclad. He was alpha—the prospect of a mate heavy with child only meant he was doing what nature had intended. And with time, she would become used to taking him. She had complained of it hurting when he rutted her, but he knew the truth in the way her body sang under his. She enjoyed their matings as much as he did.

But they weren't free, and he was incapable of protecting her from their captors already. He'd understood the full terror of his inability to save her in those precious seconds before the scent of her heat hit his nostrils when he saw her tied to the breeding post like so many females before her. If she were *pregnant...*

The bond hooked in his chest squeezed painfully, and he brought a hand from his head to rub at it, rolling his shoulders in an attempt to ease the animal instincts threatening to overtake his mind again.

"W-Why are you growling? I-Is someone there?"

351 paused and looked at the now trembling female clutching herself tighter.

Only then did he realize he was snarling, the anger roiling in his gut spilling out through his throat.

"No one," he rasped. *"Calm."*

Despite being coated in his semen, the smell of her fear still permeated the air in the cell, wreaking havoc on his nervous system. Everything in him roared to *fight* and *protect,* but their enemy was out of reach.

351 went back to pacing, staring at the bars as he searched for a weakness in them he knew wasn't there.

HIS MATE WAS quiet until one of the guards brought their evening meal.

351 snarled the entire time the man was within sight, blocking the female's body with his own. This guard was an alpha, one who'd shot 351 during their attempted escape, and he reeked of aggression.

"I don't know why you fucks act so damn ungrateful," the guard growled as he shoved the food through. "You should be dead, yet here you are, handed a fuckin' *mate.* How 'bout some goddamn gratitude, you stupid sonuvabitch?"

351 bared his teeth, his snarl deepening as he stared down the aggressor. He didn't let up until the man spat

on the floor and walked on to antagonize another alpha in one of the cages out of 351's sight.

"Is everyone here a monster?"

He turned to look at his female, frowning at her question. "Everyone... but you." She was the only one to ever show him any kindness, and definitely the only one to attempt to break him out. Even if he now wished she hadn't.

"There has to be someone who will help us," she said, even though he could see the doubt in her beautiful blue eyes. "Someone who will realize how inhumane this is."

He grabbed the tray of food and carried it over to the mattress—it wasn't how his instincts wanted to provide for her, but it was the best he could do. He crouched down by her side, ignoring how she flinched away from him when he reached for her, even if it tore painfully at the bond in his chest and made his instincts howl. Gently, he traced the curve of her cheek, yearning to soothe the broken desperation thrumming through their bond since she woke up.

Her eyelids fluttered, lashes lowering as heat rose to her face at his attentions, and a faint rose blush colored her cheeks. It reminded him of the evening she had come to his cage and cared for his wounds.

"I... should wash. Before dinner," she said, swallowing thickly as she got to her feet.

He frowned, eyes roaming her body. "Eat."

"I will. After. I'm... sticky. I don't want to eat like this." She avoided his gaze as she walked to the small sink by the toilet.

He growled, displeased that she wanted to remove his scent, but her flinching at the sound and the pungent stench of fear made him quiet. In the back of his mind, somewhere past the fog, he remembered a time before this place. A time when females prided themselves on their appearance. His mate came from that world. She wasn't a slave to her instincts like he was, despite how willingly her body responded to his call.

He watched her as she cleaned her skin in the cold water, the tightening of her nipples while she scrubbed at his semen making his cock ache. She was beautiful, his mate. He'd thought as much since the first time he saw her. He remembered the jolt of surprise that something so beautiful and pure had entered his own personal hell.

But of course, even this his captors had managed to taint with their evil.

His bond gave a searing pulse as he watched his mate return to the mattress and start eating, careful not to look at him too much. His mind was always clearer on the second day without the drugs, but right now, he wished it wasn't. Because seeing the female he'd claimed so scared and dirty, without clothes or even a blanket to warm her body... and knowing he couldn't care for her and protect her like an alpha should? That was torture.

Once they were both done eating, and she once more wrapped her arms around herself for warmth, he pulled her against his body and—despite her protests—curled up on the mattress, ensuring his body covered hers. He might not be able to protect her from the horrors that awaited them both, but he could keep her warm. And, at least for a few hours, calm.

Burying his nose in her hair to mask the sterility of the lab and the aggression of other nearby alphas, he forced a purr from his chest.

The tightness in their bond immediately eased and her body went soft underneath him, making the sound easier to produce.

He was still purring for her when sleep finally claimed him some long hours later.

FIFTEEN

LILLIAN

"Get over here, you dumb brute. I'm not in the mood!"

The angry voice ripped me from the bliss of dead sleep, underlined by a deep, furious growl rolling around me.

I blinked the sleep from my eyes and lifted my head. Once again, I found myself completely encased by hard muscle. 351.

The thunderous vibrations against my back told me with all possible clarity that the growl was coming from him.

"Lillian—get that thick alpha over here before I have to bring the taser. Trust me, no one's going to have a good day if I have to knock him out."

The vaguely familiar voice made me look over 351's bulging arm. Despite the alpha's best efforts to cocoon me entirely with his own flesh, I caught a glimpse of the speaker. Kenneth. The lab assistant—and up until last Friday, my colleague.

"What are you doing?" I asked groggily, my tongue thick in my throat from sleep.

"It's time for his injections," he said, impatient as he eyed his wristwatch. "Dr. Axell is expecting you both in twenty minutes, so please don't make this hard."

"Oh, I *am* sorry your Monday's not living up to expectations," I hissed. "Wouldn't want to keep the esteemed doctor waiting."

"It's going to be worse if you don't comply," Kenneth sighed. "Just... trust me. It's in your best interest to get that stupid alpha to cooperate."

As much as I hated my former colleague for how un-horrified he seemed, I didn't miss the warning. After what we'd gone through this weekend, I didn't doubt Dr. Axell would punish both of us if we resisted whatever sick plans he had for his newly mated prize alpha.

"You need to let him inject you," I said, keeping my voice soft to break through the alpha's unrelenting growl. "It's no use fighting. Not now."

351 didn't move, his bulk still pressing me firmly into the mattress and his growl rolling through the cell, warning the other male off.

"Please... they're gonna hurt us more if we don't," I whispered, not wanting Kenneth to hear how scared I was of what was going to happen today.

351's growl finally quieted, ending in an angry huff. He pressed his nose to the side of my face, constricting his arms around me... and I got the sense that he was trying to comfort me. Promise me it would be okay, even if we both knew it wouldn't.

In that moment, for the first time since waking up in this damned cell, I was grateful he was there with me.

Gently, I touched his arm. "Come."

He lifted off me then, slowly, reluctance clear in every line of his body as he unfolded and made his way to the bars.

"Arm," Kenneth said while I tried to hide my nudity behind my hands. I might have spent the weekend naked with 351, but this was different. This was a former colleague—a reminder of the life I'd lost. Of when I was still someone who could expect to be treated like a human being.

351 turned to the bars and allowed Kenneth to jab a needle into his bicep. He glared at the lab assistant the entire time, and I didn't miss how Kenneth avoided his gaze. It was apparent that the alpha's anger had the same effect on beta males as it did me, even from the other side of sturdy metal bars.

The cell seemed colder as I huddled up on the mattress, looking at 351 and waiting for the drugs to take effect.

It wasn't long.

Kenneth kept an eye on his watch until maybe five

minutes had passed. Then he glanced up at me. "Stand back while we collar him, okay? It's rarely a quiet affair, and I don't want you to get hurt."

I bit my tongue to stop a derisive snort from escaping my throat. If they truly cared about whether or not I was hurt, they wouldn't have locked me up with a feral alpha over the weekend, nor forced a mating. But I was too worried about what lay ahead to bicker, so I got to my feet and pressed myself up against the far wall, hands still clamped across my chest and nether region. "Can I have some clothes? Please? I don't... want to walk through the lab naked."

A twinge of what could have been shame shone in Kenneth's eyes for the briefest moment. It was gone before I was even sure that was what I'd seen.

"Sorry, no clothes. Dr. Axell's orders."

He really was a creep. I recalled Gloria's name for him—Dr. Pervert. It wasn't hard to guess how he'd earned that one.

"Stand back now," Kenneth warned, as he turned around and called to someone I couldn't see. Not that I had to wait long to find out.

Three burly guards—alphas, by the looks of them— came into view, long metal poles with collars attached in their hands.

351 let out a low snarl, his shoulders hunching as he took up a defensive stance. When they opened the door,

he charged, but they hit him with a taser, the voltage just high enough to make him jerk and lose his footing. The collars snapped shut around his neck and biceps before he regained full motor control, and by that point, it was too late. Not that that stopped the feral alpha from fighting against his bonds.

He *roared* and threw himself around, trying to break the men's hold on the poles by forcing them against the bars, but it was no use. Through much swearing and banging of metal against metal, they got him dragged out of the cell.

"Come." Kenneth held an arm out toward me. He had to raise his voice to be heard over 351's fury. "I think it's best you stay close. He's not going to want to have you out of sight."

I hesitated, eyes darting to the open door. Only the lab assistant blocked it, but there was no way I could make a break for it and make it out of the compound without being apprehended.

"Don't make me get the restraints," Kenneth said, voice a smidge softer. "Please. Just come."

I did. There was nothing else I could do, so I walked out of the cell, bare feet pattering against the cold concrete floor, still trying to keep some illusion of modesty with my hands clasped across my naked body. It didn't help much, and as Kenneth walked me by the rows of feral alphas at a safe distance from the still-snarling 351, more than one came to the front of their cage, eyes locked on what I couldn't cover. Growls, rich and indulgent rather than aggressive, filled the lab as I tried to shrink in on myself and somehow cover my nose from the assault of alpha stench without taking my hands off my chest or lower half.

Ahead of me, 351's aggression shifted from his jailers to the caged alphas. He snapped and snarled at the other ferals. Only the merciless metal bands encircling his arms and neck kept him moving forward.

We were led through a door I hadn't noticed before and down a long, echoing corridor lit up by fluorescent lights reflecting off white paint. It smelled like disinfectant, but underneath was the faintest lingering odor of alpha aggression.

When we got to three doors more or less side by side, the guards shoved 351 through the farthest one and slammed it shut before Kenneth opened the middle one for me. 351's furious growls echoed from within, and when I stepped through, I saw that we were in the same room, only he was separated from me by sturdy metal bars.

His side of the room was large and empty, made purely from concrete with video cameras mounted behind mesh casings set high in the ceilings. My side was much smaller, but equally bare. A grid in the center of it sharpened the anxiousness twisting in my gut.

On the opposite side of the bars separating me from 351 was a large glass pane much like the one between the breeding room and any observers. Dr. Axell was on the other side. He had a coffee cup in his hands as he watched us.

I shrank back against the bars before I knew what I was doing, the tightly fluttering bond in my chest pulling me toward 351 as effectively as a rope.

He made a soft noise that fully contradicted his furious and unwavering growls since I'd woken up. He pressed his body up against the bars, offering me what little comfort he could.

Ignoring the doctors, as well as the rational part of my brain, which screamed at me that a feral alpha wasn't a good source of comfort right about now, I turned around to face him, searching his eyes for some-thing—anything—that would help me get through this. Some promise that things wouldn't be as bad as I feared.

His grim expression betrayed that he'd been locked in this particular room before. And it did nothing to ease my fears.

"Hello, Lillian. I trust you've had a pleasant week-end?" Dr. Axell's voice blared through the room, making 351 jerk his head up, lip curling in a snarl.

I didn't turn to look at him.

"Ah, you're upset with me. I understand." The smirk in his voice was unmistakable, even through the scratching of the speakers. "But you should take great pride in your contributions to science. Thanks to your sacrifice, we now have a better idea of what bio-markers to look for when matching up our prospective couples. As we speak, Dr. Urwin is preparing a couple of the females for some quality one-on-one time with a few of our alphas. This really couldn't have happened without your rebellious little attempt at breaking out our prize specimen here."

I closed my eyes and drew in a deep breath, trying to find some measurement of strength. The only thing I had was the tightness of the bond in my chest, but it was enough.

"What experiments are you going to run on us?" I asked, forcing myself to look at the doctor over my shoulder. "Why are we here?"

"Ah." He smiled at me from the other side of the glass pane. "I'm sure you recall our talk about the goal for these alphas. We need them to become super-soldiers, if you will. Your role in this is to be... let's call it a *homing beacon* for 351. So for the next few weeks, we need to establish how far we can press him, what lengths he will go to and what odds he can overcome to ensure your well-being. I—" His speech was interrupted as his head jerked to the door. Cutting off the microphone, he went over and opened it, saying a few words to the person on the other side. Then he left the room, and I had a moment's relief—until the door into my section opened, revealing both the doctor and Kenneth.

351 roared a challenge out as they walked to my side, pushing at the bars so hard his muscles bulged in the process, but they didn't move.

"Calm down, subject 351," Dr. Axell said, throwing me a smile and a head-shake as if to say *"Crazy alpha."* "You need to listen, because I am going to tell you what you need to do to protect your mate. Got it?"

Despite the absolute fury in 351's eyes, he stopped pushing at the bars to get through, his snarl dying to a low growl.

Something in his quick submission made my stomach clench. Yeah, he'd been to this room before. And whatever was about to happen... it wasn't good.

"In a moment, guards will put a few objects in the room. If you attack them or try to escape... I will hurt your mate. Got it?"

351 didn't respond. He just kept his darkened eyes glued on the doctor.

"Once the objects are in place, I will assign you a series of challenges. Complete them quickly enough..." Dr. Axell brushed a finger along the side of my neck, making me flinch and 351 snarl, "...and she won't be harmed. Fail, and she will suffer the consequences."

The ominous threat sent a chill down my spine, and 351 roared in fury.

"Hm, I think we need to do a test to ensure our

alpha understands the seriousness of the situation. Kenneth, please hold the female," Dr. Axell said.

Too late, I tried to flinch away, but even though the lab assistant was no alpha, he was still faster and stronger than me. He grabbed hold of my left shoulder and right arm, twisting it up behind me until the pain immobilized me.

"Ow!" I hissed, trying to kick back at him. "Let go of me! You sick pricks!"

On the other side of the bars, 351 went ballistic. He *bellowed* and threw his full weight against the bars shoulder-first, making them twang. They didn't yield, but that didn't stop him from ramming into them again and again, howling with rage the whole time.

"Just get it over with," Kenneth hissed in my ear. He sounded... less than thrilled about what was about to happen, but that didn't make him ease his grip. "The less you fight, the less it'll hurt."

I knew he was right, but I couldn't stop myself from fighting him as he spun me around to face Dr. Axell and the taser in his hand.

Electric agony crackled through my abdomen, making my body jerk and twist as my muscles contracted. Without my conscious decision, I curled in on myself as a scream tore from my throat.

351's wrath took on a desperate note, but I was too focused on the rapid-fire shocks short-circuiting my nervous system to focus on anything but the pain.

It finally stopped as quickly as it'd begun, and I sagged in Kenneth's grasp, sobbing.

"Now let's see if our alpha here isn't more in the mood to cooperate," Dr. Axell said, his tone even and smooth like he hadn't just tortured a woman. "351—walk to the wall opposite the door and kneel. Hands behind your head."

I dragged my gaze up to meet the feral alpha's. His was black with rage, but after a moment's hesitation, he obeyed.

I swallowed thickly as he walked away from the bars and slumped to his knees, locking his fingers behind his neck. There was something about seeing his surrender that knocked whatever strength I'd found out of me. The powerful man brought to his knees by the evil of the doctor whose brilliance I'd once worshipped left no room for doubt about exactly how hopeless our situation was.

I didn't fight Kenneth as burly guards entered 351's section of the room, dragging all manner of equipment with them. It struck me, as I watched them set up what looked like training dummies and some sort of gym equipment, that they could have easily done this before 351 and I had been brought to the room. But Dr. Axell chose to wait until we were here to demonstrate how complete his power now was over the feral alpha.

When the guards were done and had exited the room, Dr. Axell addressed 351 once more.

"Let's start easy today. Please complete your training, 351. The full course. You have... thirty-five minutes. Starting now."

351 cast one long, lingering look on me still sagging in Kenneth's grip. Then he got to his feet and approached the first training dummy.

SIXTEEN

351

The second the cell door shut behind them for the night, his mate went to the mattress and sank down, curling in on herself.

She didn't protest this time when he wrapped himself around her. Instead of stiffening at his touch like she had before, she closed her eyes and buried her face in the arm he offered as a pillow.

The wetness from her lashes made the hollow in his gut expand.

He'd done everything that'd been asked of him. He'd worked through the exercises, multiple times at ever-narrowing time gaps to satisfy their captor's increasing demands, until his muscles ached so bad he could hardly move. And still, he'd continued because *he'd* demanded it. But in the end, it wasn't fast enough—he couldn't physically press his body any faster, and she'd suffered for his failure.

Her screams of agony still haunted him.

351 had refused to play the doctor's games since he got there, only ever indulging in the heat-provoked matings. He had taken every beating and sick punishment, refusing to bend to the other alpha. His conviction that he would never submit to the doctor's will had lasted until he saw his mate writhing in torment.

He could take pain—had been trained to take it for as far back as the fog would let him remember. But nothing had ever felt like the bond hooked in his chest had while the woman he was born to protect cried out for mercy, and there was nothing he could do to stop it.

That... that had broken him. Even in his drugged state, he'd known he'd been beaten. Known his captors truly owned him now. They'd taken the last scrap of him, leaving nothing behind but a void.

And her.

He clutched her tighter to his chest, ignoring the agony in his worn muscles. If they ever took her from him, there would truly be nothing left of what had once been a man, only an empty shell and the broken mind of a tortured beast.

THE NEXT DAY WAS BETTER.

They strapped them both to a chair, told him if he screamed the pain would be given to his mate instead, and sent electric currents through his body.

He didn't make a sound—couldn't, because directly in front of him sat his female with wide, frightened eyes. And he couldn't fail her again. Couldn't hear her pained cries and feel the agony in their bond.

So he endured in silence, even as his body twitched and strained while the voltage surged through him, stronger and stronger until finally, blackness took him.

They forced him back to consciousness with a bucket of freezing water and started the electricity again, but he never broke. And his mate was safe.

When they tossed him on the floor of his cell after, he didn't have the strength to move the few feet to the mattress. But she brought it over to his side and pulled and strained to get him off the concrete, begging him to move, and somehow he managed to climb onto it.

His mate curled up by his side, her slim arms wrapping around his body as she whispered *"I'm sorry"* over and over.

Her tears wetted his skin again, but this time it felt like rain after a long drought. He fell into darkness, the bond in his chest humming softly as his mate tended to his beaten body.

.   .   .

HE WAS AWAKENED by a female's hysterical sobs, and jerked upright despite protesting muscles, heart slamming into overdrive as he sought his mate.

But she was sitting on the mattress by his side, eyebrows locked in a frown as she peered out through the bars.

It took him a moment to realize the commotion was coming from out there, but he couldn't see anyone. Steel shrieked as the door opened and the alpha in the cell on the other side of the concrete wall growling accompanied the panicked female's sobs.

"What's happening?" he asked, voice low to not draw attention from their captors.

His mate turned toward him, eyebrows raised. "You can speak?"

He frowned. "...Yes. I... some." It dawned on him that the fog didn't seem nearly as thick. It was still there, lingering, cutting him off from the parts of his mind he could barely remember any longer. But... "The strain. My body..."

Her eyes widened. "All the exercise and torture—they burned the drugs out of your system much faster than normal, didn't they?" Her voice was a low whisper—clearly, she didn't want to draw attention, either.

He nodded. "I think... yes. What's... Who's in there?"

"They're bringing a woman to him. She thinks they want him to mate her without the heat-drugs, but I think... I think they're trying to establish some form of connection. Like... like us." Her gaze dipped, avoiding his eyes.

351 touched his fingers to the back of her hand, pleased when she didn't jerk away, and focused on what was going on on the other side of the concrete wall.

"Please, don't leave me in here!"

The woman's voice was filled with terror, trailing off into a plaintive wail when the cell door slammed shut. "H-He'll tear me apart!"

"If he shows sexual interest and you can't avoid it, use the oil." It was the beta doctor's voice. Clinical— detached. But 351 knew there was so much hatred under the surface of the man. Had smelled his sense of inferiority and twisted desires on him from the first time he'd brought a female to watch her mounted.

"The purpose of this evening's session is not mating. Try to talk to him. Pet him."

"P-*Pet* him?" The woman sounded incredulous.

"We want you to establish a connection with him. A friendship, if you will. And, to ensure that your goals align with ours, if he does take a liking to you, there will be no more matings with other alphas."

"But there will be with him?" she asked.

"Naturally." Just the slightest sliver of smugness was audible in the beta's voice. "But I'm sure it beats being mounted thrice daily by whichever alpha is pushed into the breeding room. Subject 195 has been selected for you based on your bio-chemistry. There's every chance you two will *hit it off,* if you will."

There was a slight pause. "Okay," she relented quietly. No doubt she had experienced the kinds of punishment the doctors arranged if they were met with anything but complete obedience. A female wouldn't have the stamina to withstand them.

"Splendid. We will fetch you at dinner time." Footsteps retreated from the cell, leaving the prisoners in silence save the general sounds from the lab.

"H-Hey, big guy," the woman whispered. "M-Mind if I touch you?"

An angry growl was followed by a screech and the thud of a body hitting metal.

"Are you okay?" 351's mate called out. To the other female, he realized, frowning.

"Y-Yeah." The other woman sounded like she was trying not to cry.

"Sit down, make yourself as small as possible. He won't hurt you if he doesn't think you're a threat," his mate said.

351 narrowed his eyes when her words brought back how she'd hunched and cowered in his cell since she got here. Was that what she'd been doing? Trying to make herself small so he wouldn't *hurt* her? Flinching when he touched her because she thought he would?

There was silence from the other cell for a bit. Then the woman squeaked again, but it wasn't followed by the sound of her body being thrown. Judging from the low grunting making its way through the wall, 195 was scenting her.

"Don't hurt me, okay?"

The woman's plea was followed by another growl, but there was more curiosity than aggression in it.

351 understood. He didn't know how long he'd been in this cell, but before *her,* it had been unbearably lonely. Even if he'd wanted to, he wasn't able to communicate with the other alphas in the lab, not after they'd taken his ability to speak. Even the rough matings were lonely—the females nothing but mindless, warm bodies, lost in their own drugged hell.

The woman in there with 195 now was the first contact the alpha had had with another human being that wasn't marred by pain and violence.

His mate flashed him a nervous look. "Will she be all right?"

351 grunted, unwilling to make promises he couldn't keep, and she didn't press him.

But the cell was quiet, save for the alpha's grunts and growls as he investigated the new presence in his cell, and 351 lost interest.

It was the first time he had some control over his own mind, and the sight of his little female curled up by his side as she stared at the concrete wall reminded him of his duties.

He needed to find a way out for her.

. . .

THE IDEA DIDN'T FORM until the beta assistant brought them their dinner.

351's hackles raised at the sight of him, a snarl forming in his throat as every instance of the pathetic man holding down his mate and helping the sick doctor torture her flashed through his mind.

But the look the beta shot his mate when he shoved the tray of food through made him pause. There was *guilt* in it.

"Wait." 351 got to his feet and made it to the bars before the smaller man had turned around, eyes wide with shock.

"Please. She... needs help."

The beta looked past him to his mate, a worried frown making its way to his forehead. "Did you hurt her?"

351 growled, as irritated with the accusation as with the beta not understanding him. "No. *He* hurts her."

There was no need to explain who *he* was—the pale expression on the assistant's face made it clear he knew who.

The beta looked away. "There's nothing I can do about that. Just be happy I don't report that your dose is too low."

351 bared his teeth. "You *can*. You won't. Difference."

"It's not that simple," the beta hissed. "Not that I'd expect a criminal to understand." And then he walked away, toward the neighboring cage.

351 roared, smacking his hand against the bars so hard they shuddered and a satisfying pain vibrated through his palm.

The cell door in the neighboring cage rolled open, the beta calling to the woman to come out as he delivered the alpha's meal.

From the short glimpse he caught of her, she seemed vaguely familiar. Perhaps she was one of the females he had been made to mount, but it was impossible to tell. They all flowed into one in his memory.

"It's no use." His mate's voice was quiet as she came to stand by his side, hands wrapped around the bars as she stared after the other woman. "Even if he *dropped* his card, we'd never make it out of the compound. There are too many guards on the upper levels. And he isn't going to risk his own skin by escorting us."

351 glanced down at her, resisting the urge to rub his chest as their bond twanged unpleasantly at the defeated look on her face.

Instincts pulled on him to comfort her, and he grunted when his cock spasmed with eagerness to replace her sadness with pleasure. They hadn't mated in days because she'd been unwilling. His nearness had made her reek of fear, and since that first time in the cell, he'd had enough control of his mind to not ignore it.

Had they been free, he would have taken her anyway, because he'd know that deep down, she wanted it too.

But here, in their shared prison... He wasn't the only man to force her into submission. The alpha doctor forced her. Maybe not with his cock, but he brought her pain and unwilling submission every day.

The thought that she would see his dominance the same as she saw the doctor's was what kept him from following his instincts to subdue her and take her up against the bars until her sadness gave way to bliss.

SEVENTEEN

LILLIAN

"What can I call you?"

It was early morning the day after Dr. Axell had tortured 351 with electricity until he passed out. Twice.

At least, I thought it was early—it was impossible to tell for certain in the underground lab, but it had been many hours since our evening meal, and the silence from the other cells suggested most of the test subjects were asleep.

351 wasn't. I could tell from his breathing. I didn't know if he'd slept at all, or if he'd woken up when I did. He seemed so attuned to me, always aware of my every move. I wouldn't have been surprised if just the change in my heart rate could bring him out of a dead sleep too.

"Alpha," he grunted after a moment's silence.

I lowered my lashes, letting my gaze rest on where his strong arm was wrapped around my midriff, pulling my back flush against his chest. It was better than when he was drug-addled and insisted on sleeping *on top* of me, but his possessive grip left no doubt as to his claim on me. In his mind, I was his mate, and he was my alpha.

My stepdad had insisted my mom call him that too.

"No. Your name," I said, fighting the conflicting emotions in my gut. The fear that had seized from the moment I woke up in his cell was still there, still tearing at my painful memories and the horror of what had been done to us. But there was also something else—some instinctive comfort in the big alpha's nearness, of his unquestioning protectiveness. He'd gone through hell to keep Dr. Axell from hurting me, and hadn't forced himself on me since that first day. Not since the drugs had filtered out of his system enough to afford him some control. They gave him more every morning, but so far the physical strain they put him through seemed to burn them out of his system much faster than before.

If I had met him outside of this compound, I wouldn't have allowed myself to fall into the biological lull of instincts murmuring that he *was* my alpha. That I should surrender to the pull of our bond hooked in my chest. But we weren't out in the real world—I wasn't free. I didn't get a choice of whether I wanted to be mated to an alpha or not, but neither did he. And right now—in this shared nightmare—the only thing that kept me from losing the last shreds of my own humanity was the comfort of his embrace. The low hum in our bond when I accepted his nearness. The scent of his pheromones in my nostrils and the warmth of his skin against mine.

There was no point fighting him when he was the only source of comfort I would ever find in this cell. And the only one who cared if I lived or died.

351 didn't answer, and I rested my hand against the back of his to urge him to speak. "Please. I can't keep calling you 351 in my head."

"Alpha," he said again, voice gravelly and rough.

"I don't want to call you *Alpha*. I know you are, but... I don't even know your name, and God knows how long we'll be locked up together in here. Please."

He growled in response, but it wasn't a threatening sound. Then, after another long pause, he said, "Zach. Barnes."

It came haltingly, as if it'd been a long time since his lips had formed those words.

"Zach," I repeated, tasting the name. I wasn't prepared for the rush of emotion saying it out loud filled me with. There was something profound about having a name for the man I'd only known as a test subject. *"Zach."*

He shivered as I whispered his name into the emptiness of the cell, clutching me tighter.

"Don't... let them hear. They will... hurt you." It was a soft murmur, somehow more human than his usual rough voice. Or perhaps I was just imagining it, because he suddenly seemed so much more human to me, now that I knew his name.

Zach.

"I won't," I whispered. And then, before I could change my mind, I rolled around in his embrace so I was facing him, that place in my chest where our bond was rooted pressed tightly to his. The link between us hummed, sending pleasant shivers through me as I looked up into his eyes. Though his face was shrouded in darkness, knew he was watching me too.

Slowly, unsure of how he'd react, I reached up to brush my hand against the side of his face. He didn't move, but his breath came out low and hoarse.

"Zach," I murmured again. How long had it been since anyone called him by his name? Or touched him with gentleness? How much humanity would *I* have left if I'd been treated like he had, for as long as he had, even without the drugs that stole his mind away?

Our bond hummed more insistently, pulling on me. My gaze flickered from the darkness to where I could just make out the outline of his lips from what little light was available in our cell.

The bond shuddered within, urging me onward, promising that everything would be better if I gave myself to him willingly. His hot breath gusted against my mouth, shooting tingles of anticipation through my body as I grabbed onto his shoulders.

Before I could lean in, something hard and *huge* rose between us, pressing insistently into my stomach.

Zach growled, a rich rumble that sent tendrils of *want* straight to my pelvis, making slickness pool between my thighs. He leant in, but instead of pressing his lips to mine, he sniffed at my throat, scenting me for readiness to mate like his animal urges told him to.

I jerked back, my heart hammering in my chest both from the sudden onset of biologically forced desire—and from realization that despite the fact that I now knew his name and that the drugs weren't as prominent in his system, he was *still* just a feral alpha.

Whatever desperation-induced fantasies I had about this alpha being capable of something more than just base desire, it wasn't my reality.

351—*Zach*—grunted at my sudden unwillingness, hands dropping to grab my hips to pull me back in close.

"No," I croaked, shoving at his bulging body to put distance between us. "Please. Not that."

"You *want*," he growled, frustration and desire thick in his voice as he forced me back to his chest with a rough jerk on my hips. His cock, thick and hard and *scary,* pulsed against my stomach. "I smell you."

"I don't! Stop!" I fought against him, bringing my knees up to push against his too-strong bulge. All it did was anger him.

With a snarl, he got to his knees and pulled me with him, flipping me over onto my front. I tried to kick, but he just yanked on my hips, turning my ass up while my face was still buried in the mattress.

I was so much weaker than him, so much smaller. There was nothing I could do to prevent this. Despite my sex shivering with anticipation of the not entirely unpleasant kind, I choked back the tears pooling in my eyes and thickening in my throat. For one unguarded moment, I'd let myself pretend everything was okay— that if I gave in to our damned bond, I would be rewarded with blissful unity. A partner in this dark hell.

What I received instead was the only thing I'd ever find in this compound:

Forced submission.

The alpha growled behind me, sending a shiver of fear and unwanted need up my spine—and then pressed his mouth to my already dampened folds.

I gasped at the unexpected touch, of the gentleness of it—and then at the shock of electric pleasure as he found my clit and sucked it into his mouth with more force than finesse.

I cried and clawed at the mattress while he sucked on me, the lewd sounds of my increasing wetness and his appreciation of my flavor a constant reverberation around us. The other alphas were waking up at the sounds of my unwilling pleasure, low growls echoing through the lab.

I clenched my eyes and shut them out, not wanting

to hear their excitement, and focused on the orgasm building between my legs.

Zach was rough with my clit, firm lips pulling and plucking at it as his tongue lapped up my slick, but my body responded as if he were playing it like a violin. Despite myself, despite my tears, heat burned in my blood and, at the final moments, I pushed back against him, grinding on his tongue and howling as I orgasmed.

He kept licking me as I slumped on the mattress, still on my knees. I panted as I came down from my high, twitching when he caught my now over-sensitive clit with flicks of his tongue, but otherwise keeping still. Hoping I could stay in my cocoon of pleasure and not have to deal with what came next.

It was a useless hope, of course. It didn't take long until the alpha was done lapping up the liquids I'd spilled in my climax, and I bit my lip as he straightened and got into position behind me.

The heated, pulsing head of his cock nestled in between my splayed lower lips, testing my body's resistance with a firm push.

I groaned, my slick tunnel eager to accept him, but still not used to gaping wide enough for an easy entry.

"Please, Zach. Please don't." I don't know why I begged him again—I'd long since given up on reaching his frayed humanity through the haze of his rut—but the ache of him as he breached my opening stoked my desperation anew. "Don't force me."

He growled in response, deep and *angry,* and I closed my eyes tight and waited for the pain of his thrust.

But it didn't come.

He clutched at my hips, digging his fingers into my flesh, but at my gasp of pain he let go with another snarl, pushing me away hard enough that I landed flat on my stomach with a grunt.

When I looked at him over my shoulder, too stunned to speak, he shot me a look I couldn't decipher in the dark and got to his feet. Shoulders tight and muscles flexing, he went to the bars, leaning against them.

I could make out his profile in the low light. He was staring into the lab, eyes fixed on God knows what. The tension rolled off him in near tangible waves, making me huddle on the mattress.

But he'd stopped.

Even in the depths of his rut, he'd stopped.

NEITHER OF US slept anymore that night. Zach stayed leaned against the bars, glaring into the lab, and I huddled on the mattress, missing his body heat, but unwilling to ask him to hold me. I wasn't dumb—whatever it'd taken the feral alpha to restrain himself, I wasn't about to push it with requests for warmth.

When our breakfast arrived, we ate in silence with as much space between us as the cell would allow, and after, Zach went back to staring out into the lab.

He growled at Kenneth when he injected him with the usual serum, but didn't put up a fight. Not until the guards came to lead us back to the test room we hated so much.

Then he fought, throwing his massive body at our captors, snarling and howling as Kenneth pulled me from the cell to follow him. It didn't help. It never did.

"Is it going to be bad today?" I asked quietly as I walked by my former colleague's side. It wasn't that every instinct in my body didn't scream at me to fight and run, but I knew better. There was no point in adding to the pain.

Kenneth didn't answer, but his jaw tightened.

I swallowed thickly as he refused to look at me, keeping my eyes locked straight ahead on the guards forcing Zach forward. Whatever was ahead, I held on to the gratitude that the alpha hadn't forced himself inside of me last night. Whatever torture lay ahead, at least I had been spared that one indignity.

I was led into the larger room of the test chamber while Zach was shoved into the smaller area closer to the observational room.

Kenneth guided me to the back wall farthest from where Zack was snarling and pacing behind the bars, and I paled at the sight of a pair of cuffs chained to a thick metal hook drilled into the concrete. They were made of steel-reinforced leather, and the chain was reasonably long, so they weren't too uncomfortable as he strapped me in. However, standing with my back turned to the large room made a sense of foreboding set in as the lab assistant left without ever speaking a word to me.

I looked over my shoulder, catching a glimpse of Zach's pacing form, but then Dr. Urwin's face slipped into my field of vision. He closed the door and walked the length of the room, a deceitfully pleasant expression on his features.

"What are *you* doing here?" I spat.

His smile didn't wither. "Why, I'm here to assist, of course. As we both know, there are certain *procedures* Dr. Axell cannot perform, and I am only too happy to help."

Sick dread nestled in my gut at the memory of what he'd said when he tied me down and gave me the heat-inducing drugs that first, horrible night. How Dr. Axell wasn't capable of preparing me for the mating because he would risk entering a rut himself.

They were going to induce another heat.

"You are a disgusting pervert," I growled as he held up a syringe, inspecting the liquid in it. "He already claimed me—this is just for your own sick amusement, isn't it?"

The beta doctor chuckled and, without pause, jabbed the needle into my thigh. I cussed and jerked, but he'd emptied the syringe into my flesh before I could move away.

"Now, now, sweet Lillian. As much as your pretty pussy is a delightful sight when it's gaping around a fat knot, we're here for *science*. Today's dose is not like the last one we gave you. It will give you some symptoms of heat, true, but nothing as severe as last time. *Just* enough to get your hormones flowing. And, you'll be happy to know, it will be much swifter-acting. No suffering for hours as you wait for your heat to break."

I frowned at him. "Why? What are you going to test me for?"

He chuckled again. "Oh, this isn't to test *you*, Lillian. I thought we'd made it perfectly clear: you are not our main interest. Your mate is. And, as you may have been able to guess from the last two days, we're currently determining how far we can push him to keep you safe. We already know the drugs keeping him feral have greatly increased his strength and endurance—but how much *more* will he be able to give us when failure means pain for you?"

"And the torture yesterday wasn't enough?" I ground out through gritted teeth.

"Oh, yesterday was *excellent*," Dr. Urwin said. He gave me a long, lecherous once-over that had Zach snarling furiously from behind the bars. "But we need to determine what sort of methods will yield the best results. Exactly what threats to your safety will give us the most dedicated super-soldier? After today, we'll be one step closer to finding out."

He left, shooting me a smirk that turned my stomach. The heavy clang of the door closing behind him left me with an ominous sense that whatever came next, the electrocution I'd endured was likely going to seem mild in comparison.

But for the longest time, nothing happened.

I remained alone in my section of the room, chained to the wall while the feral alpha paced, agitated growls rumbling from his throat at uneven intervals. But no one tased us. No one even spoke.

I knew Dr. Axell was behind the glass, watching us, along with probably Kenneth and Dr. Urwin, but they didn't *do* anything. They just observed.

The heat rising in my body was so slow, it took me a while to realize I wasn't cold any longer. I'd gotten so used to always freezing whenever I wasn't wrapped up in Zach's embrace that at first, it was a relief.

Then the delicate ache between my thighs set in.

I gritted my teeth and prepared for the onslaught of *need,* but when it came, it was nowhere near what it'd been the last time. It was a sweet, sultry pulsing in my clit and lower lips that drummed gently through my body, and I sighed and shifted my footing.

Behind me, Zach growled again, but questioning this time. *Richer,* somehow. He could undoubtedly smell me.

I flushed at the thought, remembering how eagerly he'd licked me last night. No doubt my natural scent was quite a bit of a turn-on for him.

It seemed like *Dr. Pervert* and his staff were looking to get another show, and as my clit throbbed between my thighs, I quietly resigned myself to my fate. I might fear Zach's size and roughness, but at least the drugs would ease our mating.

And, I told myself as the door clanged open again and I shakily prepared for what was to come, last night, he'd stopped himself. If he were even remotely in control of his own mind, he wouldn't touch me today, either.

Somehow, the knowledge that the man who'd claimed me as his mate wouldn't ravage me if he had any other choice made what I knew lay ahead bearable.

The pulse of desire between my legs also helped.

A loud howl, followed by several snarls from the hallway on the other side of the now open door, made me jerk up, anxiety slamming my heart into overdrive as I looked over my shoulder.

What?

Behind the bars, Zach *roared*. He rammed against them, trying to break through the solid metal with a desperation that did nothing to ease my terror.

The howls from the hallway came closer, mixing with Zach's fury until my ears rang with alpha rage.

Every hair on my body stood on end as I stared open-mouthed at the door.

No!

The speaker mounted somewhere above my head scratched to life. *"As I'm sure you've figured out by now, today's test is a little different,"* Dr. Axell said. *"May I suggest you close your eyes and think of the importance of this sacrifice you're about to make for science and our nation's defense?"*

They spilled into the room then. So many huge, naked men. Alphas, snapping and snarling at each other and at the guards driving them in with metal poles attached to their collars.

The guards released them, slamming the door shut.

Leaving me alone with five feral alphas.

EIGHTEEN

LILLIAN

They smelled me instantly.

A hush fell over them as five sets of eyes locked on my shaking form at the other end of the room. Zach's heavy body smacking repeatedly against the bars was the only sound for a few agonizing, drawn-out seconds.

Then all hell broke loose.

They were on me so fast, huge hands grabbing at me, yanking on my body.

I screamed, kicking wildly at the alpha who got between my legs, cock poised and ready to breach my pussy. Another pulled him off me, trying to take his place.

They ripped at me, unconcerned with my terrified shrieks. They fought each other like a pack of wild dogs, snarling and clawing, seeking my weeping but unwilling sex. The stench of alpha rut enveloped me, choking me with a thick blanket of male hormones.

Metallic screeching pierced the din, demanding the alphas' attention. I managed to look over my shoulder and caught a glimpse of the bars separating us from Zach lifting up.

A jolt of wild hope shot through me as the alpha leapt across the room. He impacted with the feral beast closest to my backside, slamming him to the floor with his weight. Another immediately took his place, but Zach managed to twist up and out, kicking the other male in the side of the knee so he tumbled to the floor.

Wild howls and snarls followed, mixing with the thuds of bodies colliding.

The remaining alphas seemed to deem Zach a big enough threat that they turned their focus from me to him.

It was an unfair fight from the start. They were five against one, and though they'd been fighting each other to get first rights to me, they all recognized the need to subdue the newcomer.

And yet he fought them. Punching, kicking, clawing, and biting like a beast, he tore into my attackers with a rage I'd never seen in a human before.

I couldn't see every part of the fight, couldn't see Zach most of the time as he was buried underneath the five hulking men trying to subdue him. All I could do was press myself against the wall and pray. Pray that the connection between us that I'd denied since he placed his mark on my neck was strong enough to somehow let him overcome impossible odds.

After what must have been at least twenty minutes, one of the alphas slumped to the floor, unmoving. Five minutes later, another crawled a few feet away before collapsing.

The next two followed more quickly, and then there was just Zach and one other feral left.

My heart clenched when I could finally see my defender.

Blood dripped from his eyebrow, one eye was almost swollen shut, and his already scarred body was marred with long, bloody gashes. The only consolation was that the other alpha was in a similar state.

They pulled away from the fallen alphas, getting to their feet so they could circle each other, still snarling, spitting blood onto the floor as they sized up their opponent.

If he wins this fight, I'll never turn him down again.

It was perhaps a ridiculous promise to make—but it was the only thing I had to give. I couldn't give Zach his freedom, couldn't give him any reward for saving me from the most horrific experience a woman could go through, other than my silent promise that I would submit to him. It was the only thing he had demanded of me, and as he launched himself at the last of my would-be rapists, I swore to myself that whatever he needed from me... I would give to him.

They were both tired, which was made obvious by their slower reflexes. They each landed several blows, and I winced at the spray of blood that fanned across the room when the other alpha punched Zach in the jaw. But Zach managed to spin around and push forward, using the momentum to smack his knuckles directly into his opponent's temple.

The other alpha omitted a sickly groan and collapsed as if the life had left his body. Which it might have, judging from the power of that swing.

Zach straightened, his snarl withering as he stared down at his now lifeless opponent.

"Thank you." My whisper broke through the sudden silence in the room, raspy and hoarse. "Thank you."

Zach jerked his head up, and the wild darkness in his eyes made me simultaneously shrink back and clasp my thighs tightly together as a sharp pang of want flared between them. Apparently, whatever hormones the doctors had triggered appreciated the conquering of other alphas to save me... quite a bit.

But Zach didn't seem to notice either reaction. He rolled his shoulders to ease the pain in his body and then strode to my side.

A concerned growl as he touched my back made me realize the alphas had ripped my skin in their eagerness to mount me, but it was nothing compared to the injuries he'd sustained while protecting me.

"I'm fine," I said, bringing my bound hand to his face to try and stem the blood from his split eyebrow. "But you're hurt. I'm... I'm so sorry."

He grabbed my hands and yanked on the cuffs trapping my wrists, but they were enforced with steel and didn't give.

"Don't," I said when one of the cuts on his torso began bleeding again from the effort.

He didn't obey, clearly angry with the state of what he considered his female.

"Zach," I whispered. "Stop. I'm okay." Hesitantly, following the pull of the tether in my chest, I leaned in and rested my cheek against his chest, allowing the closeness between us to settle the agitated male—and, after a little while of listening to the drum of his heart, my own frayed nerves.

He'd saved me. Again. Right then, I didn't care about our audience, or the passed out alphas scattered on the floor. I just cared that he was there, big, strong, and warm, protecting me.

"Thank you," I murmured against his thick chest.

Zach made a rumbling noise in response, and something in the rough tone made my abdomen clench.

"Oh." I pulled back, realizing too late what he'd take my touch as.

The big alpha grabbed me by the nape and pulled

me back in, bending his own head to the side of my face, nostrils flaring to take in my drug-enhanced scent. It seemed my attempt at calming him had worked far too well, letting his attentions shift. And rapidly so, based on the hardness that swelled between us.

I swallowed at the feel of it as the alpha drew his nose up the length of my neck, nibbling on my claiming mark. Tendrils of sensation went straight from his teeth to my nipples and clit, and I moaned. Everything about him, from his touch to his sounds to his scent, made the bond behind my ribs hum with excitement and slickness drip from my sex. Despite my reluctance for what he clearly had in mind, and the trauma we'd just been through, my body was preparing for him.

He maneuvered behind me, large hands brushing along my sides. He was gentler than the feral alphas who'd tried to rape me, even though the strength in his grip was unmistakable and his intentions the same.

It made it so much easier to remember the promise I'd made only moments earlier.

He'd saved me. And I wasn't going to resist him again.

When he grabbed my thighs to spread them wide, I leaned forward until I could rest my torso against the wall, surrendering my pussy to him.

Zach growled, pleased with my submission, and dragged his thumbs up along my lower lips, exposing my pink tunnel.

He didn't touch my clit this time, and I bit my lip when he pushed his cock head against my opening, clutching my hands in the shackles to steel myself for what I knew was coming. My head swam with drug-fueled hormones, heating my body, softening it for penetration, but I knew from experience that this was going to *hurt*.

As if he knew my thoughts, the alpha wrapped an arm around me, pulling my torso back so I could rest my head against his chest. It also pushed out my ass, opening my pelvis up and pressing my straining lips around the very tip of his cock.

I groaned at his girth catching in my opening, but the angle and my wetness made the stretch bearable.

Zach groaned with me and buried his face in my hair, his breath ghosting against my neck and sending delicious shivers down the length of my body.

And then he pushed home.

I let out a scream and rose to my tippy toes as he barreled through my tight sheath, forcing me wide with that monstrous cock, but the alpha grabbed my hips and dragged me down flat again, forcing his cock all the way to the bottom of my pussy with a grunt.

I gasped in agonized protest as I shook in his embrace, but beyond the pain of penetration... something else stirred.

When he'd had me in his cell, it had taken a long time for the first inklings of pleasure to drown out the agony of his size. This time, however... I wasn't sure if it was the angle, the drugs... or just my body growing accustomed to his brutal penetrations, but pleasure so sharp it made my toes curl rocked through my pelvis in equal measure to the pain of being so full.

He grunted again and drew his hips back, dragging the thick shaft and hard rim of his head through my pussy much rougher than I was prepared for, only to slam his cock back in before I was ready.

"Fuck!" My pained cry rang through the room as the alpha fucked me hard and rough, making my pussy squelch lewdly for every push through my straining opening.

But through the deep burn of his ruthless stretch, hot pleasure crackled in every nerve ending, mixing reluctant moans with my pained cries.

He was so big behind me, inside of me, taking control of my body so he could force pleasure into me for every savage thrust, and I finally understood what it meant to surrender.

The second I gave into the pleasure, the ache faded to the background, still there but irrelevant. There was just him, his scent, his touch, his brute strength, and the torturous ecstasy rolling through my pelvis.

When his thrusts became shorter and sharper, Zach released my torso and grabbed my hips instead, and this time, I knew what was coming.

I braced my palms against the rough concrete wall

and widened my thighs for him, taking the pounding all the way to my core, urging him to finish with mewled pleas.

It worked.

The swelling at the bottom of his already too-thick shaft grew swiftly, catching against my opening for every time he slammed in hard. The alpha growled in response, grinding against me, forcing the still-growing knot through my opening only to pull it back out on the backstroke.

It hurt like hell, and despite my resolve to submit, I yowled and clawed at the wall, trying to tuck my ass to escape his brutal knot. I knew it would only get bigger before it was over.

He didn't let me.

Zach clamped his teeth around the back of my neck, forcing me to still with a desperate whimper as he kept grinding his fat knot in and out of my aching channel. Finally, several strokes later, it was too big to pop back out.

Growling with unmistakable pleasure, he tightened his grip on my hips and slammed his cock all the way to the very bottom of my pussy, the wide head kissing my cervix as his knot forced the narrowest part to gape before it finally hooked behind my pelvic bone.

I *screamed,* the pain so overwhelming it took me several seconds to feel the roar of orgasm burning through my entire abdomen with a force so great my vision blackened and my knees gave in. If he hadn't kept me upright, I would have fallen—but he did.

Zach held onto me, grinding his horrific knot in just the right place to keep my conquered sex pulsing and spasming in frantic ecstasy, forcing my climax to go on and on until I forgot what it felt like to not be tied by my pussy to the brutal male. There was only him, and me, and unending, agonizing pleasure.

I HAD no recollection of time passing, only of slowly settling relief as my body's frantic contractions on the cock lodged deep in my core eased to a tremor. The fog of bliss was even slower to subside, and for a long time, I simply hung from my chained wrists, unable to think as Zach held me tight against his body, ensuring I didn't fall.

He was crooning at me, I dimly realized. Praising me with nibbles and licks against the mark on my neck.

Checking that I was okay.

I squeezed my pelvic muscles experimentally, then winced as my pussy found no give in his still-swollen knot.

Zach groaned, a pleasured sound, and I stilled, not wanting to encourage another mating. The time he'd rutted me in the cell had been all the proof I needed that the alpha was capable of multiple rounds.

But the more the blissful fog around my mind

retreated, the more aware I became of my own body—of the tired muscles and the soreness between my legs. And, most especially, of the fat knot still lodged snugly behind my pelvic bone. And it wasn't sexy anymore.

Before, despite the pain, there'd been pleasure and perverse excitement about getting plugged by the huge thing, the stretch forcing my reluctant body into a mind-bending orgasm. But now, with the desire for sex throughly fucked out of me? It was just uncomfortable.

I shifted, trying to ease the pressure in my gaping pussy, and earned a scolding growl from the alpha and a twinge from my pelvis when I accidentally pulled on our tie.

The other times he'd mated me, I'd passed out shortly after getting the knot. I wasn't prepared for *this*—the phase *after*.

Maybe it'd be different if we were in a bed, just the two of us, with no one watching and the physical intimacy of his knot tying us like the humming bond lodged in my chest. But here, now... It was just awkward, and I wanted it to be over.

A sensation that didn't exactly die down when the door behind us burst open and Zach jerked, head snapping around as a warning growl made its way up his throat.

I whimpered from the pull and he mercifully stilled his hips, but the growl only built to a snarl when guards entered the room, followed by Dr. Axell.

"Ah, the coital tie," the doctor hummed, an amused note to his voice as the guards began dragging the still passed-out alphas out of the room. "No better way of keeping an alpha in check."

"He's injured," I gritted out, trying to swallow my loathing for my former boss to ensure Zach got the treatment he needed for his wounds. "He needs medical attention."

"No worse than he's been before, but once you're back in your cell, we can provide you with some things to look after him. Some nurturing will only solidify the mating bond, after all."

The doctor stepped up beside us, careful to stay out of Zach's reach. The snarl rolling off the alpha still tied to me increased in volume, but Dr. Axell kept his expression clinical as he looked us over.

"Not that I'm sure your bond needs any more strengthening—we are *very* pleased with 351's instincts to protect you. Fighting off five equally matched rivals? No army unit has been able to get anywhere close to our results."

He shot me a small smile. "Of course, we will need to find his physical limits before we deploy him. What do you say, Lillian? Think he can save your sweet little cunt from ten alphas next time?"

NINETEEN

351

His mate was quiet while she cared for his wounds, but he felt her despair in their bond—and smelled it on her as she moved around him, dabbing stinging liquid on his skin.

He purred for her, even though it was hard to keep calm while she was agitating his many cuts and bruises, and was rewarded with a sad little smile. It made the purr come easier, and when she was done fussing with his wounds, he wrapped himself around her and lay down on the mattress. He didn't stop purring until their bond hummed contentedly.

He listened to her slow breathing, finding the sound of it soothing over the general noises from the lab and the chattering from the cell next to theirs. They'd brought the same female back to the alpha, and she was talking at him. 351 was too focused on his own female to care much for what she was saying, but her tone had lost some of its initial fear.

"The next time... don't fight them," his mate whispered. She turned halfway to look up at him, though she didn't move from her position with her back against his chest. Not that she could have, with his arm around her waist. "The next time, there will be more alphas. And more. And more. Don't... don't fight them, Zach. They won't stop until they find your breaking point. You can't... you can't save me forever. At some point, there'll be too many, even for you."

He growled, a rush of anger at her suggestion drowning out his sense of calm. Did she really think he would ever stand back and let others rut his female?

Tears glistened in the corners of her eyes as she brought a hand to his face. "I wish I could make you understand. I don't want you to get hurt again, when the end result will be the same."

He growled again and rolled her over to her front. If fighting off five other alphas wasn't enough to prove to her that he was strong enough to keep her safe, he would show her another way.

His cock rose hard and proud between his thighs as he took up position between her legs. Her cunt was still flushed red and open from their previous mating, but she didn't resist him when he reached down to manipulate the little nub that made her ready to take him.

She even arched her back for him when he pene-trated her, easing the push into her swollen depths.

He rutted her thoroughly, until she could have no more doubt he was strong enough, virile enough, to keep her all to himself, wringing orgasms from her fitfully spasming cunt that had both of them howling.

After, he lay with her, knot locked safely in her warm pussy as his cock drenched her inners with his seed, and listened to the alpha in the next cell mount the female locked in there with him.

It didn't come as a shock to him when, as the female howled in pain from taking the knot, the sound of teeth tearing into flesh mixed with the sounds of the final stages of sex.

His mate, however, jerked half up, wide eyes locked on the concrete wall. "Oh my God! W-What was that? What did he *do?*"

"Claimed," he grunted.

She shot him a quick look over her shoulder. She probably hadn't expected him to speak.

"You mean... that sound was him *biting* her?" She winced as she touched her own mostly healed claiming mark. Then her hand fell. "Wait, so he... he actually *claimed* her? Like... like you did me?"

The low sobbing from the female behind the concrete wall was underlined by a deep, pleased purr from the alpha.

"Yes," 351 grunted, tightening his grip on her hips to

still her movements. His knot had softened significantly, but it was still uncomfortable when her swollen channel tugged on him.

"But... *how?* I thought...? When you claimed me, before even... Isn't a bond meant to be... special?"

He could tell she found the notion of his neighbor claiming a female upsetting. She was probably worried for the woman—his mate had a soft heart. He brushed his nose against the back of her neck, pressing his lips to her claiming mark to calm her. She would never understand the desperate loneliness every single man in this cursed cell went through. How most of them would do anything to end it, even claiming a woman for life purely because she offered them some kindness.

"Sometimes... just available," he murmured, unable to fully explain the complexity of alpha bonding with his limited vocabulary.

"Oh," she whispered, and he felt an uncomfortable twang in their bond. But before he could investigate, commotion from the lab diverted his attention. He covered his mate with his body as the scientists chatted excitedly outside his neighbor's cell and the alpha growled furiously. 351 was unable to feel sorry for the dumb fuck so long as the scientists' attention wasn't on *his* female.

THE FOG SURROUNDING his mind only lifted enough for him to remember why he wasn't supposed to mate his female the next day.

He watched her awkwardly wash his scent from between her legs and swallowed thickly at the thought of his seed catching. If she became pregnant, his life would be forfeit.

But... it was already. He sighed at the twang behind his ribs. He'd give his life for her alone, and the evil pricks holding them captive knew as much. And there wasn't anything they could do to prevent matings when his mind was overtaken by the drugs—he was fully in his instincts' control then, and his instincts wanted nothing more than to rut her full of babies. *Constantly.*

He palmed his once-again hard cock, groaning low at the need to be inside of his woman *again.* Judging from the stiff way she was moving, she needed rest. Besides, it wouldn't be long before their captors would bring breakfast, and then another day of testing lay ahead. More than likely, she would get mated again before the day was over.

The thought of yesterday's test made his stomach churn—it was only sheer force of will, and the magnitude of his panic at seeing those five ferals try to mount her, that had allowed him to defeat them. And it had been a close call—despite her tending to his wounds, his body was still battered and sore today.

Then he remembered what she'd said while they lay together in the cell after, and his heart sank.

She was right.

They would keep pushing to see how much it would take before he broke. They wouldn't stop until he failed, and she would suffer the consequences.

The sickening knowledge that they would make him watch his mate get raped took care of the last remnants of his persistent erection.

"Breakfast."

The familiar voice of the beta assistant cut through his horror, and he turned around and snarled at the bars.

"Yeah, that's great, I'm terrified," the man said, rolling his eyes. He held up a syringe and tapped a finger against the tray of food. "Now be a good boy and offer your arm willingly, or your mate isn't eating today."

351 snarled again, wanting nothing more than to snap the man in two, but just the thought of his female not eating brought him to the bars more easily than had he been pulled by a leash.

"I must say, you've gotten a lot easier to deal with since Lillian joined you in there," the beta said conversationally as he readied the syringe. "I guess there's not much you wouldn't do to keep her safe, huh?"

The alpha glared down at him. This beta would never understand what it was like to be bonded. Under normal circumstances, 351 would have pitied him. But in here... having everything to lose was a fate worse than death.

"Too bad for you the drugs keep you from plotting anything that could get you out of here, I guess," the assistant said as he pressed the syringe to the alpha's skin. But where 351 had expected the usual prick of the needle, only the flat plastic pressed into his bulging bicep.

He stared down at the syringe as the beta pressed the plunger down, and the liquid inside trickled down the side of the alpha's arm. When he looked back up at the beta, he stared back at him with wide, fearful eyes, but a determined set to his mouth.

"Because I've read your file, and no one in here would be more capable of staging an escape than you. Sure, they were watching Lillian when she tried to break you out; they were expecting it after seeing how she cared for you. But now it's only the overnight guards keeping an occasional eye on the exit cameras on the weekends. Must suck for you to know your mind's too muddled from the drugs to save her. If you are even aware enough to realize."

He put the syringe in his pocket and pushed the tray of food through. "Eat up. You get some time off to recuperate after yesterday, but Monday, you're scheduled in for a repeat performance. I'm sure you'll need your strength for the ten alphas you'll have to fight then."

351's heart hammered in his chest as he watched

the beta administer the drug to the neighboring alpha, and then shove food through the gap in the door. The female was babbling pleas to be let out while the alpha growled possessively. From the deepening of his snarl, it was pretty obvious he had been jabbed with the needle.

351 wasn't sure why the lab assistant had suddenly had a change of heart—or if it was some sort of trap. But he knew he wasn't going to get another chance like this.

BY SATURDAY EVENING, his head was clearer than it had been in over a year.

A year.

He wasn't entirely sure of the days, but he knew he'd been here for more than twelve months. He hadn't had the capability of realizing before, but he did now.

And with it came a new kind of rage—the sort that smoldered and festered deep in his gut. He pushed it aside, and focused on his goal at hand: freedom.

Revenge could come later.

IT WASN'T until Sunday that he had a fully formed plan, and by that point, the deadline for executing it was looming.

The biggest hurdle was getting out of the cell. He'd gone over every inch of it, even considering unscrewing the toilet bowl, but the only way out was through the door. And without a keycard, it wasn't opening.

So in the afternoon, a few hours before the evening feeding, he turned his attention to his mate. He'd not spent much time with her; he had been too focused on finding a way out for them to do much more than hold her for warmth when she slept. And she hadn't tried to gain his attention, either.

The anchor in his chest twinged unpleasantly as he watched her curled up form on the mattress. She'd wrapped her arms around herself for warmth, her chin resting on her knees as she stared at the concrete wall separating them from the now pair-bonded alpha and his mate. Her blonde hair hung lank and unkempt around her naked shoulders, and even if they hadn't been tied with a pair-bond, he'd known she'd given up hope. The depression weighing on her was a near-tangible entity in the cell.

"Lillian," he said, voice gruff from not being used for days.

She started and turned to him. Though her eyes were wide with surprise, the life in them was dulled. "You know my name?"

Of course he knew his mate's name. Though... he hadn't spoken it before.

The damn bond twinged again and he rubbed at his chest. This wasn't how a claim was supposed to happen. The female should have been worshipped, felt treasured... surrendered willingly. Not like the parody of a claiming they'd gone through.

The result was a damaged bond.

He'd been too drugged out of his mind to give her anything more than the very basest of care during the vital first days. And now, instead of something beautiful and serene, the hook in his chest gnawed and twanged with her distress.

Smoldering anger flared in his gut. He pushed it down again, promising himself that the scientists would suffer for the damaged bond as well as the months of his life they'd robbed him of. *After* he'd gotten his mate to safety.

Nothing would matter if he failed.

He moved to the mattress and knelt by her side. Unable to keep his hands from her when she was so close, he stroked a lock of her hair from her cheek. She didn't flinch away, but she lowered her eyes, unwilling to meet his gaze.

Worried he'd want to rut her.

He pushed down the instinctive urge to force her into submission and remind her that, no matter the circumstances, she enjoyed their matings. And she was *his*.

There wasn't time. Not now.

"Lillian," he said again, because he liked the taste of her name on his tongue, light and soft like a kiss. "I have a plan to get us out, but I need your help."

Her eyes widened even further, some of the dullness finally receding as hope bloomed. "How?"

"When they bring dinner, you will pretend to be ill. Get them to open the door. I'll take care of the rest."

She frowned. "I don't think that's going to work. Even if they care, even if we get out of the cell, we can't make it past the guards and escape the compound."

"Leave that to me. I promise, if you get that door open, I *will* get you out of here. No matter the cost."

"Oh." She looked up at him, uncertainty in her eyes, but nodded nonetheless. "Okay. We'll try. Can't get much worse, right?"

He touched her cheek again. "If things don't go to plan... if I am held up or killed, you need to find your way to St. Halls in Georgia. Find Jerome Willis. Explain to him what's happened. That you're my mate. He'll take care of you. Got it?"

She nodded again, hesitantly. In her eyes he saw the instinctual agony just the thought of losing your pair-bonded mate brought. But he knew it was a very real possibility that he'd die for her tonight. And if he did, he needed to know that she would be taken care of.

"How are you so clear?" she asked, the waver in her voice the only outward indication of her emotional response. "They haven't tested you for days—the drugs should be—"

Noises from the lab interrupted her, and they both

turned to stare out through the bars. The tell-tale clanging of metal trays announced the arrival of dinner.

"Zach."

He turned back to look at her at the sound of his name, but though his female's lips were parted as if she wanted to say something more, she never did.

When the sound of the clanging trays came closer, he got to his feet and stepped toward the back of his cell, giving whoever came to feed them the impression that it'd be safe to open the door and tend to Lillian. "Now."

She drew in a deep breath and crawled closer to the door. Once there, she lay down on the cold concrete and stilled so completely she looked like she was dead. If it wasn't for the quiet strumming of the bond in his chest, he'd have panicked at the sight of her lifeless form.

They waited for nearly five minutes—long enough that he had to fight the urge to pull his mate off the cold floor. Her discomfort now would be worth it soon enough.

He heard the neighbor alpha receive his food, and the female once more plead for freedom, and then it was their turn.

351 sent a silent prayer to a god he'd long since stopped believing in and tensed his muscles, readying himself for the battle ahead.

"Jesus Christ, Lillian!"

The voice belonged to the lab assistant. *Good.* This should go smoother.

The beta fumbled with his keycard and smacked it against the door, abandoning the food trays. The second the door swung open, he knelt on the floor by the unmoving woman. "Lillian? Lilli—!"

351 didn't hesitate—he leapt through the room and grabbed the beta by the lapel of his white lab coat, swinging him up and around so his back hit the bars.

He groaned from impact, eyes wide and terrified as he clawed at the alpha's fingers. Whether it was for show when his superiors reviewed the security camera footage, or he really thought the alpha was about to tear him apart, 351 didn't know. He also didn't care.

He grabbed the man's keycard and threw him to the floor with a warning snarl—an unspoken threat of what would happen if he tried to move. One final look confirmed that the man was going to cooperate.

351 strode out of the cell, allowing himself a lingering glance at his mate, who was getting to her feet. "Stay here. I'll get you in a bit."

She blinked, confusion clear on her face when he shut the door behind him, locking her in the cell with the lab assistant—but for what he had planned now, she wouldn't be safe out in the open.

Moving as quickly as he could, he ran from cell to cell, smacking the keycard against every single door until nearly one hundred alphas joined him in the now crowded center of the lab.

Snarls rose from the anxiously milling crowd, but every single one of them were focused on the exit.

351 leapt through the crowd and scaled the stairs in two steps, then touched the card to the lock. He didn't have to guide them. The second that door swung open, the other alphas poured through it and into the hallway that led to freedom.

He didn't know if they'd get stuck behind more sealed doors farther ahead, but even if they did, he didn't expect anything to be able to stand between them and the smell of freedom. Not even steel.

But when he ran back to his cell, he noticed his neighbor was still there, clutching the terrified-looking female.

The smell of his fear rolled between the bars in waves.

351 spared him a single, pitying thought—clearly, he thought keeping his mate here was safer than risking her life out there among a hundred ferals and armed guards. Little did he realize the second Lillian and 351 were out of the compound, they'd be the new guinea pigs.

Lillian was dressed in a white lab coat, ill-fitting pants, and shoes that looked like they were too big for her when he returned to the cell. Next to her, the lab assistant had his arms wrapped around his body, now wearing nothing but boxers, socks, and a t-shirt.

"Got his wallet too," she said, patting a pocket in the lab coat. "There's enough cash to get us on the road."

Pride swelled within him, and he rumbled his approval at her wits. But now wasn't the time for praise. It was time to run.

"Come," he told her as he unlocked the door again. "Hurry."

The lab assistant looked like he wanted to follow, but a warning growl had him quickly stepping back into the cell again.

It was as much thanks as the beta would get for his help. He'd spent months assisting the doctors in tormenting 351—but he had made this escape possible, and for that, 351 put steel bars between the beta and any violent alphas who might get driven back here once the guards clocked on to what was happening.

351 reached a hand out, and his mate clasped it without hesitation. Her palm was small and cold against his, and he could feel the tremble in their bond from her nerves. But when he glanced down at her pretty face, she was all determination, eyes locked on the exit.

They ran through the lab and up the stairs, and were greeted with the distant sounds of snarling and fighting. A gun went off. The guards had arrived.

He kept her behind him as they ran down the hall-way, holding tight to her hand. She tripped a few times in the too-big shoes, and he had to slow his pace to make sure she could keep up. Just when he considered throwing her over his shoulder to hurry things along, they passed through a shredded metal door—and entered into the fray.

The guards had guns, but the ferals were ferocious—and outnumbered them twenty to one.

351 kept close to the wall, ensuring Lillian stayed between it and his back as he edged around the fighting to the door the guards had entered through. He swiped the card against it just as the last guard was ripped in two, and quickly stepped aside as the horde of alphas tore through it.

Once again, he waited until they were all through, shattering glass and victorious roars indicating that the path outside was clear.

He led Lillian through the destruction of what had been the reception area, heart pounding as the first tendrils of cool night air hit his nostrils. It'd been so long since he'd felt a breeze against his skin that the sensation was startling.

"Come," his mate urged from behind him, and only then did he realize he'd stopped at the threshold. "We're not free yet."

He stepped through, lifting her over the broken glass and into the fresh air.

That was when the sound of automatic gunfire filled the night.

351 snarled and ripped Lillian behind him again, following the sound to its source.

Guards swarmed from the outer rim of the

compound, bathed in floodlights, many more than had been inside. *Soldiers.*

The ferals attacked them as viciously as they had the guards, but the automatic weapons tore into the alphas' unprotected flesh and sent many to the ground in a spray of blood.

Thinking fast, 351 fell back against the building and pulled Lillian into the shadows. As fast as he could move her while remaining low to the ground, they half-crawled toward the tall fence looming against the night sky.

Miraculously, they made it through the spray of bullets without being hit. 351 didn't waste time leaping up the fence, digging his toes into the mesh to push himself up to the barbed wire topping it. Finding the strength he needed in the pulsing fear from the bond anchored behind his ribs, he tore the barbed wire apart with his hands, gritting his teeth against the pain as the metal ripped into his flesh.

Again and again he tore at it, until there was enough of a clear path that they could make it through. Only then did he jump down, grabbing for his mate.

"Your hands!" she gasped, horrified at the bloody mess.

"No time," he ground out, though he could see tendons sticking out of the wounds. But they couldn't linger. Every second that passed was a chance for one of the soldiers to spot them. And if that happened...

He had to more or less push her up the fence, grinding his teeth against the pain in his hands. But together, they managed to get her over the fence, and relief that jolted through him when she landed on the other side went a long way to numb the agony.

She was out.

She was free.

But as she stared back at him, her face contorted from a relieved, though anxious smile to a mask of terror.

"Zach! Look out!"

He didn't turn around in time. Pain blazed through his back, throwing him up against the fence with a loud rattle.

A bullet. He'd been shot before—there was no mistaking that pain. Grunting with effort, he turned to face his attacker.

A soldier with an automatic rifle aimed—not at him, but at Lillian.

"Get on the ground!" the soldier snarled. "Get down, or I'll shoot!"

351 turned his head to look one last time at the female he'd known was his mate from the first time he saw her. The woman who he would give his life for. Perhaps she truly had fallen pregnant during one of the times he'd taken her in that blasted compound.

Maybe there'd still be a part of him left in this world after tonight. It was a comforting thought.

"Run, Lillian," he whispered.

And then, drawing on the strength of the bond pulsing frantically in his chest, he threw himself at the soldier, snarling like the beast he'd been since she first met him.

The second shot hit him in the stomach, the pain blackening the edges of his vision. But it came too late. He landed on the soldier with his full weight, taking him to the ground with a battle roar.

The guard gurgled as 351 snapped his teeth shut around his throat and *tore,* metallic blood filling his mouth before his opponent could dislodge him. The guard stilled with a final, wet rattle.

351's vision tunneled, closing in, a faint rushing in his ears growing to a thunderous crash. The last thing he saw was his own blood pooling around him as he surrendered to death.

CHAPTER 20

JEROME WILLIS

Not many people knocked on Jerome's door on the best of days. And when a storm struck, no one was dumb enough to venture out into the wilderness where his cabin was located. Yet through the howling winds and branches beating against the windows of his cabin, a faint but unmistakable rap of knuckles drew his attention.

Jerome grabbed his shotgun, never more than an arm's length away, and pumped it once before crossing the floor. With a warning growl, he yanked the door open and aimed the weapon at the dumb fuck who'd decided to disturb him.

A small woman stood directly in front of the open door. Her long hair plastered to her face, and the dirty white coat covering her frail body was so soaked through he could make out her breasts and the smear of blood underneath.

Jerome kept the shotgun trained on her chest, quickly scanning the area behind her. There was no sign of people lurking in the perimeter, and his ears picked up nothing but howling wind and her too-fast breathing.

"J-Jerome Willis? You're Jerome Willis?" she asked.

He lifted his chin a fraction of an inch. "Who wants to know?"

She drew in a shuddering breath and squeezed her eyes shut for a moment, pressing her hands against the bloody place on her white coat. Whoever she was, she wasn't a threat. He knew that the second she took her eyes off him. He kept his finger on the trigger.

"Zach sent me. Zach... Zach Barnes. He said you... that you could help me." Her voice died on a whisper as she opened her terrified eyes. They were dull, as if someone had snuffed the life out of her, leaving only a doll behind.

"Barnes?" He frowned, finally lowering his weapon. He hadn't heard that name spoken out loud in... fuck, how long was I since everything went tits up? A year and a half? "Who's he to you?"

"My..." She gasped again and a flash of pain crossed through those lifeless eyes, so intense it gave a faint spasm of empathy somewhere deep in his gut. "He's my... my..." Her hand slipped in behind the coat to tear at her own flesh. Fresh blood seeped through the pale fabric.

He stared at her, dumbfounded, listening to her gasps choking off in the howling wind. Thunder rolled far in the distance, warning of a coming storm. Blood dripped from where she was trying to dig out her pair-bond.

"His mate?" he rasped. "You're his goddamn *mate*, aren't you?"

She only whimpered in response.

"Fuck me sideways," Jerome muttered. Last he'd heard, Barnes was still on death row. How the fuck he'd managed to claim a mate while locked up, he didn't know, but it was pretty clear from the woman's desperation that things hadn't ended well for his brother-in-arms. Not that any of them had expected it to.

"A'ight, girl, that's enough of that," he sighed when the blood from her wound started splattering onto his front deck. Eyes sweeping over the area once more, he put the gun by the side of the door. "Come inside—that thunder's rolling our way."

She obeyed, moving unsteadily as if she were on the brink of collapse. She looked it too. He studied her as she entered his cabin, searching for any clue that could unravel the mystery of why the fuck Barnes had decided to claim a mate before his execution. He'd been a lot of things, but cruel hadn't been among them.

"Shit," he muttered, shutting the door behind them.

If Barnes had claimed her out of selfish indifference, he wouldn't have sent her here. No, she was here because his brother had known she needed looking after once he was gone.

Seemed it fell to Jerome to pay back the squad's debt.

Rubbing the stubble covering his skull, he looked at the shivering female. She was dripping rainwater on his floor, and the blood coloring the front of her coat oozed sluggishly.

He'd given up all thoughts of ever claiming a mate after their last assignment, knew he was too fucked up to force another soul to carry the burden of his bond, but it was pretty clear he was all the hope the broken little bird had.

"I need to look at that wound," he said. "Come."

She stared at him, but made no sound of agreement or protest.

Sighing, he grabbed her lightly by the arm and walked her to the small bathroom at the back of the cabin. She sat on the side of the tub when he motioned for her to do so, but when he asked her to open the white coat, she snatched both hands into it and clung for dear life, wide eyes full of fear.

"C'mon, girl, I've seen tits before."

Tears welled in her red-rimmed eyes and she looked away, never releasing her hold on the coat.

Jerome sighed and grabbed what he needed from

the small cupboard by the sink. When he returned to her, he didn't ask. Crouching, he pried her cold fingers off the fabric and unbuttoned it easily. She didn't fight him—just sat stiffly and stared at him with unmistakable unease writ across her pale face.

He didn't bother reassuring her—there'd be no point. Right now, his goal was to assess the damage she'd done to herself and patch her up, but later, he would have to do exactly what she feared. And she wouldn't like it. Not at first.

The only thing that could save a bonded female who'd lost her other half was another alpha's claim to fill the void. That was why Barnes had sent her his way.

Jerome grimaced as he took in the deep gouges marring her rib cage underneath her plump breasts. He was pretty sure Barnes had picked him specifically because—unlike most alphas—he hated having an unwilling female beneath him. He could have sent her to any of their other brothers, and they would have happily repaid the team's debt by taking her in. Probably would have mounted and claimed her before even bandaging her wounds.

"Fuck you, Barnes," he muttered, ignoring the girl stiffening at his words. He grabbed the disinfectant and poured a liberal amount onto a tuft of cotton. When he reached for her chest to smear it on her wound, she flinched, but he grabbed her wrists with his free hand and held her in place.

She whimpered at the first sting of peroxide and hissed when he kept dabbing at the bloody mess.

It was a long while before he managed to clean her wound up enough to assess the damages fully. It looked like she'd clawed it raw for many days, maybe even a week, deepening the lacerations over and over.

It wasn't that he'd expected an invitation in the mail or anything, but knowing Barnes' execution had passed without even being told about it... He shook his head and grabbed for the bandages. Barnes had given his life. The least Jerome could do was honor his last will.

As he wrapped up her ribcage, more to ensure she didn't claw herself bloody again than to keep the gauze in place, she offered no protest, seemingly accepting his nearness despite her indecent state.

When he was done, Jerome hesitated for a moment before he shrugged out of his own shirt and offered it to her. Best she get used to his scent as quickly as possible, because judging by that wound and her deadened eyes, she'd need him to establish his bond sooner rather than later.

She pulled it on, wrinkling her nose as the scent of an alpha who wasn't her mate enveloped her, but she didn't seem too bothered by it. He'd seen mated females bite, scratch, and snarl to rid themselves of another alpha's attempt to scent-mark them. At least he wouldn't have to contend with that aspect of claiming her.

"What's your name?" he asked, brushing a lock of

her wet hair from her face. She was a pretty little thing, he'd give Barnes that, though looks had never played much of a role for alphas when it came to finding a mate.

"Lillian," she said, meeting his gaze.

"Okay. I want you to know that you're going to be safe with me, Lillian. I know things are pretty shitty for you right now, but I'll always have Barnes' back. Even now."

She nodded, gaze dropping back to her hands. She didn't believe him. But she wouldn't. Not before she had a new bond to occupy her.

He swore silently as he took in the shell of a woman in front of him. Like he did most nights, he'd planned to make himself an early dinner and fall asleep in front of the TV, if the power didn't get knocked out during the storm, but from the looks of Barnes' mate, he'd have to change his plans quite dramatically. She didn't look like she'd last much longer.

"You hungry?" Least he could do was feed the girl first.

Lillian shook her head, eyes still on the floor. "No. Thank you. I just... Is there somewhere I can sleep? Please? I'm so tired."

Jerome sighed and straightened up. "You need to eat. C'mon—you can sleep soon, but I don't want you keeling over on me, yeah?"

When she made no move to get up, he hoisted her into his arms and carried her to his living room that also hosted his small kitchen. He plopped her down on one of the two homemade bar stools by the breakfast bar and went to pull out some of the powdered soup he stocked up on when he went into town on his monthly shopping trip. He'd poured it into a pot and followed with two pints of water before something occurred to him.

"You pregnant?"

"I don't know." She looked so defeated when she answered, but despite the pain in her dead gaze, he didn't miss how her hand automatically fluttered to her belly.

Fuck.

"I've got meat in the freezer, but it'll take a few hours to prep."

"No. Thank you. I don't need... I'm not hungry."

He briefly considered ignoring her and getting out one of the deer haunches in his freezer, but decided speed was more important than substance for the moment.

She didn't eat the soup when he put it down in front of her, not until he grabbed the spoon and held it to her lips. She barely parted them then, but she swallowed when the liquid filled her mouth. It was enough that he didn't have to force-feed her, and for that he was grateful.

Once her bowl was empty, he sat down on the bar stool next to her with a sigh, leaning one elbow on the counter for support. "So... how long were you with him?"

Her voice was a hoarse whisper. "A week."

Jerome grimaced. A week. What the fuck had made Barnes claim a girl for such a short amount of time? What'd been worth the pain he'd inflicted on her? Even with another claim to dull her loss, she'd never be quite right.

"Did he... mention what would happen, once you sought me out?"

"No. Just that you'd look after me. That they wouldn't get to me."

His grimace turned to a frown. "'*They?*'"

"SilverCorp. Or I guess it might be the government now." She gestured vaguely. "I don't know if I'm of any importance to them anymore, but... they're not gonna want me to talk. Not that anyone would believe me."

"What, exactly, don't they want you talking about?" A shiver made its way up from the base of his spine, a reminder of his time in the field. It was the same shiver he'd felt when danger was imminent. Something was off. Something was way off. Why would anyone, especially the government, be after his friend's mate?

"Everything." Her body shook violently, her fingers reaching for her now bandaged ribs. She raked them over the padded T-shirt, a mindless motion born from the same despair he saw when her face contracted. "Everything they did to him. To *us*."

"Shh, okay, calm down." He slid off his chair to grab the distraught woman, pinning her arms to her sides as he pulled her against his body. She was stiff as a board, and her shaking only increased. "We'll talk about it later." Once his mark was on her neck, so she hopefully could do so without coming apart at the seams. He wanted to know—needed to know—what his brother's final days on this Earth had been like. He peered down at her nape, saw the scars from Barnes' claim marring one side, and drew in a deep breath. It was time.

The purr was hard to force out at first—the girl's trembling set his own instincts on edge, but the need to soothe her for what came next won out, and so after a few false starts he managed.

Lillian softened slowly against his chest, her eyelashes fluttering against his bare skin. Gradually, her shaking eased until she was completely still.

"He did this too," she whispered after several long moments. "He would purr for me."

"I'll purr for you now," he murmured, pressing a light kiss to her scalp. "I'll ease the pain. I promise."

The change in her happened quickly this time, as if someone had flicked a switch. She went rigid in his grasp and her small hands flew up to his chest, pushing for a distance he wouldn't allow.

"Let go of me!"

"It's the only way to save your life." He held onto her frail body, tempering her resistance with the bulk of his muscle. "You're dying—think he'd want that?" There was no point in arguing with a claimed woman facing sexual submission by another alpha's hand, but he couldn't help it. Even if she didn't hear him, he needed to say the words.

She only screamed and bucked harder when he let his hands slide down to her hips, anchoring his resolve in the feminine swell of them. *Fuck,* he hadn't knotted a woman in ages. The feel of her writhing against him had him hard as a rock, even if her desperate screeching made him sick to his gut.

"Dammit, woman! If I don't do this, you'll die like he did! You can't survive a broken mate bond! He sent you here because he wants—*ow!*" He jerked his shoulder back from where she'd bitten into his flesh.

She glared up at him, the deadened look in her eyes replaced by burning fury. "He's not dead!"

CHAPTER 21
LILLIAN

"What do you mean he's not dead?" The grizzled alpha let me drop to the floor. I took the opportunity to back away, putting as much distance between us as I dared. I knew on an instinctive level that he'd chase me down if I moved too far.

"He's not—he's not dead," I repeated, pressing a hand to my bandaged chest when the barbed wire that was my bond twisted inside. "I feel him."

God, how I felt him. All the time. I'd thought I knew pain before, thought my experiences at the compound had been excruciating.

I'd been wrong.

Jerome stared at me, confusion and disbelief mixing with relief. Despite his big cock still tenting his pants, he hadn't wanted to mount me. And for some reason, knowing Zach was still alive stopped him from trying. "You're sure?"

I laughed, a hollow sound. Was I sure? How did I explain the string covered in broken glass tying me to reality? I knew, without a doubt in my soul, that should it ever snap, I'd float away into an abyss of nothingness. It was the only reason I could still breathe, even if it made every expansion of my lungs hurt so much I wished I couldn't. "If he were dead, I would be too."

"You look halfway there, girl," he said, frowning down at me.

"He's halfway there," I whispered. "They've... they've done something to him. He's..." I didn't know how to finish that sentence, so I didn't try.

"What do you mean they've *done* something to him? He's on death row, right?"

"No, he..." I paused when I realized this man had no idea. No one did. "He's part of an experiment. The government... they contracted SilverCorp to run tests on alphas waiting for the death penalty. They're trying to turn them into super soldiers."

Jerome's frown deepened. "Barnes would just as likely sign up to be a fucking *super soldier* as he would fuck a roll of barbed wire. He's got zero trust in our military leaders after everything that went down."

I shook my head. "He wasn't given a choice. None of them were. SilverCorp developed a drug that makes them incapable of rational thought. It amplifies the alpha instincts until—"

I didn't have to finish. Jerome's dark eyes widened as they flew to the scar on my neck. "Sonuvabitch! That's why he claimed you, ain't it? Fuckers drugged him!"

"Yeah," I said, unable to fight the painful jab in my chest at the vocalization of what I already knew. Zach would never have claimed me if he'd been in his right mind, and I sure as fuck hadn't wanted him to in the first place. But that didn't change the fact that knowing I was only his mate because he'd been driven by a desperation to no longer be alone in that hellhole still hurt like someone stabbing a finger into an open wound.

"And you? Were you an inmate?" He gave me a once-over, and I couldn't really fault him for his assumption. I'd been on the road for more than a week—an inmate was probably not the worst thing someone could have mistaken me for.

"No. I was... I was a scientist there. I didn't know what was happening before I saw... They did such terrible things to them. Awful. And Zach, he..." I remembered the deep lash marks on my alpha's back after he'd refused to mate that woman, and my heart clenched. They were doing much worse to him now. I could feel it in the marrow of my bones.

I clawed at my chest as our bond wrenched again, but before I could do more than scratch at the bandages there, Jerome closed his hand around my wrists.

"And Zach?"

I shuddered, trying to focus on something other than the pain. "They tortured him. I couldn't stand it, so I... I tried to free him. But they caught me. And they... they made him..." I flinched at the urge to rub my mating mark, but Jerome's grip kept me from touching it.

"They made him claim me," I finally choked out. "And then they used me to... control him."

"God above," Jerome murmured, finally releasing me. In his face I saw the horror I'd felt too. Back when I could feel anything but pain.

"I think... I think Zach realized I wasn't going to last much longer," I said. "I don't know how he fought the drugs enough for conscious thought, but he did. And he... he managed to break me out. But they caught us, and they s-shot him. He told me to run... I didn't think I could, I didn't think I could leave him, but he... he gave his life for me. I *had* to.

"I thought he was going to die. But he didn't. He didn't die, and they are torturing him. They've... they've broken him. He's not... I wish they'd kill him. Oh god, I wish they'd just kill him so he can find peace!"

I hadn't meant to put words to that awful, desperate wish that had been haunting me since I first escaped the compound. I'd been too stunned with terror and grief to feel much of anything for some hours. I'd had a moment's relief when I realized he wasn't dead. Just a sliver of a second when my heart filled with hope as our bond sprang to life in my chest.

And then the agony had set in. The worst pain I'd ever experienced. They weren't just torturing him, but how did you explain to someone who'd never carried the burden of a mate bond that every second of every day I'd felt them tear my alpha apart, until what was left was nothing but an empty, aching shell? I didn't know what they'd done to him for our bond to hurt the way it did, but I knew whatever was left of the man whose mark I now carried, death would be the only relief he'd ever find.

I wasn't aware of my own sobs, or my desperate attempt at clawing my bandages off, until Jerome wrapped me up in his arms so tightly I couldn't thrash against the pain.

He didn't say anything as I wailed in his arms, didn't offer me anything but the strength of his body holding me against him while I fought to tear out the tether in my chest.

When I could finally breathe again, he sat me down on the bar stool next to his and went to one of the kitchen cupboards. He returned with a large glass and a bottle of whiskey.

I stared blankly at the glass as he filled it to the brim and nudged it over to me.

"Drink," he said. "All of it. It'll give you a few hours' peace."

It burned my throat as it went down, but it was a welcome pain. It distracted me from the thread of shards behind my ribs. And true to his word, it didn't take many minutes before a pleasant numbness set in.

I didn't even register the world going dark before I was taken by a dreamless sleep.

IT WAS the first time I'd slept in a week, and even though I woke up with a bad headache thanks to the alcohol, it was still worth it.

I stared blearily up in the sloped ceiling above me, the rough pine planks illuminated by faint daylight. The barbed wire in my chest pulsed, sending slow tendrils of pain through my body, but it was duller than before. He was sleeping. Or passed out. That was when the pain was the easiest to bear.

I pressed my palm to my bandaged ribs and prayed that today would be the day he never woke up. That I'd feel the tether snap. I knew the pain of it would kill me too, and I yearned for it. Yearned for the sweet relief of death I could never have so long as *he* was still alive. I couldn't leave him to suffer alone. That would be too cruel.

I lay on my back and stared up at the ceiling until my bladder forced me to get up and search out a bathroom. There was one just next to the small room I'd slept in, one of just three doors attached to the tiny landing of Jerome's cabin. When I peeked into the third, an unmade bed and the vaguely familiar scent of the gruff alpha let me know the only other room on this floor was his bedroom.

Relieved he hadn't made me sleep in his room, in his scent, I finished my business and descended the creaky stairs. The whole cabin had a handmade feel to it, and I wondered if Jerome had built it himself. It would've been a big job for one man, but he didn't seem the type to swap trades with his neighbors.

The living room was quiet, so I didn't expect the stranger sitting on the couch as I rounded the corner.

I stopped, muscles still fresh with the memories of flight tensing as our eyes locked.

He was big and burly and clearly an alpha, and at the sight of me, his blond eyebrows locked in a frown. "That her?"

"'Course it's her. How many females do you think I have hanging around?" Jerome's voice made me jerk my gaze in his direction. He was sitting on one of the bar stools, sipping from a giant mug. At my longing look, he got up and fetched another equally giant mug, pouring brown liquid from a silver Thermos.

"Can I have a look?" the stranger asked, as I closed my fingers around the steaming mug. The heat felt good against my skin—like a whisper from a past I'd long since forgotten existed.

"Sure," Jerome said, plopping down on the barstool again. "Be gentle, though, she spooks easily."

I stiffened, eyes darting to the stranger as he got up from the sofa, the piece of furniture creaking underneath him. "W-what are you...?"

"Easy now, girl. Beau's just gonna take a look at your claiming mark." Jerome nodded at the blond alpha, who'd stopped a few steps away, a hand raised in what was possibly meant as a soothing gesture.

"Why?" Shifting my grip on the mug I clamped a hand over my scar, tendrils of fear snaking through my brain. I'd spent too long having others' will forced upon me, upon my body, to voluntarily turn my vulnerable nape to an unknown alpha. This wasn't the man with whom Zach had entrusted my safekeeping.

"Because frankly, the idea Barnes'd ever claim a scientist is pretty incredible. I'd like to see for myself," the stranger rumbled.

"He's a friend, Lillian," Jeremy said. "Let him see."

I glanced to my would-be protector, but he seemed as calm as ever. Hesitantly, I removed my hand from my nape and let it hang by my side. No longer fighting it, but also not inviting it.

The blond crossed the few remaining steps between us and pushed my messy hair out of the way. Goosebumps broke out across my neck and ran down my back and arms at the sensation of his fingers skimming lightly over my raised flesh, but I managed to hold still.

When he bent his head and drew in a deep breath of my scent, I closed my eyes and tried not to think about the time Dr. Axell had let five feral alphas at me.

"Well, I'll be damned," the blond murmured. When he pulled back, his brows were furrowed. "Barnes really claimed a mate."

"Told ya," Jerome said. "She's telling the truth. He's fucking locked up in a research facility like a damn rat."

Beau shook his head, anger flashing in his eyes. "That's not right."

"So you're in?" Jerome arched an eyebrow at his friend.

"Yeah. Yeah, I'm in." The stranger flexed his hands, his anger seeping into his scent as he rolled his shoulders to ease it.

I swallowed thickly, the smell of angry alpha setting every instinct in my body on high alert. "I don't understand... What's this about? Who are you?"

"Beau's from our squad," Jerome said, a grim look on his features. "Barnes is our brother, and we ain't about to leave him behind to be a government lab rat for the rest of his miserable life."

"But he..." I frowned, trying to process his words over the steadily increasing hum in my ears. "He killed your captain... didn't he? That's why he was on death row? He's a war criminal?"

Jerome exchanged a look with Beau. "Yeah, he killed our captain."

"Then why...?" The hum vibrated through my eardrums and into my skull, making my teeth tingle. These men... they were talking about *freeing* him.

My heart pounded, but I fought against the tendrils of hope trying to spread from the dimly throbbing chord there.

"Because things aren't always what they seem, girl," Jerome sighed. He was going to continue, but Beau cleared his throat and shot his friend a warning glare.

"We made a promise, Willis," the blond said. "She doesn't need to know."

"Tell me!" I demanded, my voice sharper than I'd intended. "He's my mate. If he—if he isn't a criminal, I have a right to know."

I couldn't stop the tendrils this time. For the first time since my escape, my bond didn't hurt. Warmth spread in its wake and I pressed my free hand to my chest, desperate hope flaring against my better judgment. If I could see him again... if I could look into his eyes and know he wasn't a bad man...

Then perhaps death wouldn't be the only way out.

"We swore an oath," Beau said. "But if we get him out, maybe he'll tell you himself."

"How?" Where there had been nothing but dead flesh and pain before, a fire now burned. One last, desperate light. A chance at life not tainted by misery and darkness. And I clung to it with all my might like a drowning woman offered one final chance to breathe.

"We are not the only ones who owe our lives to your mate," Jerome said, pushing the mug away as he looked at the blond alpha. "We will contact our old team. They will come. And then you'll lead us to where they hold him. No SEAL ends his days as a lab rat. Not on our watch."

CHAPTER 22

351

It had been a long time since light touched his eyes. Maybe weeks. Months. Years. He wasn't sure. Time hadn't made sense since he'd woken up in hell.

The bulb above him tore at his eyes and he hid his face in his hands to escape its burn. But the screech of metal pushed over concrete made every aching muscle in his body tense with memories of pain.

"Get up!"

He rose at the sound of that hated voice, blind but acutely aware of the cold draft against his naked skin from the open space behind his tormentor. He no longer saw that opening as freedom. He had, in the beginning, he vaguely remembered. But he knew better now. It wasn't the cool air he charged for.

His world was pain. Pain, and the tormentor here to extract yet another ounce of it from his flesh. No matter how many times they showed him there was no point, he couldn't hold back the roar in his blood to *kill*. Every time the metal gave way for cool air, he lunged at it to maim and break apart every living thing that entered his dark hell, his instincts the only thing left in him that still resembled life.

Sharp, electric agony tore through his neck and lanced through his body. He fell to the floor with a thud, seizing as the metal collar squeezed his throat. It didn't stop until he lay limp, unable to move, save for the involuntary jerks as the electricity short-circuited his nerves.

"You'd think you'd learn," that hated voice sneered somewhere above him. "Even animals can be trained. And that's all you are, isn't it? An animal."

The words made no sense to him. They were nothing but noise. The tone he knew, though. Anger. Anger that led to more pain.

A swift kick in his already bruised ribs proved him right yet again. He groaned, unable to move, let alone defend himself.

But no more beatings followed that first kick. He lay still, waiting for it to continue, but there was nothing. Only the sound of inhaling and exhaling somewhere above him told him he wasn't alone.

"I know you're waiting for me to kill you. But I won't. You're still valuable. Only a broken man can truly be rebuilt, and that's what I'll do with you. You *will* be my soldier, inmate. Even without her, your bond is still there. I'll find a way to use it, to leash you like the dog you are. You'll never escape. I'll never let you die."

This time, one of the words made it through to his fogged mind.

Bond.

He groaned, shutting his eyes tighter at the pull in his chest. He tried to force his body to curl in on itself, to protect the soft place, that single part of him that was something other than agony.

"You understood that, didn't you?" The voice was taunting now. Smug. "Even now, all you care about is that cunt. If only you'd known how easy you'd be to control once you took her, maybe you'd have kept fighting me. Would you even have orchestrated her escape if you'd known how much worse being separated would be?"

The rise in tone indicated a question, but his tormenter didn't wait for his answer. His footfalls moved away toward the cool air. He shouted something, and then several more people entered the small cell.

351 snarled, expecting the beating he'd been waiting for, but they grabbed him under his arms instead and dragged him toward the open space.

Endless corridors of too-bright light followed. His heels dragged on the floor, skin breaking against the rough concrete. Metal shrieked and slid as they maneuvered him into new, tight spaces. On and on.

A host of scents assaulted his senses, his instincts

fighting to place them all through the fog. He hadn't smelled anything but his own filth and blood for a long time, along with the scent of his tormenter and occasionally other males. Now his nose forced images through his brain of bright white rooms with equipment and needles, vague memories of being clean, and something else. Something that made the thread in his chest hum out of tune.

Female. The word cut through just as a desperate howl rang through his ears. A female's scream.

He jerked violently, the thread turning sharp and urgent, and fought despite his leaden limbs, instincts urging him on. That sound... That *smell!* He had to protect—

"Hold him!" his tormenter snarled. "If I shock him again, he's gonna be out for the rest of the day, and I want him to see this. He's ready for the next step and we've wasted enough time."

Strong arms constricted around his limbs, so much more powerful than his own broken body, propping him upright while still containing his struggle to free himself. The sound, the *female*, still whimpered and screamed, closer now, along with wet, smacking sounds that resonated in the core of his being. He knew those sounds. His *body* knew them...

"Dim the lights."

The burn against his closed eyelids eased and he forced them open. The light still hurt, still made his eyes water, but it was soft enough now that he could fight against it.

Slowly, the world came into focus. He shuddered as a sense of recognition set in, though he couldn't remember from where. On the other side of a glass pane a rounded concrete space opened up, and in the middle of it, bent over a raised platform, a huge male hunkered down. It took 351 a second to see the female underneath —the male's body was so big it nearly blocked her out— but he heard her.

The male thrust his hips rhythmically back and forth, and 351's body remembered. Every muscle burned as he roared and fought against the men holding him back, fought as the bond in his chest flared painfully.

Protect! Protect the female!

It was the only coherent thought he'd had since he'd entered hell, but it burned like hot iron behind his ribs as his mind was assaulted with memories he couldn't quite seem to reach.

He'd failed her, he'd failed—

Just then, as if alerted by his roars, the female turned her head and he saw her face. It was pale, eyes wide with fear and flooding with tears, mouth open around a pained wail. But it wasn't *her*.

Relief flooded his body as his bond twanged, out of tune but no longer in pain.

There was something he was supposed to remember. Something important, something connected to the softness in his chest.

He stared mutely at the screaming female, every thrust of the male into her nudging at that place in his mind that was only darkness.

"Do you remember what it means to be mated, inmate?" his tormenter asked. "Do you remember how tightly that bond binds you? Maybe one day, you'll be able to remember that it is all thanks to you that we now know the parameters needed to make another feral claim a mate."

His tormentor's words made no sense. Not until the male forced his swollen knot deep into the sobbing female and buried his teeth in her neck.

Only then, and with an agony so fierce a scream tore from his chest, did he remember.

The bond was tied to his mate.

He had a mate.

And she was lost to him.

CHAPTER 23

LILLIAN

It took more than four weeks for Jerome and Beau—actual name Liam Beaumont—to gather up their team... or what was left of it. Two of their brothers in arms turned up MIA, one without a trace and the other dead. With their captain dead as well, that left five alphas making camp in the wilderness surrounding Jerome's cabin after a month had passed.

Five ex-SEALs in total, all big and gruff and insisting on sniffing my neck when they first met me. But that's all they did. Not a single one so much as touched me, except for Jerome when he changed my bandages, which I suspected was mainly to ensure I hadn't harmed myself further.

But I was too absorbed to get lost in the sweeping waves of agony from my bond and try and claw it out now. It still hurt, still knocked the breath from my lungs

—but I clung to the single ray of hope Zach's SEAL brothers had stirred in me. It was the only thing I thought about when I lay awake at night, the only thing I focused on when the barbed wire sliced through me during his waking hours.

There was a chance, however small, that they would succeed. That he would be free.

And if that failed... if the six alphas couldn't break into the heavily guarded compound...

Well, then I knew I would die while trying to rescue the man who'd risked everything to save me.

"I'd feel better if you stayed behind, girl." Jerome looked over the hand-drawn map of the area that housed the compound, circles drawn in from where I remembered guard towers being stationed. "I've got a duty to keep you safe. You know that."

"And you know I can't," I said. "It's a maze underground. You'll need my bond to locate him."

"I know," he sighed. "But if we manage to break him free, but lose you in the process..."

"We won't." Beau walked up to the wood block that served as our strategy table, casually slicing an apple with his hunting knife. "Give the girl some credit, Willis. She escaped a federally secured facility and made it all the way to Georgia on her own. We've had much more difficult assignments."

"And with a lot less at stake," Eric murmured as he trailed up behind him. He nodded in the direction of the nearest tent where Jarl and Larry were packing their few belongings up. "We're all set."

Larry had only arrived yesterday, and Eric the week before, but these guys were used to moving out with little warning.

"All right." Jerome shot me another unhappy look. "Then it's time to go."

THE FLOODLIGHTS from the four towers surrounding the compound lit up, slicing through the darkness as we crept close to the perimeter.

During the trip here, my bond had been throbbing with increasing intensity, but the closer we got, the less it hurt. It was as if it knew I was here to save my mate.

I rubbed at my chest as I stared at the fence I'd scaled what seemed like a lifetime ago. The sick memory of staring through the chain link as Zach took a bullet, knowing I'd lose him and that there was nothing I could do, assaulted my mind. It took all the focus I had not to start hyperventilating. My bond might have been calmer this close to the compound, but every other part of me was balancing on a razor's edge, panic and despair waiting for a weak moment to swallow me up.

I'd never thought I'd voluntarily walk back into this hell... but I hadn't known that being separated from the man who claimed me would be so much worse.

By my side, Jerome pointed toward the single guard patrolling the fence a good thirty feet from our hiding spot. Beau and Jarl nodded, sliding out and toward him like two silent shadows.

"Stay here. Stay hidden. We'll get you when it's done," Jerome murmured before he, Eric, and Larry headed toward the nearest guard tower.

I didn't hear any disturbances in the night, but I saw the patrolling guard fall to the ground. There was no sound of alarms being raised, no shots fired as I waited for the SEALs to dispatch the perimeter guards.

Some twenty minutes later, movement caught my eye, and my heart slammed into my throat when I spotted a soldier's uniform on the man rapidly approaching my hiding spot. But when he got closer, I recognized Beau's clean-cut face. He waved me over, touching his lips with a finger when I stumbled out of the bushes toward him.

He led me through the gates to where the others were waiting for us by an unlit section inside the chain-link, not fifty yards from the glass doors leading into the reception area. They'd cleaned up and replaced the windows since our escape attempt, I noted. It was as if it'd never happened.

"You hang back while we gain entry," Jerome said. He, like the rest of them, was dressed in the same uniform the soldiers here wore. A few of them had blood splatters staining the dark gray camouflage fabric.

I nodded, aware I wasn't here for the violent aspect of the rescue mission. It wasn't until we descended into the bowels of the compound that I'd be useful.

The five alphas made their way toward the entry area, one of them waving a greeting to what I assumed were the guards inside. The glass door opened and Jerome stepped inside, followed by the other alphas.

This time I did hear a shot, but just the one.

Was there only one guard? I frowned, trying to peer through the windows, but all I saw from my hiding spot were moving shadows. Even before the escape attempt, there'd been several guards stationed by the entry point. It didn't make much sense to decrease their numbers.

But moments later, Beau stuck his head out of the door and waved me forward, and I obeyed.

"There're supposed to be more guards here," I whispered as I finally entered the building, my old workplace, and saw a single man lying dead on the floor.

"There were double the amount of guards we expected around the perimeter," Jerome said, his gaze sliding along the reception area. "They seem to have shifted their focus to shell protection since you left, probably wanting to give their men the higher ground in case of another break-out. Which way from here?"

I hesitated, focusing on the bond. It was pulling at me, but I wasn't sure where to, except deeper into the compound. "Best bet is where they keep the test subjects." I tried to step around him to lead the way, but he placed his hand on my shoulder.

"Need I remind you what happens to Barnes if you die?" he growled. "In the middle, at all times."

I sighed and let Beau take the lead, followed by Larry and Eric. Directly behind me, Jarl closed in with Jerome taking up the rear.

"Through that door, down the hall," I said. My heart thudded unevenly as the familiar smells of disinfectant and blood assaulted me. It was like returning to a nightmare, every flicker of the fluorescent lights forcing memories of the night of my escape to resurface in my brain. Only the knowledge that somewhere deep in the bowels of this hell was the key to my survival stopped me from turning around to flee.

Beau swiped the access card he'd stolen from the dead guard on the floor over the scanner, and the doors slid open with a hiss.

None of us were expecting the sharp *pop-pop-pop* that immediately followed.

"Get down!" Jarl roared, throwing his heavy body on top of mine before I could so much as blink. Snarls erupted around us as heavy boots slammed against the concrete floors and more gunfire went off.

I shrieked as Beau fell next to us, glassy eyes wide open and a trickle of blood dripping from the corner of his half-open mouth.

Another thud of a body hitting the ground made me

twist underneath Jarl's protective cover. An unfamiliar man in a dark guard uniform stared back at me, his face contorted in pain and blood spurting from between his lips. He gurgled something and reached for me. Jarl put a bullet in his brain before he could get close.

More gunfire went off above us, accompanied by roars of agony—but it was over quickly. When silence finally fell over the hallway again, five men in guard uniforms lay scattered on the floor.

Jerome knelt by Beau's side, pressed his fingertips to his neck for a few moments, and then drew his hand over Beau's face, closing the other man's eyes. "Anyone else hurt?"

"Just a flesh wound," Larry grunted. When I looked up, he had a hand pressed against his side. Blood seeped between his fingers.

"Fuckers must've seen us enter on security cams," Eric growled as he tore a piece of fabric off one of the dead guards to bandage Larry's wound. "Fuck!"

Jarl finally got off me and helped me to my feet. When he noticed me staring at Beau's pale face, he put his hand on my shoulder. "He died for his brother's freedom. Every last one of us is willing to sacrifice our lives to get Barnes out. This was a good death. Don't feel sad."

I didn't say anything as I looked at the blond alpha who'd laid down his life to get me my mate back. I'd known him for a month—planned with him, relied on him. But I'd never really known him. I didn't know any of these men who were here, risking their lives for me and Zach. And I realized then that to me, they were nothing more than the brawn and power I needed to make my bond stop tormenting me day and night. Staring at the man who'd died to protect me, I felt nothing but indifference.

It horrified me.

Over the past four weeks, I'd thought I'd become less damaged, that the fire of determination and single-minded hope was mending the torn place in my chest where that awful tether hooked in.

I'd been so very wrong.

"Come," Jerome said as he got to his feet. "We'll retrieve his body on the way out. But first, we have a mission to complete. Larry?"

"I'm good," the injured alpha grunted, pushing off the wall he'd been leaning against with a grimace. "Let's go."

We continued deeper into the belly of the compound, our footfalls the only sound echoing around us—until we finally entered the lab where the feral alphas were held.

"Lord above," Jarl murmured as I led them through the large room flanked by cage after cage of naked men. Several were empty, but a few of the alphas had disheveled-looking women by their sides. Seemed they'd gotten more alphas to claim mates while I'd been gone.

I steeled my jaw and kept my gaze on the end of the room where Zach and I had lived together for one miserable week. But when we got there, the cell was empty.

"They kept Barnes in here?" The disbelieving question had come from Larry, but judging by his companions' tense expressions, they were all trying to come to terms with what had happened to their brother-in-arms.

"Yeah. They must've moved him after I... escaped." I touched a hand to the bars and tried to think where they could have taken him. The infirmary?

"Best hurry up and locate him, girl," Jerome grunted. "The others are waking up, and they're not liking our presence."

Deep growls rolled through the lab behind us, sporadic for now, but more voices were joining in as more alphas became aware of the presence of what they saw as rivals.

I pushed off the bars and went to the neighboring cell. The alpha in there snarled and lunged at the metal bars separating us.

"Get back!" Eric snapped, pushing me behind him as he raised his weapon and leveled it at the feral man.

"No, I need him to calm down. Please, move out of his field of vision. All of you."

They did, though I sensed their hesitation at leaving me alone with such an aggressive male. Their instincts to protect were clearly flaring, but the caged alpha couldn't touch me so long as I stayed out of arm's reach.

"Hey," I said, keeping my tone soft. I tilted my head back a little, showing the feral alpha my throat. "I'm not going to hurt you. Or her. I just need to speak with her. Can I? Please?"

He growled again, but softer this time. Less threatening. I took it as permission.

"Hey—hello?" I squinted at the dark interior of the cell and spotted what I'd been looking for—a curled-up figure lying completely still on the mattress.

Her alpha growled again at my attention toward his mate, and I dipped my head back further until he quieted.

"Are you awake? Please, I need you to talk to me. I can help you."

The woman on the mattress finally stirred. She looked sluggishly over her shoulder, but when her gaze locked on mine, her eyes widened. "L-Lillian?"

"Yeah, I'm here. Please, come talk to me. It's urgent."

She got up as if someone had pulled her by invisible strings, stumbling toward the bars with a heavy limp. Tangible desperation was painted across her dirty face as she wrapped her hands around the metal separating us. "Can you get me out? Oh please, get me out! Y-You don't know what they do to us!"

But I did know. I knew exactly what they did to her, and judging by the bruises and scratches on her hips, it was the same fate I'd only narrowly escaped.

"I will. I'll get you out, but first, I need you to tell me

where they're keeping 351." I wrapped my hands around hers, trying to force calm on her so she would tell me what I needed to know.

She hesitated, wide eyes searching mine. "Please, Lillian. Promise me."

"I promise," I said softly, squeezing her hands. "But without 351, none of us are getting out of here. Please, do you know where he is?"

She swallowed, tongue flicking out to wet her dry lips, and then nodded. "I've heard the assistants talking... there's a floor below this one. He's down there. But...there's something you should know."

"What?" I tried my best to smother my frustration with her. Every cell in my body ached to find Zach, but I couldn't rush her more than I already was. It was pretty clear from her wide eyes and pale skin that she was clinging on to reality with her fingernails. And I couldn't blame her—if I'd not made it out when I did, I doubted I'd have been in a much better state.

"They bring him up here sometimes. To watch... He's not... human anymore."

I grunted, lifting my shoulder in the direction of her mate. "None of them are."

"No, it's... it's different," she swallowed again, gaze dipping to avoid mine. "They did something to him. I think... they broke something. Something more than in the others."

I shook my head and pushed off the bars. I'd felt

what they did to him every damned day since my escape, and I was done wasting time. "It doesn't matter. How do I get to his floor?"

"I think there's a corridor past Dr. Urwin's office," she said softly. When I made to turn around, she called out to me again.

"Lillian—please, don't leave me."

"I'll be back for you," I said as I made my way across the lab, nodding to my escort to follow me. "Don't worry."

"We're not enough men to evacuate anyone else," Jerome murmured as he fell in by my side. "Even one extra would jeopardize the mission, especially with Beau gone and Larry injured."

"I know." I pointed at the door leading toward the section of the compound that housed Dr. Urwin's office. Eric and Jarl got into position, one pulling it open as the other aimed his gun at the doorway. But no guards met us, and both men filed through, checking that the hallway was clear.

Quietly, filled with the need to speak my betrayal out loud, I added, "Telling her we would take her with us was the fastest way to guarantee her compliance."

I ignored Jerome's frown as I passed through the door into the empty hallway. Once upon a time, I would have done everything to save the other women in here. They might not have been willing to become fugitives before being mated, but no one could sustain the brutality the research team subjected their mated test subjects to.

But now...

All that mattered was stopping the clawing behind my ribs from tearing me apart. The women trapped in cages with alphas they'd not chosen? They meant nothing.

THE FLOOR below where the ferals were kept was much starker than the rest of the compound. Instead of white walls and fluorescent lights, bare concrete covered every surface, and only sparse orange bulbs lit up the corridor every few yards, leaving big patches of shadow between them. It didn't smell like disinfectant down here—it smelled like mold and wet metal. Like rusting iron, or dried blood.

"Fucking hell," Jarl murmured as we walked down the narrow pathway. "Who the hell thought to install a goddamn dungeon?"

"Looks like it's meant to be a bunker," Jerome said, keeping his voice low. "In case of a nuclear attack."

"I think they planned on keeping the alphas here permanently," I said. "Once they've been trained as super soldiers. It's probably supposed to function as a military base."

"Fucking grotesque," Eric muttered.

We followed the corridor for a long while, going

down each branch as it separated into other sections. We tested every room we passed. They were all empty or filled with rusty barrels and general storage from the lab upstairs. But I could *feel* him. My bond hummed and twisted like a living worm burrowing in my chest, urging me onward, whispering that *he* was near.

Then, after searching dozens of rooms and multiple corridors, we finally stopped outside a heavy wooden door with a metal grate at the top, too high to see through but open enough to let some air into the room beyond.

And I *knew*.

"He's in there," I whispered, grabbing Jerome by the arm.

The large alpha stared at the door, assessing its strength. "We'll need something to break it down with. Jarl, Eric—go back to that room with the metal poles and get us something heavy."

Energy crackled in my blood as my heart forced it through my too-tight veins, spreading a sensation of pins and needles from my toes to my scalp as I waited, palm pressed against the damp wood.

"Zach," I whispered, the name tasting so strange on my tongue. I'd used it so many times these past weeks, but now it somehow seemed wrong, like I was attempting to personify the yearning inside of me and turn it into a person, a man.

It wasn't. *He* wasn't. He hadn't been for a long time now.

He'd told me his name was Zach after he'd claimed me, and that was what I'd called him in my head when I lay awake at night, wishing for an end to the terrible pull behind my ribs. But he hadn't been Zach since we were separated. He'd been... something else.

They've broken something in him, the woman who'd been my neighbor in hell had said.

And I knew she was right.

"Step aside, Lillian," Jerome ordered when Eric and Jarl returned with what looked like a steel four-by-four.

The door was thick, and it took five heavy thuds of the steel battering ram before it finally splintered and fell apart.

The scent that curled in our nostrils made me shudder, but not from revulsion.

It was *his* scent. Deep and potent, filled with rage and pain—but it was his. I hadn't realized how much I'd missed it until it wrapped around me like a tight embrace, filling my lungs with every breath.

A deep warning snarl rolled out from the room, underlined by a rattling of chains.

"No, let us investigate first," Jerome said when I made to step over the broken door. He put a hand on my chest, holding me back when I tried to slip past him.

Eric and Jarl slipped into the cell, using the lights on their weapons as torches.

"Holy shit," Eric gasped.

"Is he okay?" I pushed at Jerome's arm, needing to see for myself, but the big alpha kept me in place.

"Hey, buddy, it's okay. It's us. We're gonna get you out now," Eric said. His voice was controlled, strained in an effort to sound soothing, but the horror in it was unmistakable.

A roar, and a clanking of chains rang through the cell, followed by the heavy *thud* of flesh hitting flesh.

"Shit!" one of the men inside snarled, and then a body came flying through the door and collided with a heavy smack against the corridor wall behind us. Jarl slid to the floor, his eyes glazed from the impact.

"Fall back!" Jerome snapped, but he needn't have. Eric stumbled backwards out of the cell the next second, struggling to keep on his feet, eyes wide with unadulterated horror. A vicious rattle of chains, as if a large beast was straining at the end of his bindings, rang from the room.

"Shit," Jerome growled. "What the fuck did they do to him?!"

"That's not fucking Barnes," Eric said, eyes never leaving the dark door opening. "They fucked him up, Willis. They fucked him up bad."

"Let me talk to him," I said, placing a hand on Jerome's arm.

"Lillian—"

"No. No. Whatever they did, he's still my mate. Let go of me."

He cursed under his breath, but finally lowered his arm.

I climbed over the broken door, heart slamming in my throat as the darkness of the cell blanketed my vision.

A deep growl from the man trapped within resonated down my spine—it was the sound of a beast waiting for the right moment to attack, and some faraway instinct murmured about danger. But it never made it through the numb, electric buzz sweeping through my body as I approached him.

"Zach?"

A light flickered on. One of the men outside must have found a switch, bathing the room in a dim cider glow.

And I finally saw him.

My mate.

His skin was covered in so many fresh scars it took me a moment to realize it wasn't just dirt marring his naked body. Despite the low wattage of the light, he held up a hand toward the source, eyes shut tight.

They'd chained him by the throat and wrists to the wall, but with enough length that he could move around a little. I stared at the mountain of a man still covered in thick bands of bulging muscle, still every ounce the alpha I'd met what seemed like a lifetime ago.

"Zach?" I whispered again, and it was as if something in my brain slowly slid back into place, because despite the state of him, his name resonated deep in my core—in the deepest part of my soul.

He was still in there—I could feel him in my bond. Just the faintest sliver of the man I'd known in those brief moments when the drugs had worn off.

Zach.

He growled again, still such an angry sound, but I was sure I could pick out a questioning note.

"It's me—it's Lillian. I've come back for you."

Slowly, he lowered his hand, squinting against the light.

"Hey," I whispered, swallowing hard at the sight of the bruises on his face. I'd known the pain he'd undergone in the scientists' hands. I'd felt it. But seeing it...

Everything inside of me ached, but it was different than it had been. It wasn't a slicing agony tearing me up from the inside. It was this wave of emotion, like being drowned in sorrow and hurt and desperation after having been unable to feel anything but physical pain for so long. It was as if just a sliver of my own humanity returned on that wave of sadness, washing away the cold, empty hollowness that had taken over who I'd once been.

And then, at last, he saw me. Our eyes met, his narrowed to avoid the painful light, but he went rigid the moment our gazes locked, straightening to his full height.

We stared in silence at each other for three long seconds.

"Zach," I whispered, reaching out toward him as I stumbled forward, pulled by the invisible hook yanking on me from behind my ribs.

I was nearly by his side when his lip curled up in in a silent snarl, a void sliding over his narrowed eyes—and he threw himself at me like a wild beast ready to *maim*.

CHAPTER 24

ZACH

Nothing existed but pain and battle. Nothing but enemies to kill before they killed him.

And yet when he attacked the little female whose face and scent stirred up thoughts he couldn't place—images that were something other than fighting and blood—he couldn't end her life.

He dug his fingers into her flesh, pulling her up against him to crush her frail bones, but as his muscles strained to finish her, he found himself incapable.

Snarling, he stared into her wide, scared eyes, unable to grasp why she seemed... so *familiar*. What were those flickers in his mind calling to him? Why did her scent, struck through with fear as it was, fill him with... *warmth?*

He sniffed her again, closing his eyes when a tremor made its way up his spine.

"*Zach*," she said.

He frowned and looked back down at her. That word... it was like hearing someone speaking through water. Vaguely familiar, but too muddled to understand.

"Zach. It's me. I'm here." She managed to wrench a hand free from his grasp. Slowly, she eased it toward his chest.

The warmth of her palm nearly made him lose his grip on her. It wasn't painful, but the electric buzz that went through him reminded him all too clearly of his tormentor's favored tool. Fury blazed in his mind and he snarled a warning, wishing he could kill the female and end this confusing encounter before *they* returned and punished him for his failings.

"Do you need help?" The garbled speech from outside the cell reminded him of the other alphas' presence, and his anger spiked as he clutched the female tighter and pulled on his chains, challenging them to return and finish what they'd started when they encroached on his domain.

"Don't come in!" The female didn't look away from him. Slowly, she let her hand slide from his chest to the side of his face, seemingly unconcerned with the threat of his bared teeth. "Zach, don't be scared. I'll help you remember."

Her voice was so soft—as soft as her body against his. He dragged her scent in through his nostrils, filling his lungs with it, knowing he shouldn't—that feeling anything other than anger and terror would be punished until he wished for death. He should kill her now, before it was too late. Just squeeze her small body a little harder and she'd break, and it'd be over—

His pained contemplations came to a full stop when she slid her hand back down his chest and wrapped it around his cock. He jolted violently as sharp, hot tendrils of *need* rocketed up his body and down his thighs.

Pleasure.

His mind fogged as images of her face, contorted in pain and pleasure underneath him, came rushing back from the dark.

Mating.

He remembered what it felt like to rut. To fuck.

That was why she smelled so good. That was why he couldn't kill her—she wasn't to be killed, she was to be mounted. Her hand around his cock filled him with a craving that intensified with each harsh breath he expelled, urging his body to thrust. Her touch sent hot, violent yearning up his spine, licking like flames, infecting him with an insurmountable fever.

He growled again, eyes narrowed as he searched her for any sign she might attack him. That this might be a trick. There was none—and finally, from the very depths of the darkness came the knowledge of what he had to do.

She screeched when he tossed her to the floor, but

to his surprise she didn't fight when he knelt over her. Her gaze flickered from his hard and throbbing cock, but the hesitance evident in her eyes at the sight of his anatomy softened when she looked at his face. Gently, she reached out and brushed a palm over his face before she relaxed on the dirty floor, offering him... permission?

He froze, unsure how to proceed without fighting for dominance, but when she tilted her hips up, he remembered. He shredded the cloth covering her lower half, yanking it off her long limbs until the place between her legs was bared to him. He didn't think; he acted on instincts alone as the sweet call from her cunt made him bury his mouth where her alluring scent was strongest.

She yelped and jerked, hands flying to his head, and he snarled without lifting his mouth from her soft flesh. But she didn't try to shove him away, instead clutching him tighter against her as he delved in between her folds.

She tasted exactly like she smelled—divine, feminine, salty musk, and something more. Something that pulled so hard at the aching chord in his chest he struggled for breath. But what was air, when he had this? Had *her*?

He licked and rubbed and sucked between her spread lips until she was bucking and panting, her pink folds slick and flushed open, revealing her opening.

"It's okay," she whispered, her voice hoarse and breathy now. "It's okay. I'll help you remember."

He ignored her words; he didn't understand them and didn't much care what they meant. All he cared about, all he *needed,* was that glistening opening between her legs.

Her cunt.

The word rang through his brain as he fell on top of her and rocked his hips forward, desperate to be inside of her. But the broad head of his cock was too big to go in, instead rubbing up her slit, catching in the mouth of her opening.

The female shuddered and reached between them, but he pushed her hand away with a snarl and fisted his cock in one hand, aiming it at her entrance.

Her cunt resisted again, but he wasn't about to be denied. Not when every instinct in his body roared at him, promised him that *this* was all he needed to survive. That nothing would ever hurt again once he was buried inside this little female's body. With a growl and a brutal shove, he breached her, the wet sound of her pussy swallowing him drowned out by her pained scream.

"Ow, fuck!" Her hands flew to his stomach, pressing desperately at his abs, and he realized this was all wrong. She was supposed to be on her hands and knees to prevent her from scratching at his eyes and biting his flesh, but it was too late now. Electric jolts ran up his

spine, making him snarl with the reminder of the torturous shock collar he wore, but the sensation was anything but painful. Her wet inners clutched at his cock, massaging it for every fitful spasm, the tight milking making him throb and fill out even harder than before. There was no force in this world great enough to ever separate him from her cunt again. She could claw out his eyes if she wanted—he was never gonna stop fucking her.

He shoved forward, seating the full length of his cock inside her wet heat with one slow, brutal thrust, penetrating her to her very core.

Her eyes were wild, lush lips parted in a pained grimace, but she didn't claw at him. She didn't even fight him. Her hands remained frozen against his stomach, trying and failing to prevent full penetration, but she seemed to have accepted her fate.

A tendril of sharp, near-painful bliss jolted through him as he allowed himself a moment to bask in the pleasure of her wrapped around him, from the very base of his dick to the his head pushed snugly up against the end of her trembling cunt. Memories, thoughts, and sensations screamed at him, flashing images bombarding his mind, trying to force him to *remember*. He pushed it all away until there was nothing in his world but her heartbeat drumming against his cock from where they were connected. And finally, he allowed his instincts to swallow him up, leaving nothing behind but a mindless beast, no echoes of pain or torture clouding his mind.

His first thrust made her yowl and clench her fists against his abs. Instincts made him bend his head and nibble at her jawline, distracting her from the pain of his too-big cock. She still sobbed as he fucked her, her wet heat never releasing its tight grip on his girth, but she gasped and mewled in between her cries when he sucked and licked at her neck. Soon her hands moved from his stomach to his chest, flattening against his hard muscle, no longer protesting his presence inside of her.

He'd known pleasure like this before, he realized as he pounded her cunt in savage thrusts. And he'd known *her*. He stared down at her as she cried and panted, memorizing every detail of her face. The bond in his chest hummed so loudly it warred with the physical pleasure of mating, trilling a joyful tune, and he knew this was where he was supposed to be, always. Between her thighs, inside of her, making her feel every bit as wonderful as she made him feel.

He pressed his lips to hers before he'd made the decision to, kissing her as the memory of how came back to him.

She startled in response, clearly not expecting anything from him but the rough, relentless thrusts in her pussy, but soon she softened, sliding her arms around his neck. When their mouths separated, the look of shock on her face was unmistakable. Then he pummeled the head of his cock directly into the spongy spot inside of her, and she threw her head back, her entire body *clenching*.

The pleasure that rocked through his cock and up his backbone was more than his mind could take. Her pussy squeezed him to a full stop, only to erupt in a series of fluttering spasms around him the next second as she screeched and thrashed underneath him.

He shuddered and roared, his knot forming before he could move. It grew inside her already dilated opening until it was too big to pull out, and he pushed in deeper, locking it in place behind her pelvic bone while she was still riding her climax.

She screamed again, twitching to escape it, but before she could so much as push at him, he'd knotted her fully.

He groaned and rocked his hips, grinding his knot against her pelvic girdle's tight clasp. And then, finally, he came.

If fucking her had been pleasure, releasing inside of her was ecstasy. Every cell in his body flushed with bliss, his spurting cock sending ripples of raw sensation that resonated deep in his chest. He couldn't control the moans ripping from his throat, sounding nothing like any sound he'd produced in so long.

And below him, she lay, face twisted in excruciating pleasure as she was forced to ride his brutal knot, her small mewls transferring to the spasms in her cunt as it clasped him so tight, promising to never let him go.

It was then, as he stared into her glazed eyes, he finally remembered.

She was his mate.

His mate had come back to him.

CHAPTER 25

LILLIAN

Sex with Zach had always been painful, his pure size and brutality making our animalistic couplings hard to get through. But the pleasure of mating was undeniable, even if it was shameful, and when I'd seen what they'd done to him and realized he didn't remember me, I'd known on an instinctive level what I'd needed to do to bring him back to me.

I winced as Zach shifted and his knot ground against my depleted G-spot, his pleased rumble that wasn't quite a purr unhindered by my flinch as he licked at my still-clothed breasts and bared neck.

There had been pleasure, and relief, as my bond snapped into place the second his body joined with mine, but the physical aspect had not been the most powerful part of our joining by far. No rush of endorphins, not even the powerful climax he'd forced from the very depths of my sex, had dampened the soul-deep elation still singing through my entire being from finally being with him again.

And he'd kissed me.

For the first time, in the depths of the madness his captivity and torment had brought on, he'd kissed me.

Despite everything they'd done to him, he was still in there. I sighed and pressed my face against his neck, focusing on the hum of completion emanating from the thread in my chest and the pleasurable agony of fullness from where Zach's knot dilated my still-spasming sheath. Even the pain of taking it again for the first time in so long couldn't ruin the feeling of completion rolling through me in lazy waves. I'd hated his knot, once. Not anymore. It hurt to open for it, but nothing would ever tie me so completely to the man I'd thought I'd lost as the thick mass locked behind my pelvic bone. Nothing would ever quell the unbearable agony of our frayed bond so thoroughly.

"Zach," I whispered, stroking his shoulders gently. "Are you back?"

Only a light nip on my neck let me know he'd registered me speaking.

"Zach? Can you... Can you understand me?"

The large alpha kept licking and suckling at my flesh, oblivious to my question.

I bit my lip, trying to force my mind to focus through the onslaught of endorphins and post-orgasmic lethargy.

He might have calmed down, but our reunion hadn't brought him out of the darkness. "Fuck."

"Everything okay in there, Lillian?" Jerome called, breaking the illusion that it was just Zach and I in the world.

The combination of the masculine voice and my jolt of surprise cut Zach's pleased noises short. He lifted his face from my neck, lip curling in a warning snarl at the door.

"Yeah, I'm fine," I managed. "But I think—I think we need to tranq him. They keep some loaded guns in the big room with the other alphas."

Zach's snarl rose in volume, as if me talking to what he saw as rival alphas fueled his rage. When I caught a glimpse of his eyes, I *saw* the darkness creeping back like encroaching shadows threatening to take away the small respite our coupling had brought him.

"And hurry!"

IT DIDN'T TAKE the SEALs long to return with a tranquilizer gun, but by that point Zach was nearly unrecognizable. He kept snarling and spitting like a trapped beast at the doorway where he could hear them pacing, jerking on our tie every few seconds in his efforts to get to the men and tear them apart. Apparently he'd forgotten about the chains tying him to the wall, and I had to clench my jaw not to cry out from the constant tugging between my legs. I knew he wouldn't calm down if he heard my pained cries.

Thankfully, the other alphas didn't hesitate. The moment Jerome returned with the gun, he took up position at the doorway, aimed, and fired three arrows straight into Zach's back and neck.

My mate roared, lunging at his attacker and pulling painfully on my dilated opening, and I screamed. But before any real damage could be done, Zach slumped down on top of me, eyelids fluttering shut.

Boots scuffed against the concrete floor just before the others lifted Zach off me. His cock slid out of me easily, his knot deflated, leaving a wet trail of fluids dripping out of my still-open sex.

Jerome looked down at me, assessing my body for damages. He had a hold of Zach's left armpit while Jarl had the other. "You all right?"

"I'll be fine." I winced as I gathered my legs and tested my body. My abdomen was predictably sore, and I was pretty sure I'd be sporting bruises and scrapes on my back. It wasn't anywhere near as bad as I had expected when I'd first reached for his cock to remind him of who I was. He'd prepared me, rather than just tear into my dry sex, and though he'd been rough... there had been moments of tenderness.

I bit my lip, the ghost of his forceful kiss haunting me. I hadn't thought he remembered how to, nor that he had any inclination for it. But he had—so deep in the depravity of what they'd done to him, when his humanity was so far gone I wasn't sure he'd ever regain it, he'd still kissed me.

I got to my feet, taking Eric's offered hand to steady myself. It wasn't until I noticed how he studiously avoided looking at my naked lower half that it dawned on me they hadn't been watching us have sex. Heard it, sure, but not for their own twisted pleasure, like the doctors here.

"We need to get Barnes out of here before the morning shift comes in and finds the soldiers and guards dead," Jerome said, nodding at Eric. "You make sure she stays on her feet. And find her some pants."

"Wait. We can't leave yet. They've done something to him—he's... he's *different* than he was before," I said.

Jerome frowned. "How do you mean?"

"I think they've been given him another drug, perhaps even multiple. I need to find his file and see what they've given him—and if there's an antidote. I don't think... I don't think he'll be able to regain his humanity on his own." I looked at my passed-out mate hanging limply between the two alphas, and my heart ached at the many scars covering his strong body. They'd done everything to break him, and in my absence they'd finally succeeded.

THEY HADN'T PUT him on another drug.

Eric managed to hack into Dr. Axell's computer for me, and that's where I learned exactly what they'd done to him. I scrolled past the pages detailing his systematic torture, unable to stomach the clinical detachment in Dr. Axell's notes as he described his step-by-step process to dehumanize *"Subject 351"* until he was nothing but an empty shell, ready to be reprogrammed.

But when I came to his comments on the drugs they'd administered, my gut clenched in horror.

Subject 351 has been injected with 6 milliliters of the X-variant of hexatrepodamine two times a day. His reasoning skills appear to continually decline, limiting his problem-solving and ability to use tools. It is unlikely that he will ever be able to regain these abilities, and we consider the affected brain areas permanently shut down. It is doubtful if even di-hydroperalimitus will be able to reverse this effect. He is, at this point, the very basest of animals.

TWELVE MILLILITERS A DAY. When I'd worked with the alphas, it had been .75 milliliters per man per day, and it had left the alphas unable to access the majority of what made them human. If Zach had been injected with *twelve* every day since I left...

But they were wrong. He'd kissed me. Animals didn't kiss.

They had to be wrong.

"Find anything?" Eric said, interrupting my spiraling thoughts.

"Di-hydroperalimitus," I said, wiping the tears I hadn't been aware of from my cheeks with a shaking hand. "It will be in the refrigerated area where the ferals are kept. We need as much as we can carry."

He didn't comment on my tears as I led the way into the lab. The cooling section held most of the drugs used on the facility, and it was a small mercy to see three full rows of glass bottles labeled di-hydroperalimitus. We grabbed all of them and then made our way to the corridor that led to the ground floor and exit. The others were waiting for us there. Zach's passed-out form was heavy to lug around, and the SEALs were not going to leave Beau's body behind. With Larry injured, they'd needed the head start while Eric and I found what we needed for Zach.

"Lillian!"

I glanced to my right at the sound of my name and locked eyes with my former neighbor's frantic gaze.

"Where are you going? You promised to take me with you!"

I turned my head back around and stared straight ahead as I kept walking toward the exit.

"Lillian! Please, Oh god, no, you can't leave me here! Lillian!"

Somewhere deep inside, in a place the agony from my bond had muted before, I felt a stab of guilt when the door to the lab slid shut behind us, silencing the panicked woman's screams as if they never existed.

CHAPTER 26

LILLIAN

"We can't go back to my place," Jerome said as he drove us down an abandoned country road. I had no idea where it would lead us, but so long as it was away from SilverCorp's compound, it was good enough for me. "They'll have some nice images of all our faces from the security cameras—we're all gonna have to get out of the country and disappear somewhere. But we ain't gonna make it across the border with him in that state, so hopefully the drugs you stole are gonna kick in sometime soon."

"Any plans?" I asked as I slid a needle into Zach's bicep. My mate was still passed out, but a hushed growl escaped his lips as I injected him with the first dose of di-hydroperalimitus. I had no idea how fast it would work, if at all, but I reasoned it'd be much easier to give it to him while he was still unconscious. Hopefully it would be easier to treat him if the drug began to take effect.

When it took effect.

"Nothing, I'm afraid. Dishonorably discharged vets don't exactly get the kind of payout that allows for a nice backup hideout in Colombia. We'll work something out. Getting across the border's the first goal. You just take care of Barnes. Leave the rest to us." Jerome sighed, running a hand over his scalp before changing gears.

"Jerome, I... I haven't thanked you..."

"You had other things on your mind," he grunted. "And it wasn't like we were gonna let our brother rot in some fucking test facility."

"But you lost Beau. And Larry—will he be all right?" I glanced over my shoulder at the headlights following us. Eric drove the other car, allowing Jarl to care for Larry's injury in the backseat. "I didn't consider... the cost of this." Not that I would have stopped them from saving Zach if I had, but the guilt sparked by the claimed woman's pleas for help as we left the facility gnawed at my gut.

They'd all lost so much, and now they'd be fugitives as well.

"You need to understand that every single one of us will happily lay down our lives for this man," Jerome said, steel in his voice. "He did the same for us, once, but he didn't sign up for *this*. There is honor in sacrifice. In a warrior's death. There is nothing but humiliation in what they did to him, and if we'd known, we would've come for him sooner."

I looked at Zach's naked form as he lay slumped against the backseat door, unable to take my hand off his arm where I'd injected him. The contact of his skin against mine soothed the place in my chest where the bond now hummed contentedly. Despite the absence of pain, I still felt raw inside and out, and I wasn't sure that part would ever heal. Maybe the damage our separation had done would be permanent.

He'd been introduced to me as a war criminal, a convict, the lowest of scum, no better than an animal. And yet these men had all put their lives on the line to save him.

"I need you to tell me what happened," I said quietly, never taking my eyes off Zach's sleeping face. "I need to know why they charged him with treason."

"You know I can't. I swore an oath," Jerome rumbled. "If he wants you to know, he'll tell you himself."

"There is..." I swallowed thickly, forcing down the wave of despair just thinking the thought brought on. "There is no guarantee he will ever speak again, Jerome. There is no guarantee he will ever be anything more than a mindless animal. What they did to him... I don't know if I can bring him back. I'll try. I'll never stop trying. He ensured that when he put his claiming mark on my neck.

"I don't hate him. I don't hate him for being so desperate for a companion that he stole my choice and my future from me. I don't hate him for the things he has done to me because they took away his ability to control himself. But I... I want to know... I *need* to know, if the world had been different, if we had met... somewhere else. Could I have loved him? Would I have chosen him, if he had asked instead of taking?"

Silence filled the car as my voice died down. For the longest time, I thought he was going to keep quiet, and I wiped the tears threatening to spill from my eyes. I had my mate back—hours ago that was all I'd wanted, and more than I'd hoped for. How we had come to be, and how we would continue... it didn't matter. I had no right to cry anymore.

"Just because you didn't choose him doesn't mean you don't love him." Jerome's voice was uncharacteristically quiet. "Why did you try to rescue him that first time?"

"They were hurting him. No one deserves that kind of treatment, no matter what they've done. Despite... Despite everything, I would do it again."

"But why *him*, specifically?" Jerome asked, glancing at me in the rearview mirror. "There were dozens of other alphas in there, locked up and brutalized just like Barnes. Why'd you choose him?"

"I..." I bit my lip, frowning at the question. I thought back to Zach's bloody back and the pained mistrust in his beautiful eyes. And then, like a whisper, I remembered how I'd thought about him day and night, how his eyes and his body had stayed with me in my dreams. "I thought he was different."

"You thought he was different, yet you thought him a traitor and a murderer?" Jerome snorted. "It doesn't get a lot of press, not outside alpha circles... but the rumor is we're not the only ones who know when we meet the woman who's meant to be our mate. She will too, even if she doesn't always understand. Zach isn't the type of man to claim whatever piece of ass he can get a hold of just because he's lonely. I don't care what they've done to him, that shit is fused into your bones.

"You say he stole your future from you—girl, he was always your future. *You* picked *him* when you chose to free him from that fucking cell the first time 'round. So don't give me any bullshit about how you *might* have loved him if he'd been the perfect gentleman and bought you flowers before he gave you the knot and bit your neck. Love ain't like that, not for us. It's primal and it's inescapable, and what you feel for him... that's the kind of love that never, ever dies."

I gaped at his steely gaze in the rearview mirror, too stunned to respond. But his words sank in deep, penetrating the place in my chest my bond was hooked and making it hum as if it was trying to convince me he spoke nothing but the truth.

"I've been in love before," I whispered. "Many

times. It didn't feel like this—this is... it's awful. I have this *thing* inside of me, like a worm burrowing in my flesh, a parasite manipulating me, hurting me when I'm too far away from him."

Jerome scoffed. *"Beta love.* That's not real, girl. That's a beta making you feel good to get in your pants. You think your *bond* is manipulating you?" He scoffed again. "Fucking betas."

He fell silent again and I returned my attention to Zach's sleeping form. Was Jerome right? I thought back to Dr. Urwin and what he'd said to me as he strapped me onto the breeding bench. How every beta boyfriend I'd ever had had wanted to do the same to me. But that was just a projection of his own twisted desires. Right?

"On our last mission, our squad was tasked with taking a strategic vantage point. Said it was an abandoned school. Only when we got there, it'd been turned into a fucking orphanage. Mostly it was filled with kids whose parents died in the war. *We* killed their parents, and now we were going to take their last safehouse too? Wasn't gonna happen.

"Captain didn't see it that way, though. Told us to get with the program or get tried for treason. When we still refused, he shot a kid. Fucking shot him right in front of the others, and said we better get our priorities straight or he'd be forced to clear them all out. 'Cause if all the kids are dead, it's no longer an orphanage, or some bullshit like that.

"That's when Barnes pulled his gun and shot the captain point-blank. And the fuckers at home tried him for treason and judged him a war criminal, because otherwise it'd have gotten out what they'd tried to do. Barnes told us not to make a fuss. That we should take our dishonorable discharge and disappear or they'd try us too. *Tell no one,* he said. He didn't want us to die along with him. And we didn't, to honor his sacrifice.

"But every single one of us are willing to lay down our lives for him. Fuck what the brass calls us—he saved our honor that day. And our fucking souls, if you believe in that shit.

"I tell you this not to help you justify what you feel for him, whether you want to admit it it not. I tell you so if he truly never speaks again, if this is all that's left of the man who saved all those kids and his squad along with it... then at least you can tell any child you bear him what he used to be."

WE PARKED FAR down an abandoned dirt trail in a thick patch of wood. They buried Beau under an oak tree some thirty yards in, then returned to the cars to catch a few hours' sleep. Daylight meant a much higher chance of getting caught while on the open road.

Jarl took the first shift as lookout and I climbed into the backseat of Jerome's Jeep, where I curled up against

Zach. My bond hummed with contentment as my skin touched his, my eyelids fluttering shut when the last vestige of the adrenaline that'd kept me going since we broke into SilverCorp's compound left my body. He might have been unconscious, but my instincts still made me feel so much safer in his presence.

I'd slept fitfully, plagued by nightmares and anxiety since my first escape from the dreaded hellhole. Now, though, with the warmth of the alpha underneath me, I drifted off with nothing but relief filling my mind.

I WOKE up to a rumbling sound that seemed to originate from everywhere at once. It jarred me out of the my peaceful sleep, warning signals firing in my fuzzy brain.

Groggily, I opened my eyes and tried to sit up, but an iron band kept me glued to the hot surface I'd been sleeping against.

"Lillian, can you try to calm him, please?"

I looked up at the sound of Jerome's very quiet, calm voice, and saw him kneeling in the driver's seat facing us, eyes locked above me. When I followed his gaze, I realized where the noise was coming from.

Zach was awake, his lip curled to show his teeth as he let out a low, continuous growl aimed at the other alpha in the car. His right arm was clasped around my body, crushing me to his side.

"Shit," I mumbled, my brain kicking through the haze of sleep with a panicked start. None of us had thought about what might happen if Zach woke up to find another alpha so close by. "Zach. Zach?"

He didn't respond.

"Hey, it's okay. He's a friend." I gently brushed my hand up his naked side to rest it against his chest. "Zach, look at me. Everything's okay. We're safe."

I wasn't sure he understood me, but when I pressed against where his end of our bond hooked, his eyes flickered to mine.

I smiled to show him there was no threat, planting a kiss against his tensed bicep. "Calm down, big guy."

Slowly, his growl quieted, his intense stare remaining on my face. His pupils were larger than normal, but not completely blackening his irises.

"Hey," I whispered, petting his thickly muscled chest. "How are you feeling?"

He didn't respond, too busy studying my every feature as if he'd forgotten what I looked like. Maybe he had—the amount of drugs they'd given him would have been enough to shut down nearly everything but his lizard brain.

"I'm gonna take watch so he can have a moment to come to terms with everything," Jerome said. Even though his tone was still deliberately non-aggressive, Zach snapped his head around and bared his teeth. "Give us a shout if you need us."

Zach tensed even further when Jerome moved to slip out of the car, but he didn't lunge. When the door closed and we were alone again, his growl died, though he stared out the window at Jerome's retreating back.

"You sent me to him," I said, still stroking his chest to keep him calm. At this point, I was pretty sure he didn't understand what I was saying, but my voice seemed to have a soothing effect on him. "You said he'd take care of me, and he has. He got me to you—he and the others are the reason I could get you out. And... he told me what you did, before. You're a hero, Zach. Not a criminal. And I didn't know. You almost died without me knowing who you truly are."

Zach turned back to look at me, something in my voice drawing his attention from Jerome. He frowned down at me, raising a hand to clumsily paw at the single tear trickling down my cheek.

Pain lanced through my stomach and chest when I caught sight of the many scars covering his hands and fingers. I'd been there when he got them, tearing at the barbed wire until his flesh hung in grotesque strips from the bones, all so he could save me. He'd had to use his teeth to kill the soldier who'd aimed his gun at me. The doctors had done a decent job at patching them up, but they were never going to look the same again. No part of his scarred body would.

"Do they hurt?" I asked, reaching for his hand pressed against my cheek. He allowed me to take it, and

I ran my fingertips along the jagged lines. They were stiff, swollen, and when I gently pressed, a little growl rolled from his throat.

"Shh, I'll make them feel better." There wasn't much I could do to thank him for everything he'd sacrificed for me. I couldn't even guarantee I could bring his mind back from the drug-induced void they'd rendered it. But this... this I could do.

I massaged his hands, rubbing along every scar in long, smooth motions until the tension in them began to ease. I looked up at his face and smiled at his half-closed eyes, his expression full of wonder, like he'd forgotten what it felt like to have someone's touch bring pleasure rather than pain.

My smile withered when I remembered that he probably had. "It might take a while, but I think we can eventually bring some more mobility back."

Zach stretched his fingers experimentally, wincing when his tendons protested. They were still very stiff and clumsy, but at least some of the swelling seemed to have gone down.

"All right. What do you say I give you a shot of your medicine, and then we go stretch our legs and find some breakfast? We're gonna be staying here for a while." I turned to reach for the bag in the back of the Jeep that held the bottles of di-hydroperalimitus and syringes, pulling out the supplies I needed. I wasn't sure how often or how much would be the correct dosage, but I'd decided half a milliliter each morning and evening would be the best bet.

Except when I turned back around to Zach, needle in hand, his face twisted into first shock and then *rage*.

Too late I realized what the sight of a drawn syringe would symbolize to him.

"No, no! I'm not going to hurt you, I promise!" I quickly dropped the needle behind me and held up both hands in surrender. Zach glared at me, nostrils flaring. The look of distrust on his face was clear.

"Hey, you know me," I said, slowly reaching for him. His lip curled up higher in response, but when he didn't growl, I reached out to rest my palm against his chest once more. "I'm never going to hurt you; you must know that. You must be able to feel that."

His heart thudded unsteadily underneath my palm, and my gut twisted when I realized how scared he was. His anger I could take, his animalistic fury and mistrust too... but naked fear? It crushed me.

I blinked away the tears threatening to spill down my face and leaned in. When my lips pressed against his, he startled, but I persisted. Gently, slowly, I coaxed his mouth to follow mine as I guided our kiss. It was so different from when he'd kissed me, every brush of our lips light and soft and sweet, until finally some long minutes later, his heart eased to a slow, steady rhythm.

Only then did I pull back so I could reach around

for the syringe with the hand not resting against his chest.

His upper lip rose again at the sight of it, but he didn't bare his teeth fully.

"This is medicine, Zach. To make you feel better—to heal you," I said, keeping my gaze locked in his. "It's going to make you feel better."

He narrowed his eyes at me, but when I grasped his hand and put the syringe in his palm, he stayed still.

"Hold that. I need to get the rubbing alcohol."

It wasn't only out of a sense of convenience that I allowed him to hold the syringe; I also wanted to give Zach a sense of control over his fate, and it seemed to work. He sat still as a stone while I rubbed the alcohol over his bicep and allowed me to take the syringe from him again, though he never stopped watching me for any indication that I would break his trust.

I breathed deeply and evenly, ensuring I didn't give him any reason to kick into fight-or-flight mode, and jabbed the needle into his skin. He let out an angry growl at the prick of pain, but I managed to push the plunger in before he jerked away.

"Stop that," I scolded, keeping my tone light and friendly as I reached for his arm to free the needle.

I got a low growl in return.

"I know, you have every reason not to like needles." I leaned in again and kissed him right over his heart.

"When you calm down again, we'll go look for some breakfast, okay?"

I could feel his glare as I rested my cheek against his chest, snuggling close to soothe him with my nearness. Instinctively I knew his bond would work to calm him the same way mine did when we were skin to skin.

It didn't take long before he relaxed and wrapped both his arms around me. I sighed as my bond hummed in appreciation of being surrounded so completely by him.

But when he buried his nose in my hair and began sniffing at me, I gently untangled myself from his grip and pulled back. "Yeah, no, I need to pee way too much for you to start getting any ideas."

Zach rumbled at me, a questioning sound rather than a growl this time. I reached behind him and opened his door, hoping to distract him with the smell of fresh air. It worked.

The big alpha turned toward the now open door, sniffed once—and leapt outside in one jump.

I quickly got out my own side of the car, momentarily worried he'd run off, but he just stood in the middle of our impromptu camp, staring up into the canopy of trees above us.

Jerome shot me a worried look, one eyebrow raised in silent question, and I shook my head. I'd been trapped in the underground lab for a week, and the shock of fresh air during our escape had been nearly overwhelming. For Zach... it'd been much longer. He needed a moment's peace to feel the sunlight on his face.

I quietly gathered up some protein bars from the SEALs' packed rations and found a towel, a bar of soap, and spare clothes for both of us as well. Zach was still staring up in the trees, his head tilting in the direction of each bird chirping nearby. Only when I approached him did he turn his head to me, eyes locking on mine. His face held an expression so novel to him that it took me a moment to decipher it.

Joy.

I bit my lip to stop more tears from welling. I'd cried so much, but I could do nothing to temper the relief brimming in my chest.

He was capable of feeling something as human as joy.

"Come," I said softly, shifting the bundle to one arm so I could reach for him with my free hand.

Slowly, as if he wasn't quite sure how, he put his scarred hand in mine. His fingers closed clumsily around mine, engulfing them completely, and I couldn't hold back a smile. I didn't know if it was the drugs working, or if it was just a reaction to finally smelling fresh air, but there were signs. He was in there.

We walked around the Jeep, but when Zach spotted Jerome keeping watch by the other alphas' car, he jerked to a stop, upper lip curling again.

Jerome didn't react—he only looked at his friend.

"It's just Jerome," I murmured, pulling gently on Zach's hand. "Remember?"

Zach huffed, glaring in the dark-skinned alpha's direction for a few more moments before he finally deemed him non-threatening enough not to attack. It didn't stop him from ensuring his body was blocking any chance Jerome had of seeing me as my mate clutched me to his side in a none-too-pleasant death grip.

I put up with it, just thankful he hadn't decided to attack.

THE RIVER WAS REALLY MORE of a creek, only about five feet wide and three to four feet deep in the middle, with a sluggish flow and rocks covering most of the bottom.

When Zach spotted it, he gave a low sort of hum and proceeded to stalk toward it, dragging me along like a doll.

"Hey, wait up!" I called, trying to pull free from his grip as he steered us directly toward the flowing water without slowing. "We have to take our clothes o—oh *damn,* that's cold!"

I squealed the last bit, because Zach didn't let such a thing as being dressed stop him. He pulled me straight out into the icy stream, clothes, shoes, towel, and all, and only let go when the water hit my navel.

"F-Fuck!" I shuddered, trying to raise up on my tippy-toes to save my midsection from the icy cold. Only the smooth river rocks underneath us were too slippery for that sort of balancing act, and I had to reach out and support myself against Zach to not end up getting dunked.

He gave me a quick glance, ensuring I was all right, and then returned his focus to the water. It only reached mid-thigh on him, so he had to bend down to gather some in his joined hands. He stared, mesmerized at the light playing across the surface for a moment before he brought it to his lips and drank.

Despite my now numb lower half, something soft twisted inside of me as I watched the big man so fascinated with something as mundane as a river. This was his first taste of freedom, even if the drugs still held his mind captive, and despite our dire situation, I wanted him to enjoy it.

I climbed out of the river to deposit the towel on the shore before it got too wet and pulled my clothes off as well. My pants, underwear, socks, and shoes were soaked, and the bottom part of my top equally so, but since I was already mostly wet, I decided I might as well have a proper bath.

I had to grit my teeth and force myself to step back into the frigid water, and when I reached Zach, I quickly ducked under.

He turned my way at my gasps and splashes when I

resurfaced, but at the sight of my now very perky nipples, his frown changed to unmistakable hunger.

"We're not having sex now," I said, folding one arm across my chest to break his line of sight while I reached for his shirt with the other. "Come on, it's bath time."

BATHING a feral alpha determined to turn me around so he could mount me was not an easy task. But as interested in my naked body as he was, I got the distinct impression he was... *playful* about it. We'd had sex often enough while locked up in the compound, and he'd been rough and forceful about it every time. I knew he could easily force me into submission if he wanted to, and yet he allowed me to squirm out of his grip when he got a hold of my hips, as well as pull off his wet clothes so I could toss them to shore.

And I...

I wasn't afraid.

It dawned on me when I finally managed to slip behind him to rub soap on his broad back, and he momentarily paused his attempt at spreading my legs to emit a rumbling noise of pleasure.

In there, he'd been a beast. Angry, scared, violent. Out *here*... While maybe not quite human, he was... something other.

My mate.

I pressed my soap-free hand to my chest when my

bond hummed. If this was my future... if he never fully recovered... I could find happiness in this.

Zach allowed me to wash and rinse his back before he turned back around again, slipping his strong arms around my midriff.

I put a wet hand on his chest, shivering when I touched the place our bond anchored on his end. "Hey, big guy."

He rumbled in response, and I looked up into his eyes.

He looked... so different. Light. Happy.

I didn't think before I stretched up toward him like a flower searching for sun, but he met my lips without hesitation, hot and hungry—eager to devour.

I moaned, teasing him with small flicks of my tongue and shivering when he growled in response. His thick, brutal cock pushed against my stomach in obvious demand.

"I made you a promise, once," I whispered against his increasingly aggressive lips. "That I would always submit to you. And right now... I think I... want to."

It wasn't that I hadn't enjoyed it when he mated me before. That I hadn't needed him like he did me when he forced me to the floor and rutted me last night. But this time was different.

He was every bit the demanding alpha I'd known since he forced his knot into me and claimed me as his mate, his kisses were rough and his hands on my hips would likely leave bruises before we were done, but he was also... patient.

I realized then what the difference was. He wasn't afraid. He wasn't angry. He was just an alpha enjoying his mate.

He would still make me submit—but he allowed my surrender to be on my terms.

My body heated despite the cold water and I leaned in closer against him, reveling in the sensation of his scarred skin against mine. When he pulled back from our kiss, I let my hand slide down his rippling abs and close around his hard length.

Zach jerked and went rigid in response, gaze turning molten. I stroked him gently, up and down, once, and then he yanked me up out of the river and into his arms.

I squealed as he swung me over his shoulder and waded out of the river and onto the shore in three strides. At first I thought he was going to dump me on the hard rocks, but he stalked further up to where rotting vegetation had created a light layer of dirt over the years. I didn't notice the fallen tree trunk until he swung me off his shoulder and draped me across the round barrel of it, ass pointing up.

I panted, my senses alight with the smells and sounds of the woodland and the rough bark pressing into my breasts, stomach and thighs. But mostly... Mostly, I felt *him*.

He was right behind me, his presence warming my

hamstrings even though he wasn't touching me. As if aware of what his nearness meant, my sex throbbed, eager for him to take what was his.

When his hands finally connected with my skin, I couldn't hold back a wanton moan.

Strong fingers dug into my fleshy backside, spreading me open to the cool air.

"Zach...*oh!*"

His mouth against my upturned pussy startled me, but he didn't give me a chance to squirm away. This time, he kept hold of my hips as he dug his tongue into my channel, licking up inside of me as if trying to drink me. But the river had washed away most of my natural scent, and he growled irritably and flicked his demanding tongue lower down, spreading my slit until he reached my pearl of nerves.

I shrieked as he sucked it into his mouth in one hard pull, jerking up on instinct when he relieved my sensitive nub of its protective hood. He dug his fingers into my spread cheeks, ensuring I stayed in place while he sucked on my throbbing clit.

I howled into the woods, begging for him to be gentle. He ignored me, only growling low with obvious pleasure as my slick began to flow thick and rich. His teeth scraped over my swollen nub, tongue lapping up my offerings without ever giving my poor clit any respite.

My release came from deep in my pelvis, dragged

out by his mouth's merciless manipulation. Like a slow tidal wave, pleasure rose from the roots of my clit until my entire abdomen crackled with energy, my splayed legs jerking hard in preparation. He sent me over the edge with one final, deep suck, and when I screamed, he jammed two thick fingers deep in my spasming sheath.

"Shit! Oh my God!" I groaned, rocking my pelvis back to meet his digits. They spread me out so deliciously, teasing my orgasm to stretch out to small, rippling echoes that traveled up my spine.

My pussy squeezed his fingers tight as the rich sound of his desire sparked another wave of lust deep in my core. He moved behind me, pulling his fingers free with a wet pop that betrayed my body's readiness for what would come next.

I didn't have to wait long.

Zach ranged over me, the broad heat of his cock head pressed up against my opening. My lips were slick and open from my orgasm and split apart easily, allowing him access to my entrance.

I bit my lip when his girth caught in the mouth of my pussy, my body tensing in anticipation of pain even as my sex wept and softened in welcome.

He shoved forward, forcing his cock inside me, and I whimpered as tendrils of agonizing bliss seared up inside my dilated sheath. *Fuck,* that first penetration always hurt so goddamn much!

Zach groaned as my pussy clamped down around

him, trying to stop the invasion even though slick dripped from where we were joined. Another rough shove, and his cock barreled through my last resistance, seating the full length of him all the way inside of me and conquering my spasming core.

"Fuck!" I whimpered, widening my legs as far as I could to open my pelvis to him. Not that he needed it—he'd taken possession of my body now, and we both felt that mind-breaking moment of ecstasy when his head kissed my cervix.

Bent over the tree trunk, my sex was presented to him much the same way as when I'd been strapped to the breeding post, open and vulnerable—his for the taking.

Every vein in his too-thick cock pulsed with the thundering beat of his heart. It hurt to be taken by my alpha, yet nothing would ever complete me like this. He was rough, he was big—and he was *mine*.

"Fuck me! Please, Zach! I need you! Take me!"

If he was as surprised about my outburst as I was, he didn't show it. He did, however, obey.

His hips withdrew with a snap, only to smack back against my upturned ass that same second, forcing his cock all the way in again. He set a punishing pace from the start, incapable of holding back his desire for me any longer. He fucked me with everything he was, forcing me wide over and over and over, grunting with effort and pleasure.

It hurt so much—he was too big, too rough, and I... I *craved* it. Craved the pain, craved that ecstasy-riddled burn of being forced to my limits and pounded into submission. The woods resonated with the fast, wet slaps of his cock dominating my defenseless pussy and my howls for more, more, *more!*

It was the first time I'd begged not for an end to his brutal assault, but for him to be harder, rougher. My blood crackled with the rapture only he could give me, and I knew I needed everything he had. I'd been empty so long, the hollow void eating me up from the inside out, and this—being filled, reclaimed by my mate—that was the only thing that mattered now. Even if it broke my pelvis in half.

He wrung two orgasms from me in rapid succession, each one relaxing my pussy just a little more, making it a little easier to take his unrelenting thrusts. But, when that first swell at the bottom of his already grotesquely thick shaft began to stretch me, panic set in as memories of what came next bloomed in my mind.

"Shit!" I grunted, biting down on a whimper when my tortured opening gaped wide to accommodate the beginning of his knot. "Don't!"

He didn't listen—and couldn't have stopped that powerful instinct to knot even if he'd wanted to. Every cell in his body was hardwired to ensure I took the cursed thing, and when I clawed at the bark to pull myself away and kicked to push him back, he snarled at my disobedience and clamped his teeth around the back of my neck.

He bit down hard on his own claiming mark, ensuring I stayed put. I whined as trigger points made my body go lax and my will disappeared in a fog of endorphins. My hands fell limply in front of me, the claw marks I'd carved into the trunk the only reminder of my attempted rebellion.

Zach's body was hot against my back, pressing me down as he curved around me, keeping his teeth in my flesh while he continued to fuck my weeping pussy with short, hard thrusts that drove the still-swelling knot in and out of my trembling body.

Soon it began to catch in my yawning opening, and just as I thought the agony of it popping in and out would split me apart, he forced it in one last time.

I mewled in protest when he drove his hips forward with all his strength, forcing the horrifically swollen knot past my pelvic bone. The burn of it pulsed through my pelvis and deep in my bones, flickering through my entire body in one long, shuddering spasm. And then... relief.

I gasped at the flood of ecstasy when he finally seated his knot exactly where we fit together, and *screamed* when he pulled back just enough to grind my G-spot. My pelvis clamped down tight in protest, every muscle in my core tightening around his thick invasion —and I *came*.

As agonizing as it was to take his knot, nothing —*nothing*—compared to the pleasure that followed. The physicality of it, of my helplessly gaping pussy milking his cock in hard spasms until his seed bathed my cervix... it was pure bliss exploding through every blood vessel, capturing my brain and forcing pleasure into every cell. But the best part— the very best part of feeling his knot spreading me apart in ways I'd never have surrendered to voluntarily—was feeling him inside of me, around me, swallowing me up, erasing everything I'd been before he entered me, until all that was left were the parts of me that surrounded his brutal knot. The only things I sensed were my taut tissues and cramping muscles and my bones aching from being wrenched apart, excruciating orgasms thundering through me in one long, continuous roar...

And *him*.

I would never be alone again, never be whole without him. It was more than the bond tying us together; it was how much he belonged there, how perfectly he fit even though he shouldn't have. How achingly, horrendously empty I'd be without him inside of me.

CHAPTER 27

ZACH

The sun set and rose several times while they stayed in the woodland. He didn't know how long—there was nothing in his world to indicate the passing of time before then.

His days were spent sleeping, eating, sucking in greedy lungfuls of fresh air, rutting his mate, and keeping the other males away from her. Not that they tried to interfere—they seemed to accept his claim, and distantly, he knew they were safer in a group of strong alphas than alone. So he let them live, so long as they kept to the other side of the camp from his female.

Slowly, he started noticing the sun's trajectory above the trees. Soon after, he noticed a pattern with his mate. She would encourage him to mount her shortly after sunrise and shortly after sunset, and then, when he was content and docile, she would prick him with that hated needle. It took a few days before he realized she was purposely cajoling him with the sweet draw of her pussy.

The sharp jolt of realization made him stare at her as she fiddled with the needle she'd just pricked him with. She was still naked from their coupling, hair messy and nipples swollen from where he'd sucked on them. She liked it when they faced each other, and he'd increasingly allowed her to turn her front to him before he entered her, finding her breasts and the display of pleasure on her beautiful face enticing enough to suppress his instincts telling him to always mount her from behind.

With a force of will only made possible from how recently he'd emptied his balls in her snatch, he dragged his attention back from her soft body and the pleasures of fucking her. He didn't *want* to get jabbed with a needle. It went against every painful memory still caught up in the darkness surrounding his mind... and yet, he let her, because she petted and talked gently at him when he allowed it, and his body was light with pleasure from their recent matings.

He wanted to rut her from behind, but he wanted to see her face when she took him in, and wanted to suck on her nipples to make her cunt flutter on his cock.

He wanted to bring her her meals like an alpha should, but when he tried to hunt, she pleaded with him to stay with her. And he wanted her by his side more than he needed to provide his own kills for her.

She *made* him want those things.

She knew exactly what she was doing—and she was *manipulating* him!

His growl made her jerk her head up, eyes wide with concern.

"Zach? What's wrong?"

Zach.

His name was Zach. He blinked, the growl cutting off as he stared at her pink lips. She'd spoken to him many times, a steady stream of words usually falling from those luscious lips when she was around him. He hadn't understood any of them, but found the sound of her voice pleasant enough to listen to.

It wasn't until that moment when he remembered that that word belonged to him, that Zach was his *name,* that he realized he was supposed to understand. And respond.

Gently, he touched a hand to her soft mouth, tried to recall the shape it had taken as she said his name.

"Zach?" she asked again, a frown marring her pretty face now. "Are you okay?"

She lifted her hand to pull up his eyelids and spoke some more words that he didn't fully grasp, but he got the sense from them that she was concerned whether he was having a negative reaction to what she'd injected him with.

Gently, he closed his fingers around her wrist and pulled her hand to his chest where their connection hummed like it always did after he'd rutted her. It took more effort than he'd thought to make his tongue curl in the right way.

"*Zach*," he said. It came out hesitant, with the start of the word sounding sharper than it had when she said it.

His mate stilled in his grasp, her eyes widening with shock. And then, without warning, she burst into tears.

Zach rumbled in concern, reaching for her to try and make the crying stop. It pulled on something deep in his gut, unsettling him in the worst of ways. But despite her open-mouthed sobbing, she was smiling.

"You speak!" she wailed. "Oh, Zach, you speak! It's really working." She didn't resist his pull when he wrapped his arms around her, and to his astonishment, she used the new closeness to place wet kisses on his cheeks and mouth as she laughed and cried and hugged him.

He didn't always understand his female, and this whole crying-while-laughing thing was a new, disturbing development—but the bond in his chest hummed with her happiness, and that was all he needed.

"SCARED."

She looked up at him from where she crouched by the riverside, empty bottle in one hand. "Yes."

"Why?" he demanded, frowning at the unpleasant tones reverberating through their bond. Her anxiety had been increasing ever since Jerome had announced it was time to leave.

"I'm scared we'll get caught. That they'll take you away from me again," she said softly. "Or that our friends will get hurt."

"I... will protect," he ground out, irritable that his limited vocabulary made it hard to convey to his mate that she needed to stop being afraid, that there was no need so long as he was with her.

She smiled a sad little smile that didn't make him feel nearly as good as her smiles usually did. "I know."

"Then why?" he asked, his frustration deepening. The bond had been out of tune all day, and it set him on edge. She'd even cried when he rutted her—an experience he was wholly displeased with. Gasping and sobbing from taking his knot, that was perfectly fine. Good, even.

Crying, while their bond whined agonizingly in his chest? Not fine. Not good.

"I want you to see something," she said, voice gentle. Leaving the unfilled water bottle by the side of the river, she stood up and grasped his hand lightly in hers.

He allowed her to lead him into the woods in the

opposite direction of the camp. She kept walking until they came to a small clearing, where she finally stopped in front of an oblong mound of upturned soil. The afternoon sun reflected off a smooth river stone set on on end of the mound.

"We buried Beau here. He gave his life to free you. Each one of the men here have given up their lives to flee across the border to an uncertain future. They are willing to die for us—and I think, before we're finally free, more of them will. Or..." She breathed in deeply. "Or it could be one of us. And if that happens, if you die... then I can't go on. I can't go through losing you again. I won't survive it. There is... so much pain and death around us, and I don't want you to make me any promises you might not be able to keep.

"But I want you to know... I wouldn't have made a different choice, even if I'd known everything that would follow. I would still have tried to save you." She looked up at him. "I get it now. I understand this mate thing. You didn't claim me because you were lonely. You claimed me because for whatever reason, we belong together. I am proud of that. I am proud of being yours, even if you never fully recover what they took from you.

"These men... they have given everything for you because of who you are. Because of your honor, your integrity—everything you were. They'd never tell you that. They're stupid alphas who'd never show another male their emotions. But I can tell you that for them.

They love you. And I think, once upon a time, you loved them too.

"There is so much death in our world, but... we have been blessed too. I want you to remember that; we will suffer and we will hurt, and we might even die. Don't promise me the impossible—just find a way out of the darkness and share the glimmers of light with me."

Zach stared at the grave as his mate's words penetrated through the fog like a spoon parting thick molasses.

He remembered then. His brothers in arms. The many battles. The final deed that had sealed his fate.

He remembered the man he'd once been. Honorable. Strong.

Whole.

CHAPTER 28

LILLIAN

The first three nights of driving toward the border were uneventful, even if we were all on edge every time we left whatever remote bit of woodland we'd hidden in during the daylight hours. But the farther we got from SilverCorp's compound, the easier it became to breathe.

I'd almost started to believe we'd truly escaped the horrors of Dr. Axell's lab when the attack came.

WE WERE LESS than thirty miles out from the Canadian border, four nights after we'd left the camp by the river, when Jerome glanced into the rearview mirror and cursed.

"What's the matter?" I asked as Zach made a questioning noise, straightening in his seat.

"That van's been following us for the past hour," Jerome growled.

"Could just be headed for the border too," I said, twisting to look behind us.

"Doubt it," Jerome growled. "Fuck. All right—we're gonna have to take care of this before we get to the border. Barnes, you capable of shooting a gun?"

Zach grunted in affirmation, and Jerome pulled out his phone to call the rest of our group driving ahead of us.

"Larry?" he said the second the line connected. "We've got company. White van behind us—from the size of it, I'm guessing they've got a team of six to eight fighters in there. Look for a side road up ahead—something that'll give us some cover. We need the advantage, and we're running out of mileage before they pincer us in at border control."

I couldn't hear what Larry said, but Jerome made a few noises of agreement and hung up. "All right— Barnes, grab my spare gun. It's under my seat. Once we pull over, get the girl out of the car and use it as cover. We'll be drawing their attention while the guys circle back around on foot and get them from behind. You with me?"

"*Yes.*" It was a rough sound, more of a grunt than a word, but Zach's eyes reflected a grim determination as he nodded at his old friend in the rearview mirror. Despite everything he'd been through, despite everything he'd lost—*this* was who he was and would always be. A warrior.

Eric pulled the car ahead of us down a dark side road nearly two miles later. In our headlights, I could make out thick vegetation on each side of the narrow road, and my pulse quickened in anticipation of what came next.

Despite knowing what was about to happen, I still wasn't prepared when Jerome yanked on the steering wheel, throwing the Jeep around so it blocked the road, brakes screeching.

I gasped when my seatbelt bit into my throat and chest, locking me in place, but the next moment Zach slammed his hand down on the release mechanism, grabbed me by the arm, and kicked out the passenger side door. We landed on the pavement just as the van's doors flew open and a salvo of gunfire blasted through the night.

Zach draped his body over mine, smashing my face into the ground but also shielding me. His muscles worked above me, and then shots rang from right above my head as he returned fire. On the other end of the Jeep, Jerome backed him up with his own gun.

It felt like an eternity before a surprised howl penetrated the night, followed by more gunfire on the other side of the white van. The rest of our group had arrived.

The bullets stopped pelting our Jeep when our attackers turned to the ambush.

"Stay," Zach growled, and then the heavy pressure of his body lifted off me, letting the cool night air surround me instead. I pushed up onto my knees and peered around the Jeep just in time to see my mate arrive at the black-clad men. The white van's headlights illuminated his strong body as he leapt into the air like a panther and came down hard on the other side, a battle roar ringing through the night.

My heart clenched in terror at the thought of one of the many bullets finding its way into his flesh, but our bond hummed with nothing but excitement and battle lust. He was born for this.

More guns fired, but they mixed with screams of agony.

He moved like a whirlwind of destruction, tearing through the enemy with speed and strength that should've been impossible for a human man—even an alpha as powerful as he. For the first time, I saw why SilverCorp was so adamant that their sick experiment be completed. They'd wanted a super soldier, a weapon unlike any other. And in my mate, they'd created it.

He was too strong, too fast for them, pinned down by gunfire as they were. I stared open-mouthed as he ripped, tore, and shredded his way through them, human remains scattering around him like the mangled leftovers from a gruesome hurricane. It took less than ten minutes before silence spread over the deserted road, the only sounds Zach's rough, panting breath and the thunder of my own blood in my ears.

"Anyone hit?" Jerome asked.

Murmurs of denial came from around the back of the van.

"Anyone left alive?" he added.

Silence was the only response.

"Fucking hell, Barnes," Eric murmured from a few yards away. "I've seen cleaner butchering from a fucking hyena."

"Don't go near him," Jerome warned just as my mate turned to Eric with a snarl, canines bared. The battle lust still pulsed hotly in our bond.

"Shit, calm down, we're on the same team," Eric said, quickly taking a few steps back, hands raised. Zach only hunkered down in response, eyes glued to the other man's throat.

"Zach!" I scrambled to my feet and stepped around the Jeep. "Zach, it's over."

The feral alpha whipped around, nostrils flaring as he stared at me.

"Hey, it's okay. You did so, so well, big guy. You've taken out all of them—these men are our friends. Remember?" I kept my voice deliberately gentle and soft as I walked toward him, hands out.

He growled, but the sound was much less aggressive now. Some of the fire in our bond eased and he came toward me, throwing the gun to the ground with a clatter.

"I'm okay," I said when he reached for me, skimming his hands over my body to check for injuries. "You protected me well—all of you."

Another growl, more of a grunt this time, as he buried his nose in my hair and began scenting me.

I caught Jerome's gaze under Zach's armpit and flushed when he averted his eyes. Even without the hardness rising against my stomach, it was pretty obvious what Zach's battle lust was transforming into, and while the SEALs had definitely overheard us in intimate moments before, they'd always been kind enough to pretend like they hadn't. Not really an option in the middle of a deserted road, surrounded by bullet-riddled vehicles and mauled bodies.

"Zach—*Zach!*" I called, patting at his chest to get his attention, but gently enough to not trigger his urge to show me who was the dominant party in our relationship. "We can't—we have to keep moving. There could be more of them coming. We need to get away."

His growl was distinctly displeased this time, but thankfully he wasn't a complete slave to his instincts. He pulled his nose out of my hair and turned toward Jerome, still keeping me wrapped up in the protective shield of his arms. "We leave. Now."

"We can't cross the border in cars with more holes than a Swiss cheese," Jerome muttered, rubbing his scalp with a frustrated grimace. "And it's only a matter of time before someone comes across the massacre, and then law enforcement will be on the lookout for the perpetrators. *Fuck!*"

I stared at the broken bodies scattered on the ground all around us, dread settling in my gut despite our victory. Getting across the border without drawing attention wasn't our only problem. I hadn't been lying when I told Zach that more could be coming for us. More *would* be coming—he was too valuable an asset for them to ever let him go. It didn't matter how far we ran.

"They won't stop," I said. "It doesn't matter if we make it across the border or not—Zach is too important to them. So long as he's alive, we'll never be free."

I swallowed my panic and looked up into my mate's eyes. I'd do anything for this man—absolutely anything.

"There's only one thing we *can* do. Zach and I... we have to go back."

I DROVE the black Jeep all the way up to the gate shielding the compound my mate and I hated so much. My head pounded the closer we got, sweaty palms clutching at the steering wheel.

The soldier stationed there waved at me to roll down the window. I gave Zach one last glance and found the strength I needed in his gaze. He might not have understood the full scope of what I'd planned—but he trusted me.

"We're not open for visitors, ma'am," the soldier said as he looked in the window.

"I'm not a visitor," I said. "Let Dr. Axell know that Lillian Dorne has returned with test subject 351. Please."

The soldier's eyes widened as his gaze landed on Zach and he pulled out his sidearm, aiming it at my mate.

Zach growled low, the warning clear.

"Please, there's no need for that. Just call Dr. Axell," I said. "We're here to surrender."

THE SOLDIER HELD us at gunpoint while we waited for the doctor to arrive. Zach spent the entire time shielding me from the weapon with his body, a continuous growl rumbling from his throat. The soldier—a beta—did his best not to let the alpha's aggression rattle him, but I saw the relief in his eyes when two white-clad figures approached us.

Seemed Dr. Axell had brought Dr. Urwin.

"Well, well," Dr. Axell drawled when they stopped safely behind the armed soldier. "If it isn't our wayward analyst. I must say, I am very surprised to see you return voluntarily. Especially since the tactical team sent to procure you went radio silent a few days ago."

Despite his haughty tone, the sharpness in his eyes was unmistakable.

"I..." I didn't have to fake the quiver in my voice—being this close to the two men who'd ruined my life made acrid terror burn in my gut. I put a hand on Zach's broad back, a silent reminder that I would never let them hurt him again, and then dropped to my knees in the dirt, eyes downcast. "I can't go on. You *broke* him. I can't... He's too wild, I can't... I'm here... *We're* here to surrender. Please, all I ask is that you don't hurt him again. I'll cooperate, I'll try to help with him as much as I can, but please, don't hurt him again."

The two doctors stared down at me in silence for a moment.

"Bring them in," Dr. Axell finally sneered. "He followed her here—he won't give you any trouble so long as you keep the female in check."

I'D BEEN PREPARING myself for the humiliation of getting stripped upon returning to the lab, but it took everything I had to hold it together as I stood naked in front of both doctors and several lab assistants as they looked me up and down, scribbling on notepads as they went over the state of us both.

Zach caught my eye above the head of the assistant taking his waist measurement, and I managed a brief nod. Since he'd first spoken, he'd been more cognizant, almost human at times, but it was infrequent. I never knew how much he understood, how much of him was there—but right then, I saw the flash of presence in his eyes. He was there with me. Even if he was chained to the wall of the small lab they'd taken us to.

"Where's Kenneth?" I asked Dr. Urwin, trying to ignore the goosebumps crawling up my skin when he raised his gaze to mine. "Did he... make it through the riot?"

The beta doctor's lips pinched to a flat line. "He survived, but quit on the spot when we found him. PTSD, I suspect. I hope you're proud—more than sixty feral alphas lost their lives because of you, along with all our guards and more than a dozen soldiers. There is blood on your hands, *Miss Dorne.* I hope you didn't think showing up here and begging for mercy means I won't personally ensure you pay for everything you've done."

I swallowed at the menace in his voice and forced back a shudder when he let his gaze trail over my body. There was no doubt what sort of penance he had in mind.

"Ah, getting Miss Dorne up to date on everything she's missed, I hear?" Dr. Axell strolled up to us, clipboard in hand. He smiled at me with all the warmth of a glacier. "You'll be happy to know that I'll grant your request—we won't need to inflict any more unnecessary pain on Subject 351. Tomorrow, we'll run a few tests to see if any of his cognitive functions have been restored by the drugs you stole. The fact that you managed to bring him here suggests he, even without any remaining humanity, will be usable as some form of weapon.

"And as for you..." The false smile slid off his face, replaced by contempt. "You, Lillian, will make sure he follows every single order he's given. 351 paid for his mistakes after his first escape attempt. You have yet to do the same. I know you saw where we kept him. What he endured. Do not make the mistake of thinking that I won't do exactly the same to you, should your usefulness run out. Your only value is in what's between your legs and how you use it to control my test subject. Tell me you understand."

"I... I understand," I whispered.

"Good. Bring them to their old cell—give them the night to become acclimated. Tomorrow, the testing starts." He gave me one final, burning look before he turned and walked out the door.

THERE WAS an eerie familiarity in the metallic slide of the cell door closing behind us. Even the mattress looked the same—I recognized the tears I'd ripped in it the first time Zach had taken me. But something in the lab was different from our last stay. Much different.

Where there'd been maybe a hundred alphas locked

in cages, less than forty remained. And some of them were paired with females—none of whom would look our way as we passed their cells.

And the woman in the cell next to ours... I remembered her desperation when we freed Zach only two weeks ago. Now, all she did was lay on the mattress and stare blankly ahead.

"Hey—are you okay?" I called through the wall separating our cells while Zach paced the perimeter of our cage. He was checking our surroundings like an alpha would. They hadn't injected him with any more of the blasted serum, and I prayed they wouldn't get a chance to before we could enact our plan. But it was a risk we had to take.

No one answered from the other cell, and I placed a hand on the concrete wall. Guilt gnawed at my gut for how I'd deceived the woman stuck in there, but I hadn't had a choice. We hadn't been able to take them with us then.

I hoped with everything I was that she wasn't beyond saving.

———

SHOUTS and the sound of boots against concrete floors jarred me awake in the early morning hours.

I blinked sleep out of my eyes and sat up as far as

Zach's embrace would allow, looking to see what had caused the commotion.

"*Stay,*" my mate growled before he got up and went to the bars.

I turned around, kneeling up on the mattress to try to see past his massive bulk. What I spotted made my heart slam into overdrive.

"Well, well, well," Dr. Urwin said as he strolled up to our cell, ignoring Zach's bared teeth and warning growl. "It seems you weren't quite honest when you said you were ready to surrender, huh?"

"What did you do?" I whispered, eyes locked on the four naked alphas held at gunpoint by several soldiers in the middle of the lab, their hands tied behind their backs.

"Did you really think we would buy your ridiculous explanation for why you just happened to show up at our doorstep? That we wouldn't wonder where the men who helped you break 351 out were?" Dr. Urwin tutted at me, but the smugness was clear in his voice as he stared us down. "Your friends fell right into our trap when they snuck up to the compound—and you know what? We're going to keep them. We've been running short on alphas since you cost us so many."

"No!" I scrambled to my feet. Zach blocked my attempt at getting to the bars, unwilling to have me too close to the beta doctor, but I could still see the faces of the alphas they'd brought in.

"Jerome!" I cried, trying to capture the attention of the men who'd risked everything for us.

"It's no use," Dr. Urwin practically purred. "We've given them their first two doses of Hexatrepodamine. The may remember their names for a little while yet—but soon enough they'll be no more than dumb animals."

"What are you gonna do to them?" I spat. "Torture them? *Test* them?"

"Oh, we'll test them," Dr. Urwin said, and his smirk turned to a full, cold smile. "Make sure they're strong and virile. And then, Little Miss Analyst—then they are going to make you regret whatever plan you thought you had. Dr. Axell hoped we could have used you to salvage at least some of 351's functionality as a weapon for the state—and who knows, you might still... if you survive what's coming your way just as soon as we've ensured our new test subjects are nice and compliant."

ZACH FOUGHT the guards who came for us. He lunged at them, forcing his body up from the many electric jolts they sent through him to stop his assault, and did everything he could to stop them from grabbing me. It was useless—of course it was. Everything about this setup was designed to leave their test subject powerless, and in the end, they dragged both of us out of the cell like we'd both known from the beginning they would.

Zach howled in rage as they forced him through the

lab by the poles attached to the metal collars around his neck, arms, and waist. I followed with much less fuss, keeping my head down as I pattered across the cold floor on naked feet. There was no reason to fight them, not now, but I knew Zach was unable to suppress the violent instincts urging him to defend his mate. I'd begged him not to while we waited for the doctors to dole out their punishment, told him all he'd accomplish was hurting himself, but he'd just looked at me with that grim expression of his. He didn't have many words, but he hadn't needed them—because I felt the overwhelming protectiveness he had for me in our bond. The only thing I could do to protect him now was stay calm myself.

I recognized the corridor they led us down and fought down the nausea rising in my throat when we stopped by three all-too-familiar doors. They forced Zach through the middle one and took me to the third.

The concrete room that opened up made me shudder in visceral recognition, and I twisted around to look behind me. Zach was getting tied with thick chains behind bars separating his section of the room from mine. Behind him was the empty observation room walled off by thick glass.

Ahead of me, chains hung from the wall exactly like they had when they'd brought five ferals to mount me.

The rape room was probably my least favorite part of the compound.

Despite the cold terror gripping and squeezing my lungs, I still didn't struggle when the lone guard attending me strapped me in place, shackling my wrists and neck.

"You should'a stayed away, little girl," he growled in my ear, letting a hand slide over my naked backside to give it a squeeze. "You're responsible for so many of my buddies' deaths—even if you survive this, us guards've got *plans* for you, baby. Every single miserable breath you take until the day you finally die is gonna hurt."

Zach's snarl at the man's hand on my body made the guard snort and spit on the floor. "Don't worry, you sad fuck. No one's gonna want her once the good doctors are done with her."

When he left the room, I craned my neck to look over my shoulder as best I could, catching Zach's eye. "Don't fight them. Please, please remember. Don't fight."

He pulled up his lip in disgust, but gave me a short nod. The chains tying him to the wall rattled with the movement, forcing a growl of frustration from his throat, but despite the animalistic display, I knew he was still in there. I wasn't alone.

The door leading to my side of the room swung open again, revealing Dr. Axell. He wore that trademark smirk of his, and I wanted nothing more than to slap it off his face.

"I trust you're comfortable?" he asked as he sauntered over to me. The bottle of lubricant in his hand made me grit my teeth.

"You're so fucking predictable," I snarled. "How many is it gonna be this time? All thirty-something?"

He barked a laugh as he stopped behind me, uncapping the bottle. "Maybe next time. Today, we're just gonna need a warm cunt to teach our newcomers the ropes. Think your mate will get off on watching his former friends knotting what's his?"

His taunting words were followed by two oiled fingers sliding down my closed lips and, once they reached my entrance, right up inside me. I jerked, his violation making me sick to my stomach.

Behind us, Zach roared, the fury in his voice unmistakable. But he could do nothing to stop the doctor, bound as he was, and thankfully, he didn't waste any more energy fighting the chains.

Dr. Axell ignored him, finger-fucking me slow and deep, forcing slick sounds from my sheath despite my revulsion. "You'll be happy to know we've improved out methods while you've been gone. The artificial heats we induced were messing with our females' natural hormone production, so we developed an addition to the regular serum we inject the ferals with. Every alpha in here will fuck any hole they're presented with, no matter if it's offered willingly or not.

"So today, my dear analyst... today, you get to experience what it's like to take a knot while your body is screaming for mercy. There won't be an ounce of plea-sure in it for you. Just raw, delicious *pain*." His voice was low and rough, thick with perverse excitement. "I can't wait to hear you scream."

He finally pulled his fingers from my pussy, wiping the excess oil on my thigh. "There. Can't have you rip and bleed to death before our new test subjects are sated, now can we?"

I didn't offer him a reply this time. I just clutched at the chains tying my wrists as I tried to control my shallow breathing. In the distance, an alpha howled.

The unmistakable sounds of snarling, fighting alphas grew closer and closer, only interrupted by the crash of bodies and metal against concrete walls, until finally, the door to my room burst open.

They were here.

I looked up just as all four of the SEALs were shoved into the room, followed by eight guards. Their guns hung over their shoulders while they controlled the feral alphas with metal poles. The ferals immediately zeroed in on me, their fight against the other males with-ering at the sight of my naked body. Their cocks were hard already, and I swallowed thickly, sending up a silent prayer.

"I think you can release them now," Dr. Urwin chuckled as he followed into the room after the guards. "Once a feral sets his sights on a pussy, nothing's gonna distract him from it."

The guards unsnapped the poles form the metal collars around each alpha's limbs, a couple of them making crude comments about the slick state of my still-closed lips.

Dr. Axell's plan for my punishment was so simple, and yet it had all the trappings of revenge. He was going to use the very men who'd risked everything to free us to break us down. I'd long since learned that rape was his favorite weapon, and he wielded it with sick delight.

I'd been right. He was predictable.

"Now!" I yelled.

They didn't expect it.

The four SEALs reacted as one, their bodies swiveling around faster than anyone could counter. They went for the guards, for the guns hanging off their shoulders, ripping them off and putting bullets in all eight of them within a span of seconds.

Dr. Urwin shrieked and threw himself behind Dr. Axell. Jerome pointed his weapon at the beta's meat shield.

"Hands up where I can see 'em. Both of you. Jarl, help our friend out, will you? Larry, free the girl. I know she must be dying to have a little chat with our esteemed researchers here."

CHAPTER 29

LILLIAN

The look of stunned disbelief on Dr. Axell's and Dr. Urwin's faces was more satisfying than I could have imagined.

"What the hell is this?" Despite Dr. Axell's authoritative snarl, his eyes flickered between the four guns trained on him and his hands remained in the air in submission.

Not so fun to be forced to submit, is it, doctor? I gave him a small smile. "This is you losing control of your torture compound. You see, I found your antidote. And it seems it works a lot better than you anticipated—especially as a vaccine. Each of these men were injected before you 'caught' them. I must admit, we weren't entirely sure it would be enough to withstand your drug, but... it seems we were in luck."

"You'll never get away with this, you little bitch,"

Dr. Urwin spat. "No matter where you hide, we'll keep coming after you. Even if you kill us today, SilverCorp will never stop coming for you."

"Oh, but that's the thing... they will." I motioned to Jarl, and the big alpha ripped the lab coat off Dr. Urwin, handing me the garment—and the attached access card. I wrapped the white coat around my naked body. They'd used lack of clothing as one of their measures of control—had separated their test subjects from humanity by denying them the ability to shield their bodies in any way. Even though it was only a lab coat, it still felt good to reclaim a small measure of my dignity in front of my torturers.

"We're going to erase every file ever created for me and Zach, every test, every measurement. There will not be a single reminder left of our existence—and no one to tell SilverCorp who to chase down.

"And sure, SilverCorp might start the abhorrent experiment again, but they will have to start from scratch. And at that point, we will be far, far away. And no one will know we ever were here."

Dr. Axell growled contemptuously, but Dr. Urwin drew in a sharp breath, his anger replaced by fear. "Please. Don't kill me. I—I can be useful. I can help you delete everything. Just please—don't shoot me."

Dr. Axell regarded him with disgust, but remained quiet.

I tilted my head and looked at the beta who'd

derived so much pleasure from my suffering. I remembered every insult, every lecherous touch as he'd tied me down and watched me and Zach get tortured. And I didn't feel a single ounce of sympathy as he shook with the knowledge that he was going to die. Only cold, grim revenge.

"Oh, we won't shoot you," I said, crossing the rough concrete to the door without sparing the two doctors another look. "Your death will be much, much more unpleasant than that. Jerome, please sweep the building. Kill every staff member on sight. Zach and I will meet you with these two in the lab upstairs."

"WHATEVER YOU'RE GOING to do to us, it won't change the fact that you're stuck with a beast for a mate." Dr. Axell's sneer was a stark contrast to Dr. Urwin's quiet sniffling as Zach tied his wrists to the bars of one of the empty cells. Despite having a gun aimed at his chest, he seemed incapable of dropping the haughty alpha attitude. "Every time he mounts you, every time he shoves his knot into your twat, you'll think of me and everything I took from you."

"You still don't get it, do you?" I said. "You didn't *make* him claim me. You didn't *create* our bond in your lab. You took *nothing* from me, Axell. Our connection was there before your sick experiments. That's why I tried to free him. I felt it, even if I didn't know what it was. How empty your life must have been, if you as an alpha never understood that.

"Those poor souls you've forced into bonds—what they have is nothing but an ugly shadow of the real thing. So no, *doctor*. When we leave this compound, I will not think of you ever again. I will be with my mate, and I will be at peace. You may have damaged his mind, but you have not touched his soul. You cannot—because it always belonged to *me*."

There was a glint Dr. Axell's eyes that Zach must not have liked, because he was on the doctor immediately, smacking him up against the cell so hard his head bounced off the bars.

"*No.*" It was all Zach said, but the menacing tone made his intent crystal-clear: No, the doctor did not get to threaten me ever again.

He bound Axell's hands like he had Urwin's, then roughly pulled both their pants down, letting the fabric pool around their ankles and trap their legs.

"What the *hell* are you doing?" Dr. Axell asked, his voice finally betraying a sliver of unease.

"Well, doctor... do you remember how you both *enjoyed* watching all those women get raped? I do. And I remember every voltage you tortured us with, and the glee in your eyes when you told me exactly what you'd do to find Zach's limits. Do you? Because I think there's a poetic justice in how you're going to die—

fucked to death by the same men you've tortured for so long."

The whimper of fear from Urwin and Axell's defiant snarl gave me nothing but icy satisfaction. Once upon a time, I would have taken pity on them. I wouldn't have been able to order their deaths, let alone orchestrate such a gruesome method. But that part of me, the Lillian who could have shown mercy to my torturers... she'd died in their hands.

The door to the lab swung open and Jerome entered, followed by the other ex-SEALs.

"All clear," he said. "We all set in here?"

"Yes." I turned away from the tied-up doctors and walked to Zach's old cell. It was still empty. My mate followed me in and closed the door behind us. "Let them out."

"Please!" Dr. Urwin shrieked. "Please, at least give us the oil!"

I arched an eyebrow at the wild-eyed doctor. He'd twisted his neck in my direction, much quicker to accept who was in charge now than his boss.

"The oil?"

"I did for you—for all the females," he babbled. "" Please, just that one mercy, I beg you!"

"You did," I said, the memory of the lecherous words he'd said as he prepared me for my first mating with Zach echoing in my head. "Fine. Jarl, the lubricant's in the cupboard with the other basic supplies."

Jarl grunted a confirmation and crossed the lab to retrieve the bottle.

"T-Thank you," Dr. Urwin whispered.

"And you, Dr. Axell?" I asked, arching my eyebrows at the tied-up alpha.

He glared daggers at me, but finally nodded.

"So be it." I didn't care if they bled to death or not—all I cared about was that they died after experiencing the same helplessness and humiliation they had subjected so many women to. So if they wanted to lessen the pain, but increase the time it took? That was fine by me.

The SEALs applied the lubricant, any reluctance they might have had in executing such a cruel punishment dead in the wake of what the two doctors had tried to have them do to me. And then they went around to every cage still containing a lone, feral alpha, opening the doors to their cells with Dr. Axell's access card.

Out of the many who'd tried to escape the last time Zach let them all out, just over thirty remained. The rest were gone—gunned down like animals.

I glanced down at Zach's scarred hand, grabbing onto it when images of his twisted face as a soldier shot him in the stomach flashed before my mind's eye. These two men's promise to force him to watch me get gang-raped was the reason he'd made that desperate attempt at securing our freedom.

I looked back up at the two doctors as snarls erupted

in the lab. The ferals were encroaching on them, cautious of traps, and Dr. Axell couldn't hold his nature back any longer. Tied with his back to them, he twisted in his bonds, growling a savage warning at the nearing alphas.

The tension in the room snapped as if someone cut a cord. The ferals attacked as if with one mind, launching themselves at the Dr. Axell, ripping at his clothes, his hair, punching, snarling, tearing.

I had a moment's disappointment thinking they would be beaten to death, that their end would be with more dignity than they deserved, but then one of the ferals noticed Dr. Urwin whimpering, trying to curl as far away from the violence as he could. His submissive position must have finally registered in the feral's brain, because the next second, he pulled the beta up by his hips. Ass out.

Dr. Urwin managed to choke out a plea for mercy before the alpha pressed his cock in between the beta's cheeks. I couldn't see the moment of penetration from my cell, but I heard it. As did every other soul in that accursed lab.

Dr. Urwin's scream rang through the room and echoed off the walls, and in it was the agony of every woman who'd been forced to bend over his breeding bench. Eyes wild with desperation, he tried to climb the bars he was tied to, but the alpha behind him gave him no quarter. He pulled Dr. Urwin down with a rough jerk, the smack of flesh hitting flesh ringing through the air, announcing the moment he was taken to the hilt.

The alphas tearing at Dr. Axell stilled, every pair of eyes on the beta doctor and the alpha making him his bitch.

A vicious snarl tore from one of the ferals by Dr. Axell. He grabbed the alpha doctor by the hips, jerking him into position. Dr. Axell howled and tried to kick out, but his legs were trapped in the fabric around his ankles. He fought as best he could, but it was no use. The feral gripping him by the waist pushed forward, forcing his hips flush with the doctor's, and his furious growls turned into high-pitched whimpers.

Zach looked down at me, and in his gaze I saw the same cruel satisfaction flooding my own veins. How fitting that the doctor who had gotten off on forcing every test subject he came across into submission was finally made to surrender himself.

We hadn't discussed this, hadn't planned for it to happen—but deep down, we'd both known how we were going to make our tormentors pay for what they did.

"Come," Zach said, nodding at the frenzy in the lab. Every single feral was focused on the two doctors, waiting their turns to finally extract their own revenge. "Free now."

I squeezed his scarred hand and smacked Dr. Urwin's access card over the lock. "Let's end this."

IT TOOK a long time to search through every electronic nook and cranny for any and all mentions of mine and Zach's stay in the compound—everything from my employment file with HR and the contract in which they forced me to sign over my life, to Zach's daily physicals and the many reports of our successful mating and the others it had led to.

For the first time since our friends had overpowered the guards, I hesitated, the file of my neighboring female and her alpha hovering over the shredder. Images of Lea, the woman, covered several of the pages, including close-ups of the bruises her alpha had given her alongside descriptions of her depressed state.

"What are we gonna do with the mated couples?" I asked.

Zach didn't respond immediately. The grim expression on his handsome features made me shake my head. "We can't. It's not like the staff here—we can't kill them. They've... They've been through enough."

"They... not like...us," he said, taking care to form each word. "They claimed... because desperate."

"So we can break the bond?"

"No." He shook his heads. "Only death."

"Can we bring the women, at least? If their bond isn't like ours, maybe they'll be able to—" My voice died when he shook his head again. "Zach, there has to be another way."

"Ask... her." He nodded at the file I was holding.

I frowned, remembering Lea's pleas to free her when I came for Zach. I'd been numb to her distress then, but now... she was a broken husk of a woman. And I'd left her to that fate.

The thought of killing her made an uncomfortable ache rise despite the icy satisfaction of extracting revenge over the doctors.

I didn't deserve what they did to me.

But she hadn't, either.

THE SOUNDS of sex were still unmistakable when we entered the lab, but there were no more grunts and cries from either doctor. When I glanced over to the cell where they were tied, I could only see their bound wrists through the throng of feral alphas waiting for another go at their tormentors.

"The beta passed out about an hour and a half ago," Jerome said as he crossed the lab to meet up with us, gun still in hand. He nodded toward Jarl, who was stood off to the side of the violent orgy, keeping an eye on things. "Alpha doc clocked out about thirty, forty minutes ago."

"We'll check for a pulse before we leave," I said, drawing in a deep breath. "But first, we need to decide what to do with the mated couples."

Jerome arched an eyebrow. "I assumed we'd give them a swift death. Can't leave them here for Silver-Corp officials to find, can't bring them—and to be honest... it's gonna be a mercy."

"A mercy?" I snapped. "Killing innocent women who got mated against their will is a mercy?"

"Trust me." He placed a hand on my shoulder, ignoring Zach's narrowed eyes at the contact, and nodded to a cell nearby. "Even if we pretend we could free them, that's what they have to look forward to."

I followed his gaze and swallowed thickly at the sight. The snarling ferals gathered around the doctors had blocked out the sounds from the cell housing an alpha and his claimed female. She was on her hands and knees on the concrete floor, tears streaming down her dirty face. And behind her, her mate was pounding away at her pussy. Judging from the tight grimaces she pulled, she wasn't experiencing much of the pleasure I did when I was underneath Zach like that.

"Third time he's on her since you left," Jerome grunted. "The excitement's getting them all riled—all the mated alphas are like this."

"We could treat them with di-hydroperalimitus, like we did Zach," I whispered, unable to look away from the woman. Her face broke into a pained wail, bleeding fingers scraping against the floor as she tried to escape. It was in vain—her alpha grabbed her by the hair and pulled her back, forcing his knot into her.

"We could," Jerome said. "And if that's truly what you want to do, if you think it's worth the risk to you and Zach, we'll try to bring them with us. But I need you to understand that not every bond is like yours and Zach's. Not every claim ends happily. You've seen their files—if you think these fuckers can be redeemed, if you think they'll stop raping their mates if they regain some humanity... we'll bring them."

I opened my mouth to say something, anything, but I couldn't. As much as I wanted to believe that there was a chance for these couples, that if Zach had been wrongfully convicted so could the others... I knew that wasn't the case.

Even in the depths of his feral state, Zach had never mistreated me like these alphas did their mates. Sure, he'd been rough and forceful... but not like this.

"Ask," Zach said, voice gruff but also gentle.

I swallowed thickly and made my way to the cage where the mated pair were tied together.

The male looked up with a growl at my approach, but his features softened when he saw I wasn't another alpha.

"Hey," I whispered at the woman.

She'd collapsed on the floor, her mate stuck inside of her but not caring for her like Zach always did for me, after. She rolled her eyes up to meet mine, slowly as if she even opening her eyelids cost more energy than she had.

"Do you know who I am?"

"Lillian... Dorne," she rasped. "The one who got away. Yeah. We all know."

"We're breaking out. Again. For good this time. And I'm going to give you a choice: You can come with us, alone or with... with him. Or... we can... end your suffering." I bit my lip, forcing strength into my voice. "But what we can't do is leave you here. We can't leave any trace of their experiment succeeding."

"Can you... break the bond?" she asked.

I shook my head, and she squeezed her eyes shut and drew in a deep breath. "Then... then my life is over anyway."

"There is a drug... We can reverse some of what they did to him," I said, wrapping my hand around the bars, wishing I didn't already know her answer—but it was written all over her face.

"He's vile," she whispered. "It's not the drugs—I can feel him, *inside* of me, all the time. Before, he was... he killed *babies* while their mothers watched. And then he raped them. And I can *feel* it inside of me, the *sickness* in him. In me. Please, if you can't break the bond... please, just kill me."

She reached out a hand and placed it around mine still wrapped around the bars. "Please."

I breathed in deeply and nodded. "Okay."

Jerome came over to my side, gun in hand. "I'm sorry," he murmured.

The feral in the cage didn't take his appearance as easily as he did mine—he growled again, rising up off his mate. Their tie tugged harshly on her, and she winced.

"Just tell me one thing first," she said, not taking her eyes off me. "Tell me you'll let the doctors suffer until their last breath."

"They will," I said, placing my free hand over hers. "They did."

She nodded once and closed her eyes.

Jerome fired a single shot, and the woman's hand went slack between mine as a spray of red bloomed from the exit wound in her temple.

Her alpha let out a furious howl laced with pain so intense I almost felt bad for the baby-killer—but another shot ended his misery before he could move from his dead mate. He slumped down on top of her, his big body shielding hers from view.

I GAVE every woman there the same choice, and every single one chose the same. Some with bitter tears, some with relief—but every one chose death. When we got to Lea and her mate, I clung to Zach to keep from crumpling to the floor. It had been easy to order the death of the staff in the compound, but this—this wasn't easy. Because there was no justice.

"Lea," I called as I crouched by our neighboring cell.

Only her alpha moved within, emitting a low rumble that wasn't quite a threat.

She was lying on the floor, eyes open but unresponsive.

"Lea, I need to talk to you. It's important." I remembered her desperation for freedom when I'd liberated Zach, and I pushed down the wave of guilt at seeing the empty husk she was now. Could I have saved her then?

Her alpha approached, but he didn't growl at me. Instead he wrapped both hands around the bars and stared, and on his face I saw the naked plea as clearly as if he'd been able to speak.

He was scared for his mate.

I remembered him from when Zach had helped me escape—he'd clutched her to his side, protecting her. Terrified she'd get hurt. What had these two been through in the scientists' hands?

I knew the answer too well.

And this man—I didn't know what he'd been before. I didn't know if he was a serial killer, a rapist, an arsonist... or falsely accused. But he hadn't mounted his mate in the excitement like the others.

He'd been too worried for her.

But when she'd been able to, she'd tried to escape him. She hadn't found pleasure in their bond.

Only pain.

I spared Lea a long look before I put my hands gently over the alpha's.

"Him first," I whispered.

The alpha slumped to the floor, trailing a smear of blood. Lea didn't so much as blink. Jerome's bullet bit into her skull the next second, finally ending her suffering.

Zach wrapped his arms around me as I got to my feet, lifting me up into his embrace without a word. We didn't need any—I knew he felt my sorrow in our bond as keenly as I felt the warmth of his concern.

"We need to get rid of the bodies before we leave. There can't be a trace of the claimed women left," I said.

Jerome nodded, waving Eric over. "We saw an incinerator on our sweep. You find clothes for us—we'll clean up here." He glanced at Jarl, who nodded in return. "And then we're done."

"And the doctors? They're dead?" I asked.

"They're dead," he confirmed. "And we'll want to have steel doors between you and the ferals before they get tired of mauling their bodies. It's time to leave this place."

I'D BEEN KEPT up by the cold rage, and the rush of vengeance, but as we made our way toward the exit of the compound dressed as staff members, I had nothing but sorrow and anxiety left. The horrors I'd experienced in SilverCorp's lab would haunt me for as long as I lived, but I knew I'd get through it—because Zach was with me.

I glanced up at my mate, who silently supported me as we made our way through the long, white corridors. I hadn't fully understood how lucky I was that he had been the one to brand his claim into my neck until tonight. How unique our bond was. I'd accepted that we belonged together, that I was no longer whole without him. But I'd thought... Some part of me had still assumed that what I felt for him, that warmth of completion in my gut when we were together, that it came from the biology of his claim. That all women felt this with their mates, even if it might take them a while to accept their lot.

If today had proven anything, it was that I'd been wrong.

The kind of bond I had with Zach—it was the real thing. There was no forcing it—and despite everything we'd gone through,... I hadn't sacrificed my life when he marked me.

I'd come alive.

Zach looked down at me, his attention drawn by the flicker in our bond. And in his eyes, I saw the truth of our connection.

He *loved* me.

The drugs had taken away so much of his humanity —but they'd also taken his ability to deny his emotions like I had for so long now.

"I love you, too," I whispered.

His expression softened, if only for a moment, as he squeezed my hand tighter. Then we arrived at reception, and his focus shifted.

"Okay, I've got the keys to a couple of staff members' vehicles," Jerome said, turning to look at us all. "It's close to regular leaving hours, so the hope is that the soldiers won't look too closely as they let us out the gates. Eric, Jarl, and Larry, you guys take the first car. Zach, Lillian, and I will take the second. We'll make sure to stick close. Don't let them close the gate between us—if we get separated, we won't be able to regroup.

"We'll swap cars at the meeting point. It should be dark once we get there, so we'll head directly for the border and stay on the road until dawn. Everyone on board?"

There was an affirmative murmur from our small group, and then Jarl stepped forward, leading the way outside.

We walked toward the staff parking lot, locating the two vehicles by pressing the unlock function on the key fobs. I got into the passenger seat next to Jerome to make the arrangement look more normal than if he'd been chauffeuring us both in the back, and we rolled toward the gate after the blue Ford Jarl was driving.

"Showtime," Jerome murmured as Jarl pulled to a stop by the gate. A soldier leaned out the small booth and Jarl rolled his window down.

"You're the first out—is anything going on down there?" the soldier asked. "We usually see a small trickle earlier than this."

"*Fuck,*" Jerome mumbled. My heart jumped into my throat, adrenaline coursing through my veins and overriding my exhaustion.

"Bit of an incident with the alpha lab," Jarl answered. "It's under control now, but it was all hands on deck for a while."

"We didn't hear anything," the soldier said, and I didn't miss how he peered into the car. "Usually do, when the ferals get unruly, after the shit-storm a couple of months ago. Any idea why the docs forgot the new policy?"

Jarl's answer was too low to make out, but it seemed to have appeased the soldier, because he straightened back up and spoke into his radio for a moment before the gate opened with a clank.

"Oh, thank God," I murmured, relaxing in the passenger seat as the wave of adrenaline eased ever so slightly.

Jerome pulled forward as the blue Ford drove out the gate, stopping next to the soldier.

"You guys have any more info on what went down in there?" the soldier said after Jerome rolled the window down.

"Oh, just the usual," Jerome replicd with a shrug. "Couple of ferals getting into a fight—one of the techs forgot to keep two of the more combative ones away from each other. They smashed up some lab equipment. Nothing worth calling you guys over, but a mighty big mess to clean up."

The soldier frowned. "Really? That guy just said it was about a female."

"Oh, yeah—might've been that too. We're just the guys who scrub the floors," Jerome said.

"And you're the first to leave?"

Shit.

"Didn't know there was a girl on the cleanup crew," the soldier continued, peering into the car at me. "What's your name, sweetheart?"

"Vivienne Dixen," I said, flashing him what I hoped was an easy smile. It was the name on the staff member's badge I'd taken. "I'm in IT, though. I'm just catching a lift home."

But the second my eyes connected with the soldier's, his face froze. "The fuck you are!" he hissed. "You're *her!* That fucking cunt responsible for the last breakout! Get out r—"

He didn't get to finish his sentence. Jerome pulled his gun up and shot him point-blank between the eyes. The sound rang through the car and echoed across the compound.

"Fuck!" I screeched. In the distance, more soldiers were running toward the gate. "Drive, before they close the gate!"

"It's no use," Jerome hissed. "They'll be on us before we get anywhere. We need a distraction." He twisted around in his seat, locking his eyes with Zach. "There is no time to say everything I hoped I'd be able to tell you once your mind returns, Barnes, so I'm going to just say this: What you did for me, for all of us—you saved our fucking souls. You've earned your freedom, brother. And your mate's. Stay with the others—let them help you protect her. And name your first kid Jerry, a'ight?"

And with that, he kicked the driver's side door open and leapt out of the car, aiming his gun at the closest soldier sprinting toward the gate.

"Jerome!" I called after him, but he didn't pay me any mind. He shot the soldier and dove for cover from the rain of bullets that followed. Then he ran back toward the building we'd escaped from, drawing the rest of the soldiers with him.

He'd sacrificed himself so we could escape.

I threw myself into the driver's seat and slammed the car into gear, barreling out of the gate before anyone could think to check if Jerome was alone or not.

In the rearview mirror, I saw the alpha who'd taken me in when I had nothing left to live for fall to the ground, clutching his side. He twitched in the dirt until another round of bullets bit into his body.

Then the road curved, and my view of the compound was obstructed by the trees surrounding it.

EPILOGUE
ZACH

Six Months Later

"Fuck's sake, why is it so fucking impossible to wipe your feet before you enter the house?"

The sound of Lillian's sharp voice made Zach look up from the engine he was messing with, the usual pang of love vibrating through his end of their bond at the sight of her pretty face.

The two alphas she was scolding on the porch to their shared home murmured an apology, and she—apparently dissatisfied with their easy capitulation—spun around with a huff and stormed in through the door.

"Well, I'll be damned," Larry hummed by his side as

they both looked at Eric and Jarl creep off the porch, suitably chastised. "Guess your missus is a nester."

Zach arched an eyebrow at him in question.

"Oh, come on, man. Since when has Lillian given two shits about anyone tracking dirt in? And that pile of blankets she's been dragging around the house all day? She *screeched* at me when I tried to move it off the sofa this morning. Told me I'd make them stink." Larry shook his head, re-focusing on the engine. "Don't worry, I'll get the guys out of your hair for a few days. We'll go on a hunting trip or something. Need some more meat for the stores before winter hits, anyway."

Zach frowned, getting the distinct impression he was missing something important. He stared back at the door Lillian had disappeared through. He remembered the blankets. She'd made him sleep on them, despite his complaints that he was warm enough. In the morning after they'd gotten up, she'd carefully folded them and hissed at him when he tried to help her.

She'd been very short with him all day, but he'd been too preoccupied with needing to fix the damn engine and chop enough wood to get them through the harsh Canadian winter to pause and check if something might be wrong.

A low buzzing at the base of his spine made him push off the open hood with an irritated grunt. He'd promised her he'd protect her, and while yes, that also meant providing her with shelter and heat, he'd been neglectful in not asking if she was okay.

Words still came hard. Complex thoughts and ideas came hard. Making sure his mate was happy and and well-cared for? That was not only within his capabilities —it was his primary concern in life.

She'd accepted him as her mate, nursed him back to health, and never shown him anything but love and respect despite his irreparable damage. She didn't think less of him because he couldn't tell her how seeing her skin glow in the morning light spilling in through their bedroom window made his insides feel weightless with happiness, didn't lose her patience when he didn't understand her if she used words with too many sylla-bles. He owed her everything—his life, his strength, his protection—and most of all, his attention if she was unwell.

"Enjoy, you lucky bastard," Larry called after him, getting a chuckle from Jarl. Zach didn't stop to ask them what they found funny, and he didn't care, so long as Lillian was all right. They were his friends, his brothers —the men who'd sacrificed everything to save him from hell, and his bond to them was unwavering. But nothing and no one mattered like she did.

He took the stairs to the porch in one stride, pushing open the door to the log cabin with too much force, making it bang against the wall loud enough for the glass to rattle.

"Lillian!"

She appeared from the living room, but instead of the usual joy radiating from her beautiful face at the sight of him, her lip was curled in a snarl. "What the hell do you think you're doing, barging into my house like that? Get your shoes off before you muddy the floor! I spent all day cleaning!"

"*Ours,*" he said, instincts rearing at her choice of words. She was *his,* she *belonged* to him, and he would never allow her to have a home that wasn't also his. He pushed down the rush of anger, kicked off his shoes, and crossed the floor. The second he was within reach, he grabbed her chin and tilted her head up, studying her face for signs of sickness.

Her skin was flushed and warm to the touch, her pupils dilated, and the buzz at the base of his spine was just starting to tip into full-blown panic when she wrested her chin out of his grasp—and *bit* him!

Zach yanked his hand back with a growl, an unexpected pain blooming in his index finger.

"Stop manhandling me!" she snapped, her outraged expression twisting to discomfort as she put a hand to her lower belly. "God, I feel shit enough without you rolling up and getting all handsy on me."

It was then as he stared at her rubbing her abdomen, face scrunched up in a cute scowl, that he finally realized what was happening with his mate.

The smell of soap had been too overwhelming to

pick up those first delicate traces in the air. She'd cleaned, all right, despite Eric washing the floors just two days prior, and when he glanced into the living room he could see she'd washed all textiles she could get her hands on as well, including the curtains, and placed them all around the living room in neat stacks and piles.

Ridding what she planned to be her nest of all scents of the alphas they shared their home with.

His lips quirked up in a pleased smile, the throb in his finger numbed by the rush of hormones flooding his blood.

"What are you grinning at?" she asked, once more aiming her fury at him. "Is it f—*oh!*"

Her voice died on a whimper when he closed the rest of the distance between them, forcing his body flush with hers as he bent his head to sniff her neck.

Yes. There it was—her scent flowered against him, filling his nostrils as he drew in greedy lungfuls of her beginning heat. Pure and full, it rolled through his veins and filled his mind. She'd been in heat the first time he mounted her, but it hadn't been right. Her smell, powerful as it'd been, had been laced with chemicals. The doctors had injected her like they had injected him, forcing her into heat.

This time, there was nothing but her natural, all-consuming, intoxicating scent.

He growled against her neck, licking at her skin to

taste her. His cock throbbed hard and urgently in his pants, more than ready to sate her—

His thoughts cut off when another pinching pain bloomed from his chest where she'd bitten him—*again*.

"I said, stop manhandling me!" she growled, pushing at him to try and put space between them, but this time, Zach wasn't caught by surprise.

There were many things he would never be able to give his mate, many things she did or said he would never understand without her help. This—this was not one of them.

Lillian screeched when he hauled her over his shoulder, her small fists pummeling his back as he carried her into the living room in a few strides, inspecting her piles of fabric. Without putting her down, he grabbed several of the soft piles, including the blankets she'd demanded he sleep in last night, bundled them under one arm, and headed for the stairs.

"What are you doing?!" she howled, trying to rip the cloth from his grip. "Stop touching them, you're gonna mess them up! Give them to me!"

Zach ignored her until they got to the bedroom. There, he placed her back on her feet and threw the bundle of cloth on the bed. *"Stay,"* he said before he left the room again to get the rest of her fabrics.

When he came back, so loaded with cloth he had to twist to see around it, she'd started arranging the previous load in an oval shape on the bed.

She was so absorbed in her task she didn't even look up when he returned, nor did she acknowledge him when he deposited the rest of her fabrics in the yet unused pile.

She muttered to herself as she worked, her jerking movements displaying her irritation when something didn't come out just right. More and more frequently, she'd pause to wipe sweat off her forehead, the rich scent of her heat only enriching with each passing minute.

Zach watched her quietly, knowing she needed this time. He hadn't been through this stage before. The many females he'd rutted through their heats in the laboratory were only in his presence when they were past ready for penetration, but his instincts guided him now.

Finally, some long minutes later, Lillian stepped back from the bed, staring at the misshapen oval she'd created out of an uneven mix of blankets, pillows, cushions, and curtains.

A faint memory made him bite down on a smile. An old, mated sergeant had taken it upon himself to explain to the younger alphas in their team what mated life was like. They'd all been young and stupid and pretended like they knew everything there was to know about females, but his words had stirred up urges that had little to do with knotting a freshly fucked pussy.

Zach remembered when the sergeant had explained about a woman's first heat and how it would usually take her a few times before she would know what to do. How it was her alpha's job to see her through, reining in his own instincts to mount her before she'd been allowed to prepare.

Looking at the floral curtain fabric sticking out of the wall she'd created, it was plenty obvious that his mate wasn't great at this. Yet. She would go into heat plenty more times, and every time, he'd be there to see her through.

"What the hell am I doing?" Lillian's confused whisper made him close the distance he'd been keeping, soothing her with a hand on the small of her back. She didn't try to squirm away this time.

"Nest," he rumbled.

"What?" She finally turned to look at him, brows knitted in confusion.

"Heat," he explained, running his free hand over her damp forehead, wiping the sweat away.

Understanding broke behind her blue eyes, but instead of relief, terror stirred in their bond and flashed across her face. "Oh, no! No, it can't be! W-What are we gonna do? I... *Fuck!*"

Gently, he pulled her in against his chest, placing her cheek where his bond hooked. The purr flowed easily from his chest, rumbling into her in powerful waves until she slowly began to relax. He knew why she was scared, knew into his bones why the word *heat* brought nothing but terror for her.

All she'd experienced was the twisted version the doctors had put her through, and all the pain, humiliation, and fear that came with it.

"Lillian," he murmured. "Look... at me."

She lifted her head, and despite her dazed look from his consistent purr, tears dripped down her cheeks. He wiped them away with the pad of his thumb.

"I.... will.... protect. *Always,*" he said, ensuring she understood his absolute conviction in every word. "Don't cry. Don't... fear. Just *me* here. Just us."

"Just us," she whispered, swallowing thickly. There was still hesitation in her gaze, but the panic in their bond was easing.

He held her against him, petting her hair and her back as he did his best to ignore the painful throbbing in his cock at her increasingly mouthwatering scent, until finally she began to fidget. Her body was hot and slick with sweat, and soon her annoyance flared in their bond again.

"God, I'm so fucking hot!" she hissed, squirming out of his grasp. "I know they call it '*heat,*' but this is ridiculous."

Zach reached for her top, wanting to ease her suffering, but she smacked his hand away. Shooting him a dirty glare, she turned back around to stare at the misshapen nest. "And this is all wrong!"

"Again," he said, even though he was more than happy to mount her on top of the mismatched pile of curtains and sofa cushions. But she needed this—he knew that with every throb of the bond in his chest.

Lillian huffed, a frustrated little sound, and attacked the bed again. Every scrap of fabric landed on the floor and she began anew, starting with the blankets that smelled like him.

IT TOOK three more tries before his mate was content with the nest of blankets she'd built for them, and by that point, Zach's resolve to allow her the time she needed was crumbling. His skin was too hot and too *tight,* his cock ached for relief with a deep, throbbing pain that went all the way into the marrow of his spine, and every breath perfumed with her scent was torture worse than any he'd experienced at the hands of the doctors.

He paced back and forth behind her, rolling his shoulders and flexing his hands to ease just some of the tension pulling at him like a howling hurricane. He'd long-since abandoned his clothes, and his swollen cock bobbed with every step he took, precum leaking from the bloated tip in a steady stream.

His head throbbed in sympathy with his aching dick, a red haze of need clouding his vision, vivid fantasies of rough-fucking the damned female who was making him wait flickering before his mind's eye. But still he held on, clinging to the singular strand of sanity that remained in his hazy mind.

She needed him to wait.

"Alpha."

The soft sound of her voice, like a hot breath brushing against his eardrum, made him snap his head toward her.

His mate stood by the side of the bed, clothes soaked through with sweat and eyes wide and unfocused as she took in all his naked glory. Her gaze darted down his strong body, her pink tongue peeking out to wet her lips when she reached his crotch.

And the last vestige of his self-control snapped.

She shrieked when he threw himself at her, clawed at him as he shredded her clothes, but the bite of her nails only fueled his need.

He tossed her on her back in the nest she'd built, growling low in his throat, reminding her of his dominance.

"I need..." she croaked, crawling to the edge of the bed, reaching for him. "I need you!"

He pushed her back down again, following this time. She swiped at him, clawing bloody streaks into his chest until he forced her onto her stomach.

Snarling, fighting him for dominance, she tried to resist, but he pinned her neck to the mattress as he climbed between her thighs. She needed him to prove his strength, prove that he would be a worthy father of their offspring—and he was going to do just that.

His mate kicked, but he pushed her legs wide with his knees, forcing her to show her flushed and pouty pussy to him.

The scent of her slick hit him fully in the face, and he groaned, his cock weeping. He wanted to bury his mouth there, lick every drop of her desperation from that beautiful little snatch, but he didn't have enough strength left.

Lillian snarled like a wild animal when he forced her up on her knees, trying to twist around to bite and claw at him, but he kept her in place, head down and ass up. Ready to take her alpha.

Wet heat met met his cock as he pressed it up against her opening, shooting electric jolts up his spine. Lillian froze beneath him, her angry snarl dying to a series of needy whimpers. On instinct, she widened her knees and pushed her ass up, submitting her swollen sex to him.

Zach pushed through her tight opening with a hoarse cry, the pleasure of her slick walls so intense it bordered on pain. That first push inside of her was always overwhelming, all his focus centering in their carnal connection the moment she surrounded him, but *this*—this was something more.

She didn't cry out in pain when he penetrated her anymore; their many matings in the months they'd been

together teaching her body how to open for him prop-
erly. But now, in the throes of her heat, her every nerve
ending was overcharged with sensation, and they both
howled when he bottomed out deep in her cunt.

Her inner muscles clamped down on him and she
jerked against his hold on her neck. Zach kept her down,
gritting his teeth through the initial full-body shudders
of bliss.

And then, *finally,* he fucked her.

His mate screamed as he pounded his cock into her
trembling cunt, the squelches and fast slaps of skin
against skin constantly vying for dominance over her
high-pitched yelps and squeals. Everything was wet,
tight heat and pleasure so intense he couldn't stand it,
but nothing in this world was powerful enough to make
him stop fucking her. It was agony and it was ecstasy,
and when her pussy erupted in a series of hard, fluttering contractions around his cock, Zach thought he
was going to black out from the pressure.

His vision tunneled and he roared and kept
pounding her cunt until his cock swelled hard and fast,
stretching her opening wide.

White-hot relief blazed through his pain as he
pushed his knot through her pelvis, locking it in place.
The first spurt of his seed shot deep inside of her, the tip
of his cock nestled right up against her cervix.

He collapsed on top of her, groaning incoherently as
he bathed her womb in semen, ecstasy shuddering

through him in rhythmic cramps. Underneath him, his mate whimpered and panted, rocking with him while she rode her orgasm out on his dick.

They lay like that for a few long, blissful moments before Lillian grew restless again.

Zach was used to her accepting multiple matings, but rarely did she ask for more after her first knotting. This time, however, she began twisting underneath him within minutes, hips jumping impatiently. When her pelvic bone caught on his still-swollen knot, she growled at him, her temper rising as her heat reignited.

He ground her G-spot with his knot, riding it hard despite her yelps of pain when his thick knot pulled too far. When his knot finally deflated enough for him to thrust, he fucked her again, longer this time, giving her exactly what her body craved.

Again and again he rutted his howling mate. The only respite she got was when he brought her water so she wouldn't dehydrate. Even then she fought him, wanting his cock and dominance more than she wanted to slake her thirst.

But his job wasn't to give her what she wanted. It was to ensure she got exactly what she needed.

Through the four days it took before her heat broke, she drank as much water as he demanded, even slept a few hours on the second day when he coaxed her to rest with his cock still buried deep inside her. And every single time he knotted her, she was on all fours, ass up and face down—submitting to her alpha exactly like she was meant to.

HE FELT it in every cell of her being when his mate, sometime after noon on day four, slid down flat on the mattress underneath him with an exhausted groan. Her heat was finally sated—and so was her temper. There was no more fight left in her body, no more fire burning in their bond.

Complete and utter calm hummed through him from her scent, from their bond, from the feeling of her soft curves underneath him, and from the relaxed grip of her pussy around his aching cock.

His every muscle hurt from the prolonged mating, but it was a pleasurable ache. Pride at having cared for his mate so thoroughly swelled in his chest, and he nuzzled at her nape where his claim was branded into her skin for eternity.

She made a soft little noise in response, and he gave her nape a few licks before turning them both over to their sides.

"I love you, Zach," she whispered, and though he couldn't see her face, he heard the deep emotion in her voice. "More than I ever thought I could love someone."

She'd told him before—often when they would lay like this, his knot still hard inside her.

"I love... you, Lillian," he murmured, pulling her

tighter to his body, needing to feel as much of her as possible despite having just spent days with her in bed. "Always."

They lay quietly, processing the experience of her first true heat in silence.

At first, Zach simply enjoyed the sated lethargy, basking in the physical pleasure and the gentle hum of elation in their bond. But slowly, as his mind wandered, the implications of mating a female through a true heat set in.

An alpha, like any beta, could get a woman with child without a heat, but the chances were so much higher during. He remembered the terror he'd felt at the thought of bringing a child into the world with her while they'd been captives in the lab, knowing the doctors would not hesitate to use an innocent life to twist him into the weapon they craved.

But now... here, they were free. And he wanted... with a yearning he hadn't known he was capable of... his seed to take root. He wanted his mate to bear their first child, here, in the sanctuary they and their friends had carved out deep in the Canadian woods. It would be safe here. Cherished. Protected.

Always.

Gently, he slid a hand down her body, curving his palm around the lower part of her stomach. He would never forget the cost of this beautiful life he'd been granted. He would never stop being grateful.

Lillian's hand came to rest on top of his, her soft touch soothing.

"Jerry," he said, stroking his thumb over the small swell of her abdomen.

"Jerry," she agreed.

Arlington County, Virginia

Bright light seared his eyes. There was nothing but empty whiteness—not a tunnel, like they said. Just bright, fluorescent nothingness.

"You're awake." The voice came from his side, clear as day. Clearer than any voice he'd heard before, and so close the speaker must have been within reach.

He jerked, trying to reach for them, but his arms wouldn't move. Frowning, he tried again, but still nothing. It didn't feel as if he'd been restrained—his muscles simply didn't respond.

Growling, he tried to open his mouth to demand an explanation, but he couldn't unclench his jaw to speak.

"Be calm," the voice said, and this time a face

appeared above him, outlined in the light like an angel descending.

But this was not heaven—that was the only thing he was sure of.

"Voice activation engaged," the speaker said. "You can talk now."

"Where am I? What is this? Why can't I move?" Words flowed from his lips in one long string, tumbling out as if they'd been pressed against a gate that'd suddenly been yanked open.

"You are at the Pentagon. This is a testing facility." The light suddenly dimmed and the face above him turned into a dark-haired woman's. She wore glasses, and what he could see of her shoulders and chest was covered in a white lab coat. "And you cannot move your limbs because I have not authorized it."

"What?" He yanked on his arms again, tried to kick his legs free, but again, nothing happened. "What have you done to me?!"

"Tell me what you remember from before you woke up here."

"I..." He tried to recall where he'd been before he woke up, but no memory returned.

"What is your name?"

"I am..." His voice died when no word came to his lips. "I don't..." Had he ever had a name?

"Remote control engaged. Sit up, AX1."

Without his permission, his body moved, muscles

engaging, contracting as he sat up. There was a mirror on the wall opposite where he'd been laying. It took him a moment to realize it was in fact a mirror, because he didn't recognize the person looking back at him.

If it was a person.

The thing in the mirror had dark skin and the face and general appearance of a man. But where flesh should have covered the right side of his body, metal gleamed. The transition between flesh and chrome was seamless, giving the appearance of a being that was neither human nor machine, but something in between.

The woman smiled, though it held no warmth. "All you need to know, AX1, is that you were on the brink of death, and we brought you back. We have spent millions of dollars and countless man hours ensuring you could walk again, talk again. We made you stronger than you were, faster... better in every way. And all we ask in return is that you serve your country as the soldier you were made to be."

CONTINUE WITH ALPHA TIES

AX1's story continues in

PROTECTOR
ALPHA TIES III

Get free bonus chapters and news about upcoming books by signing up to Nora's newsletter:

WWW.NORA-ASH.COM/NEWSLETTER

THE OMEGA PROPHECY

MORE DARKLY DELICIOUS OMEGAVERSE

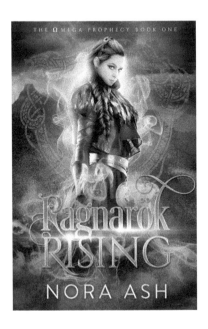

Five possessive Alpha gods and the end of mankind. That's my fate.

I always thought the end of the world was a myth. But then, I also thought Norse gods were make believe too.

They're not.

Five of them are coming for me. They claim I will only survive if I surrender to them, body and soul. But they don't realize it's about so much more than carnal servitude. I am so much more than they could ever suspect. So much more than even I knew.

I am the only one who can stop Ragnarök from covering the world in ice and darkness. The only one who can save gods and men alike from annihilation.

And in the shadows lurks betrayal so deep it will change the fate of the world...

ALSO BY NORA ASH

ALPHA TIES

Alpha

Feral

Protector*

THE OMEGA PROPHECY

Ragnarök Rising

Weaving Fate

Betraying Destiny

DEMON'S MARK

Branded

Demon's Mark

Prince of Demons*

ANCIENT BLOOD

Origin

Wicked Soul

Debt of Bones*

DARKNESS

Into the Darkness

Hidden in Darkness

Shades of Darkness

Fires in the Darkness

MADE & BROKEN

Dangerous

Monster

Trouble